The Vow

Eliana Vazquez

Copyright

Copyright © 2024 by Eliana Vázquez

Cove Design and Internal Design © 2024 by Eliana Vázquez.

Cover Design by Daniela at Ever After Cover Design

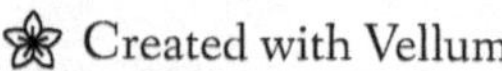 Created with Vellum

ALSO BY ELIANA VAZQUEZ

Fated Lovers Series
The Muse
The Vow

Poetry
The Evolution of Love

To Lila, thank you for your immense support and love for my characters.

The Vow

PLAYLIST

Mind Over Matter - Young the Giant

Whenever I Go - One Republic

Hotel - Montell Fish

Friends - Chase Atlantic

Cinnamon Girl - Lana Del Rey

Scared to Start - Michael Marcagi

You And Me - Niall Horan

Souvenir - Selena Gomez

Love Is a Bitch - Two Feet

Habit - Still Woozy

I Feel Like I'm Drowning - Two Feet

Tell Me You Love Me - Demi Lovato

Young and Beautiful - Lana Del Rey

Wildest Dreams - Taylor Swift

Home - Good Neighbors

Dandelions - Ruth B.

Content Warning

This book contains depictions of severe anxiety, panic attacks, body dysmorphia, and disordered eating. It also portrays verbal and emotional abuse by parental figures. Additionally, the story explores a consensual Dom/sub relationship that includes breath play, which can be dangerous if not practiced safely and responsibly. Reader discretion is advised.

Chapter One

Eloise

Present Day

At twenty-two years of age, I never saw myself in the position of having to run around my penthouse just to try and get away from my overbearing mother. I wouldn't have allowed her to come in if I knew she'd be chasing me around my home.

"Eloise, please just listen to me!" My mother pesters as she follows me down the hall.

"This helped me get pregnant when I was having a rough time, too."

I groan in mortification.

This could not be happening right now.

"Mother, I don't need any of your remedies," I shout,

reaching out to the nearest door and quickly entering it and locking it before she could catch up to me.

I hear my mother's body hit the door and can't help but let out a chuckle. It served her right to come into my home just to pressure me into having a child.

I was fortunate not to have heard anything from them when William and I had made our six-month mark in our marriage. But now that we would be making a year in a couple of weeks, their persistence to ensure I got pregnant was becoming consistent.

It was all because my marriage hadn't been enough, in their eyes. My father agreed to merge his company with Wren Technology, which guaranteed him one less company in the competition and a *son* to take over for him. Of course, my marriage had not been enough to settle the agreement. My father wanted to make sure that our company stayed within our bloodline, and that's where my uterus took part in his plan.

It's not that I didn't want children; I just didn't think this was the right time to bring in a child—not that it even mattered. To have a child, you'd need to actually partake in the activity that leads to the making of one, and William and I had only ever done it once.

And that had been a mistake.

"Eloise, honestly, stop acting like a child. This is a normal conversation to have. All you have to do is rub the oils on your—"

"Absolutely not, mother!"

A deep chuckle has me peer my head up to look over to the desk in the middle of the study.

William sat there in all his glory, laying back on his desk chair as he looked over at me in amusement. His dark hair was slicked back, and he was dressed casually in his jeans and black shirt. His beard was longer than when I had first met him. After our wedding, he had let it grow out and maintained it at that length. It made him look older, but I liked it. His blue eyes radiated from across the room. There was something about William that made you feel like he knew exactly what you were thinking.

Help me, I mouth at him, my mother's rant continuing from the other side of the door.

William lifts himself up from his chair, walking over to me. I assume he's heading towards the door to speak with my mother, so I move out of his way. But his arm shoots out and blocks my way as he corners me into the wall. I look up to face him, his eyes dragging down my body. He did it quite often; I wasn't sure if it was because he liked what he saw or hated it completely.

Regardless, I was too scared to ask.

"How long has she been pestering you about this, blondie?" His voice is strict, and I swear I can hear a bit of annoyance in it, too.

"I don't know, a couple of weeks ago," I reply.

"Eloise." I can hear the sternness in his voice as he continues to look at me. His overbearing presence makes me feel even meeker.

I had entered his study because it was the first door closest to me, and I thought he wouldn't be home today. It was Tuesday, which guaranteed that he would be in the office. But I was obviously mistaken.

"Like three months? Maybe... I'm not too sure." Actually

I'm positive it's been three months but maybe if I sound confused or unsure he won't be as angry with me.

"God, blondie, why didn't you say anything before?" He groans, pinching his nose in a stressed manner.

I only give him a shrug in response, not wanting to get into any detail about how I didn't want to be more of a disruption in his life than I already was.

William had given up a lot just to satisfy our parent's wishes to marry us. Before we married, he had been engaged to Jasmine Monroe, a beautiful woman I could never compare to.

Especially not in his eyes.

"Eloise, it's going to be a year, and you still aren't pregnant. You have to fulfill your duty as his wife." My mother's commentary only has my stomach tying a tighter knot that will possibly end up with me vomiting my breakfast. Her commentary is durable as long as I'm the only person in the room having to hear it. But with said husband, who I lacked fulfilling my wifely duties with, standing right in front of me, it makes me even more anxious and embarrassed.

William lets out a curse under his breath and reaches for the door handle. He unlocks it and opens it to find my mother and her many remedies in hand.

Mom stops her, ranting as she looks up at William. He practically towers over her tiny frame, but then again, he did the same with my own, being that he was 6'4. That had been something I found out on our honeymoon. Our drunken banter led us from talking about our height and our feelings to speaking only with our bodies in the hotel room.

But it had all been a mistake, just something that happened in the spur of the moment.

"Oh, hello there, William; Eloise hadn't told me you would be here today." My mother glares over at me through the tiny space William left between him and the wall.

"It's because she didn't know; I intended to go to the office, but all my meetings for today were canceled, so working from home today seemed fitting," William answers, his eyes practically staring into my mother's soul as the silence grows thick between them.

"Clarice, do you think I'm unable to fulfill my husbandly duties in getting my wife pregnant?" William asks, puzzling me with his question. He had never spoken to my parents like that.

"N-no." My mother stutters, realizing she's crossed a line.

"Great. I suggest you never bring that topic back up again in this house. When Eloise and I decide to have a child, we will make sure it happens. Until then, no more harassing my wife."

With that, William closes the door to the study, leaving my mother out there on her own. Hopefully, that was more than enough for her to get the hint to leave.

William turns to face me again, remaining silent before stepping toward me.

"Blondie, what did I say on our wedding day?" William murmurs.

I shrug, recalling his private vows to me.

"That you were not my parents; you are my equal. That you'd always take my side." I recall.

"Correct. So the next time something like this happens, you let me know instantly, okay?" William demands.

A short nod is all William needs to return to his desk. I

make my way back to the door, but his voice stops me from leaving.

"Oh, and blondie, let the chef know what you want to eat tonight; we're having dinner."

I furrow my brows in confusion, "we have guests coming?" I didn't know we would have people coming over tonight. Usually, William would add it to our calendar so that it wouldn't catch either of us off guard. But nothing has been put on the agenda for this week.

"No, it will be just you and me," William states, looking through the paperwork on his desk and not bothering to look up at me for one second.

We never had dinner together, not like that.

Not just us.

"I don't really eat dinner unless—" William lifts his gaze up at me, his eyes darkening at my words.

"Eloise... pick a dish for tonight at six."

"Okay," I manage to murmur as I step out back into the hall, away from my husband's intense glare.

Chapter Two

Eloise

Eleven Months Before

"Eloise, where are you going?" Charlotte, my maid of honor and best friend, asks me as I make my way out of the room, running down the hall towards the direction of the opposite wing, where William's room was.

Charlotte's hand wraps around my wrist, holding me back. "Hold up, where are you leaving to?" The fear in her eyes told me she thought I was about to make a run for it. But hopefully, by the response I'd receive, I wouldn't have to make a run; I'd just be let go of this arrangement overall.

"Jasmine is here." I turn back around, not wanting to get into the details of things. I needed to find Jasmine and get my answer.

Jasmine was William's ex.

Before our parents had bargained away our love life, he was devoted and determined to marry her. But for some reason, he chose to save his company rather than be with the woman he loved.

It hadn't been my intention to try and call off the wedding. Nothing I would say would make a difference. I was a pawn to my parents, nothing else.

But when William and I were out on one of the pre-planned dates that were set up for us, Jasmine happened to be there. The minute I saw William's eyes land on her, I knew that she would be my only chance of leaving this marriage of convenience.

I tried everything that would get William to see that what we were doing was wrong and that his love for Jasmine was way more important than money.

But he was committed to his deal with my parents. I had invited Jasmine to come to the wedding, but when I didn't receive a response, I did the only thing I could think of: I showed up at her apartment and begged her to help.

Even though she had promised to be here today, I hadn't actually expected her to show up.

"What's she doing here? How did she even make it past security?" Charlotte questions, trying to catch up with my fast pace. I pause to look at her.

"I asked her to come; I asked her to come and speak with him."

Charlotte's eyes widen but are quick to change into a stare of pity. "Oh, Eloise." She grabs my hands and brings me closer to her.

"I don't need your pity, Charlotte."

Charlotte and I had been friends since we were children. We grew up around each other, thanks to our fathers, who were both very successful men in the tech industry.

Her brother, Ulysses, wasn't a stranger either. Ulysses Hawthorne had been one of my firsts, and having him at the wedding made it even more awkward. I wouldn't go as far as saying we were in love. But there were definitely feelings between us, and the plans for my life had ruined any chance of exploring them.

"I just don't want you getting your hopes up, Eloise."

Charlotte looked magnificent in her pastel yellow dress. The color scheme hadn't been something I would've chosen, but it didn't look horrendous, especially not on her. Her voluptuous figure fit the dress perfectly, and the dark waves of her hair framed her face effortlessly. The hairdresser barely had to do anything to it.

"Charlotte, I have to try."

Charlotte gives me a nod and turns back to the room that was designated for us. At least if my mother came and found me missing, Charlotte could come up with an excuse to calm her down.

I walk over to the end of the hall and spot Jasmine right at the end of hers, having come out of William's room. The slightest shake of her head lets me know that this wedding is going forward. I was going to be marrying William.

There was nothing that could be done to prevent it. If Jasmine couldn't convince him, no one would.

His mind had been set; I would be William Wren's wife.

CRYING IN A RANDOM ROOM OF THE MANSION HADN'T been how I thought my wedding would go. After getting my response from Jasmine, I walked back to my room, but the minute I felt my hands clam up and my chest tightened, I knew a panic attack was beginning to brew.

I found the first vacant room I could find and locked myself in it. I slide myself down the door and sit on the floor, bringing my knees closer to my shaking body.

Breathe in, "one," *breathe out.*

Breathe in, "two," *breathe out.*

Breathe in, "three," *breathe out.*

I continued the same breathing patterns, focusing on my breaths as much as I could. I disregard the yelling of my name from outside the door as people begin to search for me. At this very moment, I didn't care about the way I looked or if people were worried that I had gone missing.

I just wanted to fucking breathe.

A sob breaks out from me, and I can't help but continue to let the tears stream down my face.

I close my eyes, continuing to try and control my breathing.

Come on, Eloise, you're okay, you can do this.

I listen to the noises within and outside of the room, trying to focus on something else distinctly that will help me calm down. The sound of the air-conditioning is prominent in the room. It's the first thing I can really focus on listening to, other than my mother's screams.

That's one.

Finding a different sound became much harder, especially with the chaos outside. I open my eyes and look out the window where birds are flying around the tree. Their singing brings me some comfort as my anxiety begins to mellow.

That's two.

Even when my anxiety felt better after two searches, I still searched for a third sound to make me feel secure. I close my eyes again, and try to focus on another sound.

The sound of slow-paced steps walking towards the door catches my attention, and my heart picks up once again. A light knock sounds from the door, but I remain still. The knob jiggles above me, but no words are said.

It was seconds before I finally heard his voice from the other side of the door.

"Eloise, are you in there?"

I open my eyes and lift myself off the floor. I couldn't ignore him, could I? He was probably just as annoyed as everyone else who now had to search for me.

"Eloise, open the door, please. It's just me out here; I'm not upset."

I reach over to unlock the door and open it. I step aside and let him slide into the room. He looks at me before closing the door and locking it. I looked like a mess. I wasn't too sure how much of the makeup was waterproof, and my dress was all wrinkled now. The minute my mom looks at me, she's going to have a heart attack.

"Are you okay?" William asks.

How did I answer?

No, William, I'm not. The reason being that I don't want to marry you.

"It's bad luck to see the bride before the wedding," I say instead, trying to change the topic away from my breakdown.

God, I wish I had looked at a mirror before opening the door. I probably looked insane.

William lets out a chuckle before taking a look down at my wedding dress. Not trying to hide his stare from my breasts that looked bigger than they were, thanks to the tightness of the bodice and the square-cut neckline.

"You look beautiful." William's eyes return to meet mine. I can't help but grip the fabric of my dress to calm my nerves.

"Th—thank you." I manage to murmur, looking down to stop him from being able to see the flush in my cheeks.

"How did you know I was in here?" I asked him, curious about how he was able to find me while everyone else still seemed to be in search of the hidden bride. William clears his throat, making me look back up at him. I noticed the slight discoloration in his cheek, though it was practically gone. The last time I saw him, he was beaten up pretty badly. He hadn't told me what had happened, but I also didn't ask him to.

He looked handsome in his tux. He was clean-shaven, and his hair was pushed back. But I like the way he lets his stubble grow out at times. It made him look... sexier.

"I didn't," William responds, pulling me out of my daze.

"What was that?" I ask, having forgotten what we were talking about.

"I said, I didn't know what room you were in. I went down the hall and tried opening each door." William admits, taking a step closer to me.

"Oh." I managed to say it, but I'm not sure what exactly to say about his reveal.

"Eloise, I am not your enemy," William assures, taking another step closer to me.

"I never said you were."

And it wasn't like I saw him as an enemy. That would be harsh and somewhat irrational of me to think. William was as much a victim in this marriage as me.

"You don't have to say it when your actions have said it all. You've been trying to stop this wedding from the moment we saw Jasmine at that restaurant; why is that?" William's eyes seem to darken as he looks right at me. Even though I had heels on, which made me even taller than I was, he still managed to tower over me.

"I think that's a stupid question," I remark, not thinking my words through before letting them slip off my tongue.

Crap.

William doesn't seem to mind my retort, though, because his lips pull into a playful grin. "I guess it is." He responds, leaning in closer to me.

"Do you have your vows?" He whispers as if someone were around to hear. I only shake my head in response. My mother had hired someone to write the vows. I had told her I wouldn't have minded writing them myself. It would at least make this marriage feel somewhat real. But she thought I was being ridiculous.

"I see," William sighs. His eyes still linger on my own. His blue gaze seemed to calm me more than any technique had.

"Well, I still want to give you mine now. Away from all the people if you wouldn't mind." William brings the palm of his hand between us, gesturing for my own hand to go on top of it.

I bring my hand to his, and William holds it firmly, pushing the engagement ring from side to side with the pad of his thumb.

"Eloise, I know you're scared and that this isn't how you pictured your life going. Trust me, I had a whole different plan in mind. But, just because the plan has changed doesn't mean it's wrong." I look over to the window, swallowing the lump forming in my throat and blinking away any tears that were daring to fall from my glistening eyes.

"Eloise," William grabs ahold of my chin to have me face him. "I vow to be your partner. This marriage may be out of convenience, but we can learn to care for one another. I am not your parents; I am your equal. I vow to be on your side, to defend you, to honor you, and to care for you. You will be my wife, Eloise. And a wife should not have to hide from their husband. You will always have me."

William's words give me the calm I need. A singular tear strides down my face, but he's quick to wipe it away. He brings my hand up to his mouth and gives it a kiss before letting it go.

"Come on, we have a wedding to attend." William moves away and walks over to the door, unlocking it and pulling it open.

He looks over at me and nudges his head for me to walk out. I try to straighten out my dress as much as possible before walking right out towards my mother's voice at the end of the hall.

There was no more delaying the wedding. I was going to marry William, and maybe things wouldn't be as bad as I thought.

Chapter Three

Present Day

Dinner wasn't going quite as planned. Not that I had planned much of it. This was our first dinner together as a married couple. A dinner that involved no one but us. Which was quite embarrassing when you think about it. Eloise and I were going to make a year as a married couple, and we had never had dinner together.

I'll be the first to admit it was mostly my fault. I had never stepped up to ask before today. To be quite honest, I wasn't entirely sure why I had asked her to have dinner with me in the first place.

I knew she never had dinner; she had a specific diet that was drilled into her mind by her parents, and the only time I ever saw her break from it was when we had essential dinners with potential business partners or acquaintances. But even then, I noticed that she would remove a meal from her scheduled routine to allow herself to have dinner.

But despite having asked her to have dinner with me, she barely touched anything on her plate. In fact, the meal that she had asked the chef to cook for us wasn't something she enjoyed.

I take a sip of my wine as I focus on Eloise from across the table, picking at her steak.

She hated red meat.

I don't think I had ever seen her eat anything but fish for protein. Occasionally, she would eat chicken, but even that was odd.

"Why did you ask for steak?" I finally question.

Eloise sets down her utensils and looks over at me, giving her shoulders a shrug.

"You like steak, no?" Her face looked concerned. Fearing that she had made the wrong choice for dinner.

"I do like it," I reassured. "But you don't."

Eloise takes her bottom lip in between her teeth, obviously unsure of what to say.

"Next time, please, just choose something you enjoy too." I encourage.

I hated how much Eloise shelled herself. Her parents had used her as a puppet throughout her life to get what they wanted. Having her break away from that mentality of feeling the need to put other people before herself was tough.

"Do you want children?" I blurt out before even thinking the question through. The way her mother chased her down today with concoctions to help Eloise become pregnant made me sick. They treated her like cattle they needed to breed.

Eloise and I had structured a practical relationship after our honeymoon. We fell into a system that worked for us. We each had our own lives. We had separate rooms, friends, and agendas. We never interacted as a couple unless we had to.

But even if we had tried to join our lives together and potentially be an actual couple, I don't think it would've been that difficult. Eloise was mesmerizing, and despite being an heiress, she wasn't arrogant.

The times that I had crossed paths with her she always seemed to keep to herself. The only person I ever saw her with, other than her mother, was Charlotte.

Other than them, Eloise seemed to always be *alone*.

Knowing this about her never really bothered me, but something about today irked me more than I would've wanted it to. Having to hear her mother's words and the way that Eloise had been dealing with this sort of expectation from her mother for months riled me up. I wasn't her best friend, Charlotte, but I was still her husband. I wanted her to be able to come to me when she needed help. If I hadn't decided to work from home today, this would've continued.

It also didn't help that the reason behind this issue was because of our lack of intimacy. It wasn't that I hadn't thought of sleeping with Eloise. Of course I had, I wasn't blind.

Most nights, I stirred awake in bed just thinking about that night.

The only night.

But that had been done out of anger and heartbreak.

And Eloise didn't deserve that. She deserved a loving marriage.

"Yes, I'd like to have children. Maybe not right now, but someday." She replies, setting down her utensils.

I nod my head as I take a bite of my meal.

"I mean, I wouldn't be opposed to having children now; I just haven't finished school yet. I would've liked to finish that before having children." Eloise shifts uncomfortably in her chair.

"Eloise, relax. I'm not in a rush to have any kids myself." It only takes that sentence to leave my mouth for Eloise to let out a breath of air and relax in her seat.

I reach my hand across the table, unsure of what compelled me to do so, and bring her hand into mine. Eloise's crystal blues meet mine, and for a moment, we are just met with silence until I speak up.

"Eloise, you are allowed to be your own person. You do not need to please me. You need to be honest with me. I will be by your side with every decision that you make. Just speak to me, come to me, and I'll be there."

Eloise only gives me a slight nod and mutters a thank you before pulling her hand away from my own.

"I didn't know you still wanted to continue school."

Eloise had gone to Columbia and gotten her bachelor's in pre-law. But after she graduated, she didn't make any attempts to apply to any law school. Not that it mattered; I could very well support both of us and our children if we ever had any.

Eloise gives me a shrug, looking anywhere but directly at me.

"Eloise." My voice comes out stern despite wanting to be

as calm as possible. I wasn't meant for this. I had never been too good with emotions. I wanted to be Eloise's friend, but I didn't know how to be one. But maybe that was the problem this whole time. I had tried being her friend and maintaining a composed relationship with her.

But she's not my friend.

She's my wife.

"Our anniversary is coming up. I think that a trip is more than deserved. Pick anywhere you'd like to go for that week." I set my utensils to the side, lean back in my chair, and take in Eloise's surprised reaction.

"Anywhere?" She asks, her eyes brightening at the thought of traveling anywhere she desires. She looked as ecstatic as a child on Christmas. I didn't think anything could impress an heiress who had probably received it all in life.

"And from now on, Tuesdays and Fridays, we will be having dinner together. Be sure to have the chef make something you like. I'd like to see you enjoying your meal next time, blondie." I say, giving her the pet name that, for some reason, always made her cheeks blush. And that, in return, gave me some sort of fulfillment.

I was determined to make Eloise happy.

Chapter Four

Eloise

"That must mean something, right?" Charlotte asks, in between bites of her salad. It had been four days since the first dinner with William. After that, I steered clear from the penthouse as much as possible. The only other time I had seen him was on Friday night when we had dinner together, just as he had suggested. "It seems like he actually wants to build a relationship with you." Charlotte encourages.

As much as I wanted to agree with Charlotte, the last thing I needed to do was to get my hopes up at the idea of having this marriage work out. It would all be a fairytale if William and I fell in love with each other. But the world didn't work like that. Sure, William and I could form an amicable relationship, but love was a far fetched idea for us.

"I don't know, I think he's just trying to make things

easier between us... *you know*." I trail off, not wanting to say the actual thought in my head out of embarrassment.

"Am I supposed to be catching something in your words?" Charlotte asks, reaching for her water to take a sip.

I lean my body toward her and look around before speaking. The last thing I needed was for one of my mother's socialite friends to get ahold of the news.

"I think he's being nice in hopes of me being comfortable enough to get pregnant with his child."

Charlotte's fork falls onto her plate. The noise caused heads to turn over at us. Charlotte and I were having lunch at the Maplewood. All the socialites could be found here at some point of their day. It wasn't my usual choice to spend my Saturdays. But Charlotte's fiancé, Dev and Ulysses, usually came here to use the tennis court to their advantage. So Charlotte had begged me to come along for lunch while the men enjoyed their time on the court.

"You think he's trying to butter you up to have sex with you?" Charlotte clarifies.

"Well, yes, but mostly for the outcome of a child." I was aware that William had said otherwise. But he wasn't someone I trusted yet. Besides, trust wasn't something I handed out for free; he needed to earn it just as much as anyone else. Just because we were forced into a marital predicament didn't mean that he was guaranteed anything.

"Hm, I don't know Eloise. I think he just wants to make things work."

I shrug my shoulders, unsure of what exactly to say. If I let my guard down, it would only cause disappointment in the end. I was better off waiting to see what William's intentions were before I filled my head up with stupid, happily ever after ideas.

"Who really wants to make things work?" Two chairs pull up next to our table as Dev and Ulysses sit on either side. Dev leans over to lay a kiss on Charlotte's lips. They were perfect for each other. Charlotte had met Dev while studying abroad in London. At the time, Dev was working on his start-up company, which had become quite successful after two years in the making.

The two had fallen for the other instantly. Enough to commit to a long-distance relationship. That is until Dev's company took off, and he was able to move out to New York, branching out his company along with his move.

Something Ulysses and I would've done as well, if my marriage hadn't gotten in the way of our relationship. Not that it mattered. Ulysses wasn't someone I was in love with; he was just someone I grew comfortable around. Ulysses continues to stare directly at me as he awaits a reply to a question that I had completely forgotten that he asked.

"Nothing," I mutter, suddenly finding enough appetite to take another bite of my salad.

"Nothing?" Ulysses furrows his brows as he looks between Charlotte and me.

I stared at Charlotte, ensuring she kept this conversation between us. The last thing I needed was for my ex-boyfriend to learn that my marriage was in disarray.

"If she said nothing, then it's nothing. Stop prying into our conversation." Charlotte reprimands, giving her brother a playful slap on the arm before leaning into Dev's arms. It was also best that nothing was said in front of Dev, though I'm sure Charlotte probably told him about our conversations. Dev and William ran in the same circles. They'd met up countless times to network, and now that Dev was engaged with Charlotte, they both seemed to make more of an effort to be friends.

When it came to Ulysses, though, William had made his feelings for him quite clear. He couldn't stop Ulysses from being around Charlotte and me when we hung out. But he didn't allow us to be alone together.

Ulysses rolls his eyes at Charlotte, choosing not to start an argument with his younger sister this time.

"How's William, Eloise?" Dev asks, picking at Charlotte's salad looking for the protein.

Ulysses's eye roll doesn't go unseen as I answer Dev. "He's fine; we're actually planning a trip for our one-year anniversary." I'm not entirely sure what made me want to give out that information, but it had spilled out before I could stop myself.

"That sounds wonderful, where to?" Dev asks.

"I'm not too sure yet; I haven't decided."

I had been in between a couple of places I hadn't been to yet. So, I hadn't made a concise decision. But I would have my choice by William and I's next dinner together so that he still had time to make the arrangements.

"Well, the Maldives are a great place to visit during this time of year," Dev says.

"Oh, the Maldives, that could be where we go for our honeymoon." Charlotte lifts her head from Dev's shoulder to look at him. "But you hate the ocean." Dev points out, brushing his dark hair back.

Charlotte sags in her chair and gives him a shrug. "Who cares? Most of the activities of a honeymoon are indoors anyway." Dev gives Charlotte a sly smile, raising his eyebrows, intrigued by Charlotte's statement.

"Hello, her older brother is sitting right here." Ulysses points at himself, his face showing his disgust towards the lovebirds in front of us.

"Hey, don't act like I didn't have to swallow my vomit each time I was around you two." Charlotte remarks, pointing over at Ulysses and me.

I'm silent in my chair, not giving much of a reaction. But I know the comment bothered Ulysses. I hadn't done the best job at breaking the news to him when I broke up with him. I didn't think he would take the news as badly as he did. Ulysses was a good-looking man. His light brown locks and hazel eyes wooed every woman who crossed paths with him.

But the day I told Ulysses about my engagement to William, he took off running to my parents' home, asking them to take back the agreement with William's family and have me marry him instead. But, my father was a man of his word, and I think, despite the arrangement, he genuinely took a liking to William.

"We can go to India," Dev suggests, bringing the conversation back to the honeymoon.

Charlotte scrunches up her nose, giving me a look that says, *is he being serious right now?*

I can't help but laugh, and Charlotte soon joins in with her own fit of laughter..

"What's so funny about my country?" Dev questions.

"Nothing, baby, just that I'm not really interested in hanging around your family for our honeymoon. We can go to India any other time."

Charlotte and Dev continue to bicker about the best

honeymoon destination while Ulysses and I remain silent while watching. Ulysses clears his throat before looking over at me.

"I miss that." He says, his voice in a hushed tone, obviously not wanting Charlotte to pick up on our conversation.

"Miss what exactly?" I ask.

"Your laugh, our relationship, us," Ulysses whispers.

"Ulysses, I'm married." Somehow, even though I was in a public space with Charlotte and Dev right next to us, I still felt like I was doing something wrong.

"Isn't it odd?" Ulysses questions.

His stare burns through the side of my head as I just continue to focus on Charlotte and Dev from across the table. I extend my foot and kick Charlotte, trying to catch her attention to get me out of this situation. Charlotte peers over and looks at Ulysses, getting my hint.

"What was that?" Charlotte asks, gaining her brother's attention. I let out a breath of air. The pressure that began riling up in my chest diminished.

"I just think their age gap is odd," Ulysses mutters.

I can't help but feel embarrassed at his sudden opinion of my relationship. I hadn't known it was any of his business in the first place.

"Ulysses." Charlotte reprimands.

"It's really not that big of a deal." Dev follows.

"What, he's like thirty?" Ulysses argues.

"More like twenty-eight. I guess you could say I look thirty with the beard, but Eloise doesn't seem to mind it too much." Heat rushes to my face as William's voice sounds from behind me. Charlotte's eyes widened at William's sudden appearance, her eyes glancing back and forth from William to me.

I look down at my watch, remembering how I had asked him to pick me up at around three since he would be around Maplewood at this time.

I turn to face him, expecting to see a somewhat angry William after getting caught speaking to Ulysses. But William's face remains stoic as he looks over at Ulysses, his hand reaching out to touch my bare shoulder.

No one dares to say a thing to William, not even Ulysses, who had a lot to say about him before he got caught. I sigh and place my hand on William's to get his attention.

"You came early." William had actually been right on time, and that in itself was early. I was used to having to wait an extra hour if needed for him to wrap up his meetings.

"Yeah, my meeting ended earlier than expected." I clear my throat and stand up from my chair, feeling more than ready to leave.

"Charlotte, Dev, it's always good to see you. We will have to schedule dinner soon after Eloise and I's *first-anniversary getaway*." William's tone was not missed in those final words of his statement.

In other words, he was telling Ulysses to back off.

"Of course, Eloise was just telling us about it." Dev says, "Let us know what you end up choosing, Eloise. Maybe Charlotte and I can add it to the long list of places we can go to for our honeymoon." Charlotte gives Dev a playful slap as they continue to discuss their wedding.

I look back at William, who just gives me a nod to follow. I say my goodbyes and walk right behind William out of Maplewood and towards his car.

THE DRIVE HOME HAD BEEN UNCOMFORTABLE. WILLIAM had driven himself today, so the ride home consisted of me in the passenger seat staring out the window while William drove us home. Both of us listening to one of his preferred podcasts. But the minute we got home, the anger in his demeanor was apparent.

I step out of the elevator, following William towards the door, which he unlocks and opens so that I can enter ahead of him. William closes the door and saunters over to his study, ignoring my presence completely.

"You're upset," I state, following him toward the study.

"Well, I can't say that I'm too thrilled, blondie."

William's voice is low and intimidating, but being that he still called me blondie rather than Eloise meant that he wasn't exactly angry with me.

William pulls out his bottle of Whiskey from his desk and pours himself a glass. "Is it because I'm not allowed to be around Ulysses?" I blurt out the question, not caring if it brought on an argument. William pauses his pour and looks back up at me, sealing the bottle and returning it to its drawer.

"First of all, I never said you weren't allowed to be around Ulysses. You have your own free will, Eloise." William saunters over to me, taking a sip of his drink before hovering over me. "Secondly, I will admit that I did share my preference of not wanting you two alone together. Regardless, the issue is not that you were with him. The issue is that the prick has a lot to say." William's jaw tightens, defining it more.

I swallow and open my mouth to speak, but I'm not entirely sure what to say. I should have defended William rather than look at Charlotte for support.

"I should have said something. I'm sorry."

"That's not the issue here, blondie," William murmurs; his breath smells like whisky, and I've never been much of a fan of the brown substance, but suddenly, I was craving a taste of it.

"Then what's the issue?" I dare.

I had no clue what had gotten into me to have taken a step closer to William, challenging him. William's eyes darken as his lips turn into a smirk.

"There's no issue if it gets you acting this bold."

Was he flirting with me?

I bite back my smile as I look up at my husband, taking on his stare.

"Do you think he's right?" William asks.

"About your age?" I furrow my brows together, unsure of where his question was coming from. Sure, William was older than me, but that never put me off.

William only nods his head, awaiting my response.

I let out a sigh in frustration. "Of course not, William. Ulysses said that out of jealousy. If he and I were six years apart while we were together, age would not be any of his concern."

My relationship with William wasn't exactly what I pictured when we got married. I didn't expect a separate bedroom, separate meals, a separate lifestyle, and a lonesome marriage. William seemed to be trying to make this work.

Regardless of what his intentions were, I didn't want to lose the chance of making this marriage work because of a stupid comment that came out of my ex-boyfriend's mouth.

William downs the rest of his whisky before looking back down at me. He reaches out his hand, cradling my face with his palm. My skin rises, and the intimacy between us feels just like that night. The only night that William had touched me.

"How did you know I liked your beard?" I ask, breaking through the heavy silence between us. He had brought up my liking for his beard at the Maplewood, but I hadn't realized that my liking for it was so evident.

William licks his lips, a smirk appearing on them as he looks down at my own. The pad of his thumb grazes my bottom lip, and the look in his eyes tells me that he's contemplating stealing a kiss.

But William doesn't kiss me. Instead, he lets go of me, my skin feeling the loss of his warmth. "I didn't, blondie. But it's good to know." Is all William says before walking right past me, out of the study.

Leaving me alone and yearning.

Chapter Five

Eloise

Eleven Months Ago

Our honeymoon had been a gift from William's father, Donovan. And as beautiful and exciting as it was to be in Fiji, it was also quite dull. I had underestimated how awkward it would be to spend my days with William. In the beginning, he tagged along with the activities that were set up for us. But after the third day, it was just me waking up early to get to my activity of the day while William lingered in bed. And by the end of the day, when I'd get back to go to bed, he would be out.

He was enjoying his time at the bar, being that he came back each night smelling like whisky. I was counting down the days to the end of this honeymoon. But the days seemed to be going by slower than ever, even with all the different activities I had started doing on my own.

Today, I decided to skip out on the plans that had been set up for us and stay around the resort to catch up on some reading. I was also tired of the embarrassment that came with having to tell the guides of our activity that my husband wouldn't be joining us.

I open the bathroom door, trying to remain as stealthy as possible so I don't wake William up. I grab a towel from the counter and head outside towards the private deck of our bungalow. I remove the crochet dress from my body, fold it, and place it neatly on the deck.

The waters were crystal clear, but the waves had picked up compared to other days. I opt for the pool instead, rather than risking a drowning incident. I plunge into the water, surrounding myself with the coolness. I close my eyes and allow myself to float in the water. The sun was warming my skin, and the sound of the ocean was bringing me some form of peace.

Was this how our marriage would always be?

Would it always feel this... lonely?

"You're here." William's voice startles me up. I open my eyes and put a hand up to my forehead to shade me from the sun. William stood over the pool in nothing but his trunks. My breath hitches as I take in his toned body. William moves to the side, allowing his frame to block the sun from hitting my face.

"I am."

William looks around, focusing his gaze on the ocean. Probably contemplating taking a swim within the rough waves rather than being in the same vicinity as me.

"I can go," I let out a sigh and begin walking towards the stairs of the pool.

"No, don't," William says. The sound of his body diving into the pool grabs my attention. I turn around to face him. He wipes away the water from his face, dragging his fingers through his hair before peering over at me once again with that icy blue stare.

"No activities today?" William asks, lowering himself into the water. I roll my eyes at his audacity to ask the question. "Not much to do when an activity for two turns to one. After a while, you get tired of the pity stares." I mutter.

I had exaggerated; there weren't any looks of pity. Not when I had told anyone who asked that William had a nasty food poisoning. William clears his throat, looking anywhere but at me.

"Right... I'm sorry about that." William's voice sounds sincere, but I only shrug, not interested in his pity.

If he had actually been sorry, he'd have tried to make the best out of this trip. I wasn't asking for his love, just common respect.

"Eloise, this is new to me." William moves closer to me, but I don't do anything to fight off the distance.

"Oh, I'm sorry, William. Is this my fifth rodeo or something?"

William leans against the edge of the pool, this time hovering over me. This was the closest we had ever been, without counting the kiss at the altar, which had been nothing but a quick peck.

What woman wanted a peck on the lips on their wedding day?

"I know... you're right." William's stoic face breaks into a grin. There was something about his smile that made your stomach fill with butterflies.

"What is it? What did I say?" I ask, approaching him.

"Nothing... It's just nice to see you like this." William peers down at what I can only assume is my breasts.

Was he checking me out?

"Like what? In a bikini?" I chuckle.

"No—well, yes— no, wait. That's not what I was referring to." William closes his eyes, taking a moment to pause and gather his thoughts. I think this was the first time I had ever seen William Wren flustered.

He lets out a sigh, looking back down at me, his eyes focused on my own this time. Trying not to look anywhere below my neck. Not that I would have minded. He was my husband, and divorce wasn't in our contract.

"I was referring to your attitude. You're always so posh. I don't think I've ever seen you speak out to someone with such a tone... I like it."

I can't tell if my cheeks immediately heat up from the sun, his comment, or the embarrassment of having assumed he was checking me out. I clear my throat and give him a nod before scooting towards the edge of the pool where the stairs were.

"Did I say something wrong?" William moves towards me, trying to grab my wrist to stop me from leaving. But I'm too quick and out of the pool in seconds.

"No, not at all. I just want to get started on my reading." I lie, not wanting to continue this uncomfortable interaction. I think this had been enough socializing for one day.

"Reading?" William asks as if he had never heard of it before.

I pick up the towel and crochet dress, drying myself off a bit first before putting the dress on. "Yes William, you know... reading. Like a book, with words."

William lets out a chuckle, swimming to the other end of the pool before looking back over at me.

"There's that attitude I like so much."

William sends me a wink before thrusting himself into the pool's water, his defined back muscles clenching with each movement as he continues swimming laps in the pool.

I make my way back inside the room, water dripping from my still-wet body. But it didn't matter. I was grabbing my stuff and heading out towards the beach to enjoy my day.

After all, even if I spent it alone, my birthday deserved to be celebrated and enjoyed.

I SIT DOWN IN THE LOUNGE CHAIR, MY BOOK IN HAND. I had barely gotten any time to sit down and enjoy a book these past couple of weeks. Today, I was going to enjoy everything about beginning a new book and finishing it all in one day while I lay myself comfortably on this chair and drank as many margaritas as I could intake.

It was rare for me to ever drink. My mother always said I looked like a pufferfish after a sip. But right now, I didn't care what I looked like or what my mother thought. If my husband could drink his problems away, then so could I.

I hadn't minded my birthday landing on the date of our honeymoon. Every year, I spend it the same. It was just

Charlotte and I and a piece of chocolate cake that I had to promise my mother I hadn't eaten. I wasn't keen on lying, but that lie was always worth it.

I open my book, taking a sip of my drink simultaneously. The book at hand had been a recommendation from Charlotte, and usually, on my trips, I would always bring *Metamorphosis* by Franz Kafka. It had become my comfort read after all the years of re-reading it. I had first read it in middle school, and after that, my father came up with the idea to collect a version of the book in every country we traveled to.

I was aware that it was a tactic my father had come up with, so I wouldn't complain about having to travel with him for boring networking events. But it had become something that I had actually looked forward to with every trip.

For some reason, that story always stuck with me. Maybe because even at thirteen, I had already realized that if I had turned into a roach, I would be worth nothing to my parents.

"This seat taken?" I look up from my book, my eyes meeting with a tall man, tattoos covering his body. His nipple piercings do not go unnoticed. He stood over the vacant lounge chair, his dark hair pushed back, the ocean's salty water dripping off of his skin.

"Um, no, it isn't," I respond as I return back to my book.

The man takes a seat in the lounge chair next to mine. I try hard to focus on the words that are written on the page but can't help but get distracted by the feel of his stare.

Maybe I should've just stayed inside the bungalow all day.

"My name is Ben," he says, bringing his hand over to me. I turn to face him, looking down at his hand. I reach out and shake it, "Eloise." I say.

As intimidating as he looked with all his tattoos and piercings, he didn't seem like someone I should be worried about. He was obviously on vacation, just like I was.

"I couldn't help myself from coming over to speak to you," Ben says, un-grasping my hand from his hold.

"Is that so?" I bring the book up to my face this time rather than settling it on my lap. Just so my wedding ring could give him the answer he was looking for.

"Ben, stop harassing the girl, and let's go." A man with shaggy blonde hair calls out from across the beach.

"Yeah, Ben, stop harassing my wife and run along with your friend." The sound of William's voice sends goosebumps throughout my body. I look back at the sound of his voice. Ben gets up from the seat, gesturing for William to take over.

"Hey, sorry, man. I didn't know she was married."

"By the way, the rock on her finger is reflecting on your face, I doubt it." William retorts.

Ben gives him a shrug before turning back over to me and giving me a wink as he passes by me and walks over to his friend.

"Does that happen often?" William asks, taking a seat beside me. I rest my book on my lap, turning my body to face him. I don't think I'd be catching up on any reading today.

"Do men come up and speak to me? Oh yeah, all the time." I exaggerate, the sarcasm in my voice doesn't go over his head as he laughs.

"I wouldn't be surprised if it did, you really are beautiful, Eloise," William reassures.

He had said as much on our wedding day, but it still felt

good to be acknowledged as beautiful by someone who wasn't in love with you.

"So you've said." I allow a smile to play on my lips, probably one of the realest ones I've actually given him.

"And will continue to say, until death do us part." William teases, I can't help but cringe at the stupid vows we had to repeat. I had always thought those vows were beautiful and monumental to a wedding. But, now, they felt stupid and untrue.

"Do you want to go to the bar and get drunk?" William asks, stopping my thoughts from spiraling into a tornado of anxiety.

"Tired of doing it all on your own?" I tease, a grin spreading onto his face. His eyebrows raised in astonishment at my snarky response.

"It makes it less concerning if someone is getting drunk with you." William reasons, knowing that it'd just mean that instead of one drunk at the bar, they'd have two.

"Why the hell not?"

Chapter Six

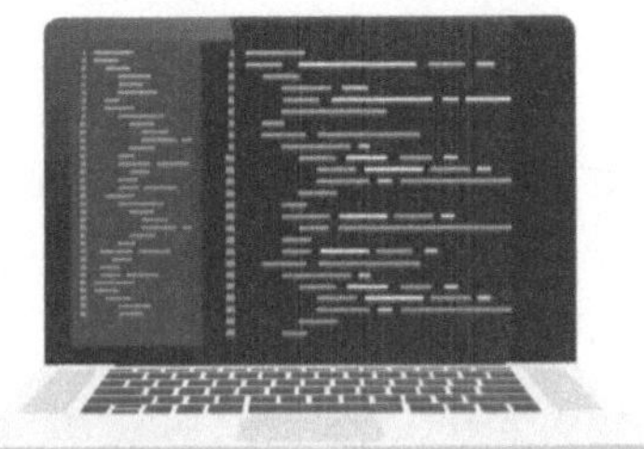

William

"Are you already drunk?" Eloise giggles, placing her head against my shoulder. I wasn't sure if it was the tequila or my actual feelings, but god damn, it felt nice having her this close.

"I promise you I'm not drunk, I just get bloated... like one of those fish, what are they called?" Eloise scratches her head as she peers up at me with those sky-blue eyes.

God, she looked unreal.

Eloise denied having many suitors after her, but she was oblivious to the looks she got. Every man that got the chance let their eyes linger on her. The only reason most of them didn't come and speak to her was because they knew their place. Eloise was a woman who was worth millions, and she was a woman who deserved those millions, too. Despite her wealthy upbringing, she seemed to be a sweet woman.

Guilt ranged at my chest as we stood there, finally getting along after days of ignoring her purposefully so as not to feel the shame that gnawed at me every time she appeared in my field of view.

My ex-fiancée, Jasmine, had appeared to me before the wedding as a favor for Eloise in hopes of having me call off the wedding so that Eloise could get the chance to actually marry someone that truly loved her.

But I had let my greed get the best of me. I needed the opportunity that came with marrying Eloise, which was merging our companies in hopes of me taking over once Eloise's father retires. Which, according to the man, would be very soon.

"Pufferfish! It's called a pufferfish!" Eloise exclaims, appearing as if she had just had a breakthrough.

"I promise you that you don't look like a pufferfish." I roll my eyes at her degradation.

"Liar, my mother told me herself." She declares, laying her head back down on my shoulder.

"Could I get some water?" I ask the bartender.

"And a chocolate cake!" Eloise practically bursts out of her chair, causing stares from the others sitting by the bar. But I didn't fucking care.

"Okay, let's settle down, blondie." I bring my hand around her waist, sitting her back down on the stool.

"No, I don't want a blondie. I want a chocolate cake." She pouts.

"I'm not ordering you a blondie, I'm calling you blondie," I explain, not knowing where the sudden nickname came from. It was the tequila taking over. Maybe I should make that two glasses of water. The bartender walks over, and I open the bottle of water for Eloise. Handing it over to her, she takes a couple of sips as I pick up a menu by the bar.

"Are you hungry? Do you want something to eat?" I could go for something to eat myself. I wasn't too sure if the food here was any good, being that most of the time I was here, I had only ingested alcohol.

Eloise lets out a giggle as she shakes her head.

"No, it's my birthday."

Her birthday? How drunk was she?

I highly doubted that she would have her honeymoon around her birthday. But then again, I wasn't sure that she had drunk enough to begin making up stories.

"It's your birthday?" I ask, wanting to clarify the truth.

"Mmh, I turn twenty-two today." She takes another sip of her water as I turn over to the bartender, placing an order of food to sober Eloise up.

"Why would you choose to have your honeymoon land on your birthday?" I ask, not entirely believing the birthday reveal just yet.

Eloise chuckles, shaking her head at me as if I had asked the dumbest question known to man.

"I don't know how to reveal this to you, William, but... I don't get much of a say in any choices in my life. Not who I marry, when I marry, and certainly not when I go on my honeymoon."

Fuck me.

It was her birthday.

"Do you have a chocolate cake?" Eloise asks the bartender, who looks like he's already had enough of us.

"I have a lava cake." He answers.

"Add it to the order, please." I cut in, the bartender gives me a nod as he walks over to the register to add it to the system.

"Will you share it with me?" Eloise asks, pouting her lips at me. For some reason, it was turning me on more than it should. I look down at my drink and take another sip. Eloise was my wife, there was nothing wrong with finding my wife attractive. But the engagement ring Jasmine had given back to me the other day was burning a hole in my pocket. Maybe that was just the guilt of all the lies and deceit, or maybe it was just the guilt of feeling attracted to Eloise despite having been in love with Jasmine.

"Usually, Charlotte and I share it. But, being that she's not here, you can take her place." Eloise explains, but I can't help but think how lonely it must be to share a cake with just your best friend for your birthday. Surely, she must've had bigger celebrations.

"What else do you usually do for your birthday?"

Eloise at me questionably, confused by my simple question.

"That's it."

"That's it?" I ask, I don't think I can remember a birthday where I wasn't getting shit-faced or celebrating with friends and family in some way. Sure, as I got older, I cared less about it. But Eloise was twenty-one, well, twenty-two now. And she never had a celebration.

"What about gifts?" I ask, surely she at least got a gift from her parents.

"Hm, oh, I got a tennis bracelet from my father for my sixteenth birthday." Eloise takes a second to think the memory through before pursing her lips and looking back up at me.

"Then again, it was after I had caught him cheating on Mom with his secretary, so I think it was just something he gave me to keep quiet." She mutters.

Jesus Christ.

What the hell was wrong with them?

"You wouldn't cheat, right?" Eloise asks, her tone apprehensive. I hadn't thought about being with anyone other than Jasmine for a long time in my life. When I was forced to break up with her because of this marital agreement, I had gone out days after my break up and slept with anyone I saw. I wasn't proud to admit I had slept with my one secretary, but that wasn't something I was admitting to Eloise.

That had been a mistake of the past, and Calliope had agreed to forget about it and never bring it up again. After what Eloise had revealed to me, the last thing I wanted was for her to think she married someone that was just like her father.

Regardless of my feelings, I would have to learn how to love Eloise. Divorce wasn't an option within our agreement. Cheating would only make both of our lives even more miserable than they are.

"Eloise, I do not plan on being unfaithful." I declare, hoping she would believe my word. Though Eloise's face looks hopeful, I can see a grain of doubt within her eyes. But that didn't matter; trust was something that would have to be earned over time. Even though we had been on a couple of dates, there wasn't much we had ever spoken about. Most of the time, we talked about our day and if we had been enjoying the meal on our plate. We never made an effort to get to know each other, but I think now more than ever, some effort has to be made.

The bartender comes back and lays the food right in front of us, which we gladly dig into. I don't think I had ever seen Eloise scarf down food like that. It felt good to see her drink and eat without a care. She deserved that. Not the diets and overbearing lifestyle shoved down her throat by her parents.

"Why are you staring at me?" Eloise asks, her mouth full of fries.

I let out a laugh, brushing the strand of her that had fallen in front of her face.

Why had I done that?

"I like it." Is all I say, giving her a shrug and eating along with her.

Out of everyone my father could've married me off to in hopes of saving our company, I was glad that Eloise had been the one.

I could learn how to love her, especially when she was so easy to care for and so deserving of it all.

"Wait, be careful," I say, pulling her closer to me. Afraid that one wrong step would have her falling off the deck and into the dark waters.

"I'm fine, hurry, open the door." She pleas, laying her head against the side of the bungalow, looking up at me. My breath hitches as I stare down at her. We had just come back from the bar where we had shared a tiny piece of lava cake for her birthday. I wish I had known before the trip that it was her birthday, I would have tried to make it better. But then again, I hadn't even tried to make our honeymoon that special. I had spent my days alone at the bar and would come late to bed just so that I wouldn't have to deal with the consequences of my decision.

But I was starting to realize that Eloise was anything but a consequence. She had been a gift from fate that I didn't deserve.

Everything about her radiated beauty.

Her long blond hair, unlike most days, was a bit messy and wavy from her time in the water. The freckles that appeared on her nose from being out in the sun and those eyes of hers held so much sorrow within them, and for some reason, I wanted to be the reason that they found some joy.

"Why are you staring at me like that?" Eloise's voice pulls me back from my thoughts. Her teeth graze her bottom lip, before I can even think it through, my hand lifts to palm her cheek, and the pad of my thumb pulls her lip away from her teeth.

I really shouldn't start something that would only further complicate matters. But the alcohol in my system said otherwise, and the way she looked at me with that lustful gaze only encouraged my actions. I press the key card against the doorknob, and the green light on the lock lights up and unlocks the door.

"Fuck it."

I grab Eloise by the waist, bringing her closer to me. Opening the door, I bring her in, and push her up against it. My lips hover over hers, my eyes asking for the permission I need from her. Eloise grabs my nape, pulling me down to her. My lips meet hers in a passionate and I quickly I lead my hands down to her round ass, which had looked so fucking tempting to bite when she walked out of the fucking pool earlier today.

I hoist Eloise up, her legs wrapping tightly around my waist. Our lips move in sync, her tongue flicking the bottom of my lip for entrance.

I walk us over to the bed, and set her down and immediately pull my shirt off. "Get that dress off, blondie. I want to see all of you."

Eloise removed the dress, leaving her in the skimpy white bikini I had wanted to tear off of her the minute I saw her floating in the pool.

"You are so fucking beautiful," I growl, sliding my pants down, leaving me with only my underwear. I tower over Eloise, my finger teasing the fabric of her bikini. Her nipples harden from just my touch. If that's all I had to do to get her body to react this way, then how would it react when my cock was buried deep within her wetness.

"More," Eloise moans.

The sound escaping her lips was captivating. I needed to hear more.

"More what, blondie?" My nails scratch against her outer thigh, moving inward, spreading her legs apart. The fabric barely did anything to cover the wet mess between her legs. I bring my lips to her thigh, licking and sucking on the sensitive skin. Eloise instantly pushes herself towards me. But as much of an appetite as I had for her, I would wait for her words. I needed to hear her beg.

"William, I need to feel something, I need to feel you, please." Eloise peers down at me, her hair looking more like a lion's mane, and I am more than happy to be her prey. I untangle the strings on the side of her hips that were holding the fabric together and slide it right off of her. Revealing her glistening pussy.

My dick hardens more than I ever thought fucking possible at the look of her looking down at me with those pleading eyes. Begging me to lick that pretty cunt of hers.

"You want to feel something, baby?" I whisper against her thighs, pressing a trail of kisses as I lean in closer to her pussy.

"Fuck, yes. William , please me." I take a bite of her thigh, and a yelp escapes her lips. Before she can say anything, I wrap my lips around her clit. My tongue licked her pussy from the entrance back up to her clit. Eloise's hands grab onto my hair, leading me up and down. Trying to take some form of control as she rides my face. Her moans cause my cock to harden even more within my briefs.

I gaze up at her, our eyes meeting as I please her cunt, grazing my teeth against the little bundle of nerves. I reach my hands up and push her top off to reveal her perky tits awaiting my touch. I bring them into my hands and knead them as I flick my tongue in and out of her pussy; following the movement of her hips as she grinds up against me.

"William, please. I want more." Her voice shakes, telling me I'm close to getting her exactly where I want her. I release my hold on her tits and bring my fingers back down to her pussy. Inserting one in as I focus on sucking and teasing her clit. Eloise arches her back towards me. My name leaves her mouth repeatedly as I move my fingers faster, deep inside of her. Her pussy tightens around my fingers, only getting wetter and tighter the faster and rougher I fucked her with them.

"William, please. I need your cock inside me." Eloise bites down on her plump bottom lip that's been driving me crazy all fucking night. I couldn't help but picture how good the crown of my cock would look lying right on the entrance of that beautiful mouth of hers. "Be patient for me, baby," I whisper against her mound, leaving a kiss on the bundle of nerves that she keeps pushing closer to me.

I fucking loved seeing her like this.

Reckless.

Determined.

Yearnful.

Eloise's eyes darken as she looks down at me. This was probably the first time I had ever seen a hint of anger or frustration on her face.

"William, if you won't put your cock in me, the least you could do is eat my pussy right and make me come." Ferocity looked remarkable on Eloise. But no one spoke to me like that, especially not in bed.

I lift myself up, my hands trailing up to her hips before turning her around, her ass instinctively raised in the air. My hand smacks against her pale skin, and it immediately begins reddening.

Eloise lets out a yelp but doesn't complain, instead, she arches her back even more, pushing her ass closer to me as if asking for more.

"Fuck, you're a good girl, aren't you?" I praise, rubbing my hand against the smoothness of her round ass.

"That depends on how you treat me, sir."

Sir.

Fuck, I liked the sound of that.

My left hand travels down her spine, sending shivers

down her body as I stop at the nape of her neck. My fingers clenched around her hair, pulling her up in what had to be a torturous position.

Eloise lets out a hiss in pain but doesn't ask me to stop. I stop the rubbing motion on her ass and lead my hand down towards her cunt, that's currently dripping in need of my cock. But I wasn't going to give in that easily, even though my hard-on wanted nothing more than to be inside of her. I insert two fingers inside her sopping, wet pussy. A moan escapes Eloise's lips as she clenches her walls around my fingers.

"I like hearing those sweet moans coming out of your mouth, blondie." I quicken my pace, inserting a third finger to stretch her open.

Eloise's eyes meet mine as I continue to stretch out her cunt, pushing my fingers deeper into her. I had fucked many women, but something about Eloise made my heart falter.

That fucking stare.

Those fucking eyes.

She was sweet, sweet girls didn't get treated like this during sex. But, there was something about Eloise that made me want to corrupt the sweet billionaire heiress.

"Open your mouth and stick out your tongue," I order, as I feel her thighs beginning to clench and shake, letting me know that she's close. I remove a finger and quickly follow the same rapid movement, watching as Eloise comes undone. Before she can close her mouth on me, I let go of her hair and wrap my hand around her throat before hovering over her face, my spit running off of my lips onto her tongue.

Eloise breaks into a grin, biting her lip seductively as she falls onto the mattress coming down from her high. But I haven't forgotten how much she needs my cock in her.

I pull off my briefs and set myself behind her, giving her ass a hard slap. Eloise lets out a shriek, bringing her ass back up to me.

"Did I say you could rest?" I growl.

I grab my cock and place the tip against her entrance, gliding my hands up her back, I make my way back to the nape of her neck to bring her back up.

"Are you on the pill?" I ask, inching myself a little more inside of her.

"Yes, sir."

Fuck me.

That's all I needed to hear, I slam my cock deep within her pussy. Eloise's moans collide with my own as I slide in and out of her. Feeling her wet cunt grip onto my dick made me want to stay inside of her forever.

"William, harder." Eloise brings her ass back onto me, following the same rhythm as my thrust. I let go of her hair and hold onto her hips as I thrust even harder into her.

"Touch yourself, baby. I want to feel you come on my dick."

Eloise brings her hand down to her clit as she holds herself up, still maintaining her arched position. My movements begin to get faster as Eloise's moans fill my ears, her walls hugging my cock perfectly. It feels like this pussy is meant to be mine.

"Oh fuck, William, I can't." Eloise stops touching herself, but a slap on her ass has her back in the same position in seconds. I grab her neck and hover over her, bringing my lips to her ear.

"You're going to cum on my cock, Eloise. And I'm going to fill this pussy up the minute I feel those walls spasm around my cock. Am I understood?" I whisper, grazing my teeth against her earlobe.

"Oh god, yes." She squeals, rubbing her clit even faster, my thrust becoming even sloppier as I try to hold the load that's waiting to spill inside of her.

"Yes, what?" I growl.

"Yes, sir, I understand." Eloise shrieks, her walls tightening around me as she screams out my name. I release my load deep inside her cunt, something I had never once experienced. But now that I have it, I don't think I will be able to stop.

Eloise collapses on the bed, her body rising with each breath. Nothing is said as we both catch our breaths and then proceed to make it under the covers.

I lay on my side while Eloise lay on hers.

No words, no cuddles, no glances.

As if nothing had happened.

IT TOOK ELOISE A FEW MINUTES TO FALL INTO A DEEP slumber as I just stared at the ceiling fan above us. There was nothing to say or do that would've made our interaction any less awkward. And now that I was beginning to sober up, sleep became something difficult to obtain.

Every night I drank to forget, and it allowed me to drag myself back to the bungalow where I could finally fall asleep.

That hadn't been fair to Eloise, but then again, this marital contract wasn't meant to be fair to either of us.

But how could I complain? I had agreed to it. I broke off my engagement to marry Eloise just to save my father's company and to guarantee my position as the CEO once Eloise's father stepped down from it.

I somehow ended up winning even though I had to lose some. So maybe I didn't have the right to say it was unfair to me. Not when I could've stopped it.

I get up from the bed and retrieve the pants I had been wearing from the floor. I slide them up before making my way out onto the deck. The sea was calm compared to previous nights, but the darkness still made it look intimidating despite the lack of waves crashing.

Jasmine's ring remained in my pocket, and for something so tiny, it felt heavier than it should. I remove the ring from my pocket and peer down at the glimmering diamond. I had promised her forever and failed because of my greediness. Now, I had let my greediness affect Eloise. I had slept with her like she wasn't my wife.

I wasn't in love with her, and I didn't know if I ever would be. And sex would only complicate this relationship even more.

I vowed to be there for her, and I would be, but right now, I couldn't be a husband. Even though Eloise deserved it all, I just couldn't give her that right now.

The ring shone against the moonlight before I threw it into the ocean. I couldn't give Eloise what she deserves at this moment.

But this was a start.

Chapter Seven

Eloise

Not even a day had passed after we came back from our honeymoon before my mother began bombarding me with calls. After that night, I woke up in an empty bed. But I hadn't expected there to be a warm body embracing me the next morning. Not after the post-orgasm clarity had kicked in, and we had realized what we'd done.

Nothing was said between us. When we arrived back in New York, we were taken to the penthouse we had purchased. He had thought the home was of my choosing, but Mother had been the one to pick it out. I hated having such an enormous place, especially when most times, it would just be me in the home. The emptiness within it would just emphasize how lonely I really was.

The only good that came with the home was the room that my mother had made into a library for me. I hadn't even realized that my mother had noticed such things about me.

William hadn't seemed to mind the home; we both seemed to have come to an unspoken agreement when it came to choosing a bedroom. He had given me the master bedroom, while he decided to stay in the guest bedroom a couple doors down. I hadn't expected sex to resolve our issues, but I didn't think it would push us further back.

"Hello, mother," I mutter, picking up the unwanted call.

"Oh great, Eloise, you must tell me. How was everything? How were the Maldives?" She chirps.

"Fiji, mom. We went to Fiji."

"Hm, are you sure?"

"Well, being that I just came back from my trip there, I'd say I'm pretty sure." I rub my temples and take a seat on the enormous sofa that was quite ridiculous for a home of two.

"Then who was it that went to the Maldives? I could've sworn that someone had gone on a trip to the Maldives. Give me one second; let me ask your father... Harold!" I move the phone away from my ear to protect my eardrum from my mother's shriek.

"Mother, is this necessary right now?" I sigh into the phone's receiver, hoping that she'll take the hint at my disinterest in being on this call.

"Oh god, Eloise, it'll only take a second. Not everything is about you, you know? You can wait a few seconds to figure out who went to the Maldives, and then we can get back to your trip."

I don't bother to respond as she continues to shout for my

father on the other end of the line. I contemplated hanging up, but it would only earn me another phone call that would be much longer than the one I was currently on.

"That's right, it was the Bloomberg's daughter who went to the Maldives for her own honeymoon."

"Penelope got married?" I question, shocked at the fact that Penelope had found a man that met her standards. She had a new man wrapped around her finger every week. By the end of the week, she'd discard one and move on to the next.

"Yes, Eloise, must we gossip about other people's lives? I would much rather hear about your own time away with William. Tell me, how were the Maldives?"

I don't bother correcting her this time. The quicker I told her about my stay in Fiji or, in her case, the Maldives, the quicker I could end this call.

"The trip was beautiful, we enjoyed our stay there. The bungalow was nice, and the food—"

"Oh Lord, please tell me you didn't go outside your restrictions, Eloise. You know what carbs do to you." I swallow the lump that had begun to grow in my throat. I sigh into the receiver, counting to three in my head before a panic attack could arise.

"No, Mother, I didn't eat carbs," I mutter.

"Oh good, I was beginning to get worried."

I roll my eyes at my mother's fear of carbs and her even larger fear of me gaining weight.

"I mean, there's not much to it. We went out scuba diving and to the beach—"

"You went scuba diving? I specifically told Lorena not to

add that to your activities. Not for nothing ,honey, but swimwear isn't the best look on you and then adding scuba gear to it doesn't make it any better."

My mother had won many awards throughout her life, most of them being from beauty pageants. But one award that had been difficult for her to achieve was mother of the year. I wipe away the tears that run down my cheeks and clear my throat before speaking again.

"Mom, you know what? I think it's best if I go."

"Eloise, there is no need to cry. I'm sure William barely noticed how the swimsuit looked on you. Besides, what really matters is that you didn't drink. You know how your face begins to bloat, and you end up looking like one of those pufferfish." My mother lets out a hearty laugh as if she had told the joke of the year.

"Goodbye, mother." I hang the call up before breaking into a sob. My chest tightened with every breath I took.

It's okay, Eloise.

Breathe in, "one," *breathe out.*

Breathe in, "two," *breathe out.*

Breathe in, "three," *breathe out.*

"Eloise, is everything alright?" I open my eyes and find William's deep blue eyes looking down at me. I open my mouth to respond but nothing comes out but a sob.

"Fuck." William sits down on the sofa, bringing me closer to him as I continue to count my breathing. I feel the pins and needles develop in my hand, rising up my arm.

Oh God, this was a bad one.

I look around the room and begin focusing on different items. My breathing is picking up.

"Hey, hey, hey, Eloise." William's voice leads my eyes

back towards him. I focus on his lips as he begins to speak to me again.

"Hey, I'm right here. Breathe for me." William holds me in his arms, rubbing circles on my back for comfort. "Count with me, blondie."

Breathe in, "one," *breathe out.*

"Good, just like that." William soothes in my ear.

Breathe in, "two," *breathe out.*

"Just like that, blondie. Just focus on me, focus on my voice." William runs his other hand through my hair.

Breathe in, "three," *breathe out.*

We lay there together for what feels like hours,if not days, but I knew it had only been a couple of minutes. Despite having come down from my panic attack, William continued to comfort me.

"Do you get them often?" William murmurs as if he were aware that his regular tone of voice would cause the attack to rile back up again.

I open my eyes to peer up at him, I give him a nod, not yet feeling like speaking. I didn't want to talk about my panic attacks. I went to therapy for that. I was doing well at controlling them for the most part, my parents just had a way of making them worse.

"Would you like to talk about it?" William asks.

"Not really." I manage to croak, clearing my throat right after.

I try lifting myself, but William puts his arm over me, stopping me from leaving. "I have nowhere to be." He clears his throat and slides his hand into mine.

"You can stay if you'd like. I won't ask you any more questions. When you feel like speaking about it, I'll be here."

William's words had my heart skipping a beat and even though his words seemed friendly and caring I had to remind myself that William and I would never work out.

I wasn't who he wanted. Nevertheless, I took him up on his offer and laid back down in his embrace. Later that night I woke up tucked within the warm sheets of my bed.

Chapter Eight

Eloise

I paced back and forth across the living room of my home, trying my best not to pick at the gel manicure I had recently gotten done. My mind was in a complete disarray after the other night, and what made it worse was that after the incident with William I hadn't seen him again the rest of the week.

I knew he arrived home after ten every night, and then he would leave at six every morning. If my drunk state of mind on our honeymoon hadn't scared him off, my panic attack sure as hell did. I can't believe I didn't think of taking the call in the privacy of my own room. My cheeks begin to heat up at just the thought of the embarrassment that I had gone through.

"Do you think he's cheating?" Charlotte suggests, her

voice low as if the tone would make the idea of him cheating more bearable.

"Already?" I utter, taking a seat right next to her on the couch.

Had I scared him off enough to provoke cheating?

No, William wouldn't do that. He had stayed loyal to Jasmine for many years, and even when he was forced to take on a relationship with me, he had done the right thing and broken things off.

Not that she had deserved it.

But still, he had chosen a contract over someone he loved. And although I was his wife, I wasn't someone he loved. So what was stopping him from doing whatever he wanted?

"I don't think there's an actual time or best moment for when a person can cheat on their significant other." Charlotte rubs circles on my back as I try not to freak out over something that isn't even real yet.

"What do I do?" I sigh and lay my head on Charlotte's shoulder as she continues to comfort me.

"I'm so sorry, Eloise." I knew Charlotte didn't have the answers, but I didn't want her pity either. I wanted her anger and her confidence. I wanted her advice.

"Should I stay up and wait for him tonight?"

"And say what? Dinner got cold on the table? You two don't even have dinner together." Charlotte reasons, pushing her long hair to the side. If I had Charlotte's hair and curves, I probably wouldn't have to sit and worry about my husband staying out all night. Before I can help myself, my eyes begin to brim with tears.

"No, no, no, don't cry." Charlotte brings me into her arms, rubbing circles on my back to soothe me.

"My life is a mess, Charlotte. My wedding was horrendous, I didn't even get to marry the man that I loved, I don't even want to speak about that honeymoon, and now my husband is ignoring me instead of trying to make things work." Charlotte continues to coo and tries to soothe me as I try my best to control my emotions..

I had thought that marriage would be my escape to happiness, that I would somehow be gone from my parent's demands and I'd be happy with someone that actually cared about me. Someone that wanted a future with me. But instead, I only married someone that wanted to be part of my family, who wanted my father's business.

"Do you want me to stay over? We can stay up late and wait for him to arrive. That way he won't question why you're waiting up for him. As soon as he arrives I'll leave and you two can talk to one another." I move away from Charlotte's embrace and take a moment to really think things through before lifting myself back up.

"No, I have to get over this. Crying won't solve any of my issues, and neither will thinking about the possibilities. I'm his wife, I need to speak to him." I walk over to the bathroom to fix my appearance and. Charlotte quickly follows and leans against the bathroom's vanity as I try to fix what I can.

"So, does this mean you're going to confront him when he comes home?" Charlotte asks.

I peer over at her from the mirror after adding the last swipe of mascara to my eyelashes. "No, it means I'm heading over to the office now to confront him." I drop the mascara back into my makeup bag before zipping it up and dropping it back into the drawer of the vanity.

Charlotte's eyes practically jolt out of her eyes at my declaration. "Are you sure that's a good idea?" Charlotte questions, following me out the door.

"Charlotte, we are talking about a man who does nothing but work and socializes with his male coworkers on days that he isn't working. If he's seeing anyone, it's definitely someone from his office." As much as it killed me to come to that conclusion it was also the only rational reasoning I could find. Besides, when my own father was out late at night, it was known that he was in hotel rooms or just back at the office with his secretary. And even though my memory was a bit hazy from that night at the bar I could've sworn William had promised he'd never do such a thing.

But, the one good thing my mother taught me was to never confide in a man. They'll be the first to betray you, especially after they've taken all that they can from you. And she had said that to me after downing two bottles of chardonnay, I could only imagine what my father had done.

"I guess that makes sense," Charlotte mumbles to herself as we wait for the elevator.

"But are you sure that this is what you want to do?" The elevator door opens as I look at Charlotte.

"I refuse to end up like my mother."

Charlotte reaches over and grabs ahold of my hand, leading me into the elevator.

"Then let's go find his sorry ass."

I RUSH THROUGH THE HALLS OF THE MAIN FLOOR, trying to get inside the elevators quick enough before I change my mind. Charlotte had given me a pep-talk on our way over here. But now that I was so close to William's office my confidence was beginning to diminish.

"Oh no, I know that face." Charlotte groans, holding on tightly to my hand, almost as if she were afraid that I'd turn around and run back home. "You can't turn back now, remember why you're here, Eloise. You deserve respect." Charlotte encourages, pulling me into the elevator before the doors can even open fully.

"I know, I'm just nervous. A part of me almost feels as if I don't have any right to ask him what he's been doing. We aren't really together." I bite the inside of my cheek to distract myself from the thoughts that are currently running through my head.

What if this was a stupid idea?

"A marriage license is as real as it gets, Eloise. He made a vow, in other words, a contract. And he, as a businessman, should know the importance of following said contract." Charlotte lectures as the elevator doors open onto William's floor.

Charlotte pulls me out of the elevator and takes a look at the large desk over to the right that has a curvaceous redhead that had to only be a few years older than me, if that.

"Oh my god," the words leave my lips as I process the truth. "I think I may vomit."

I needed to get out of here, this was a mistake. The last thing I needed to do was cause a scene with my panic attacks. I turn back towards the elevator but Charlotte only pulls me back to her side.

"Don't get ahead of yourself, Eloise. Just because his secretary is pretty means nothing. The only way you'll know the truth is by asking him." Charlotte's reasoning makes me relax a bit, even though a voice in the back of my mind, which I like to call a woman's intuition, somehow knew the truth already.

Even if William was a good man, he wasn't a man in love. And just because a man isn't in love doesn't mean he doesn't have desires. And that redhead looked like she could fulfill all of William's desires.

"Well, don't just stand there. Walk over there and demand to see your husband." Charlotte pushes me forward, smacking my butt for reinforcement. I look back at her arching a brow to question her odd behavior.

"It felt right," Charlotte responds with a shrug.

I can't help but chuckle at her nonsense. But, that nonsense was making me feel a bit better about marching over there to ask to speak to William. I take a few steps, stopping right in front of the secretary's desk. She's typing away at her computer and from the looks of it, she might not have a great peripheral vision because she doesn't question me.

I clear my throat, but she continues typing; ignoring my presence completely. So maybe her peripheral vision was just fine.

"Hello," I sing, awaiting a response from the redheaded woman. The clicking of her keyboard finally comes to a halt as she turns over to face me.

"Do you have an appointment?" She asks her voice monotone, her demeanor cold.

"No, I'm—"

"No appointment, no meeting." She looks back at her computer, completely ignoring my presence again.

Is this how she spoke to everyone, or was this just exclusively for me?

"Right, but I'm—"

"God," The redhead turns back to me, her eyes looking anything but friendly. Her dark stare held anger and annoyance.

"If you don't walk back to where you came from lady I will call security." She threatens.

I give her a slow nod, watching as her shoulders relax and she turns back to her computer to ignore me.

If this was how William's secretary always acted with other visitors, then William would most definitely keep her for reasons other than her work ethic.

I look at the giant doors that are a few feet away from the desk. If I remembered correctly from previous visits, that was William's office. I look back over at the secretary, who now seemed to be thoroughly entertained by whatever email she had immersed herself in. Obviously, it was more important than speaking to me, let alone hearing me out.

I look back at the door one last time before making a run over to William's office and opening the door. The secretary's footsteps are right behind me, but she doesn't make it enough to stop me from entering the door.

"Eloise?" William questions, looking down at the time and back over at me. Almost as if he had been expecting me.

"Is everything okay?" William stands up from his chair and looks over at me, now frozen in my spot.

His secretary runs in and stops directly between William and I. She reaches over, setting her hand on William's arm, and inclines her chest forward showing more cleavage than I ever could.

"I'm so sorry Mr. Wren, I told her you were busy but she just ran in here." Somehow even when apologizing she made her voice sound seductive. I look between William and her, the boiling anger of seeing the two ate away at my anxiety. As much as a part of me thought it wasn't true, the way William looked at his secretary with those same lustful eyes I saw on our honeymoon told me all I needed to know.

"That's alright, Calliope. Eloise is my wife, she's allowed to enter at any time." Calliope takes a sudden step back, cheeks heating up at my introduction.

"Oh, I didn't know, I'm s—"

"Of course you didn't. You didn't give me a chance to speak," I remark.

Calliope opens her mouth to respond but William steps forward, gesturing her off to the side. "Calliope, give us a moment, will you?" He asks, pushing her towards the door and closing it shut as soon as she's out of the room. William stands there for a moment, facing the door. I don't say anything. Instead I wait with him. He knows he's dug his own grave and now I'm waiting for him to get in it. I walk over to his desk and take a seat right on it as he takes his time looking for a stupid excuse.

"Eloise," He groans, turning himself back around to look at me.

"William," I reply.

William lets out a puff of air before walking over to his desk and taking a seat on his chair.

"What are you doing here?" He asks, leaning back to look up at me. And for some reason, looking down at him like this, calm but burning with anger on the inside made me feel godly.

"A wife can't stop to visit her husband at work?" I question, the sarcasm in my voice not going unnoticed.

"Of course, but then again, I barely see my wife at home—"

"Well, who's fault is that?" I bite down on my lip to stop myself from exploding from anger.

He had made a promise to me on our honeymoon.

Hell, he had made a vow at our wedding.

"Eloise—"

"I refuse to be like my mother, William. You don't have to love me, I'm aware that you never will. But I deserve respect."

William's hand falls onto my bare knee and I cursed myself for having worn a skirt today. "I understand that I've been a little distant, but I don't think that would be seen as disrespectful." William reasons.

"Is fucking your secretary respectful?" I blurt out, unable to suppress my anger. William's hold on my knee tightens as he looks at me..

"How did you find out?" William asks, his eyes look sorrowful but I wouldn't say there's any remorse. He seems to be more upset about having been caught than cheating.

"I'm not an idiot, nor am I blind." I smack his wrist away

from my leg and get up from the desk to leave. There was nothing else I had to say, not after his admission. But, William gets up and cages me in between his arms. I try pushing his arm away to leave but he doesn't budge.

"William, let me go. This was hurtful enough." I try holding back any tears that are daring to escape. Somehow I kept finding myself in vulnerable moments with William and I wouldn't give him that anymore. William grabs my face and makes me look right at him.

"Listen to me, blondie." He says, his voice calm but stern.

"Don't call me that." I spit.

He didn't have the right to call me any pet names, not when he was treating me like this.

"Eloise, it isn't what you think." He whispers as if his tone would somehow calm me down.

"So, you didn't fuck her?" William winces and takes a moment to contemplate his response.

"Yes, but not while we were together." His hands remain on my cheek, rubbing the pad of his thumb across my skin. At some point, William's touch had become comforting and I wasn't sure when that had happened but just that it felt good to have someone bring me that peace.

"Well, not while we were married." He corrects, cringing at his admission.

"So, you had a relationship with her before we got married?" I ask, trying to get his story straight.

"Yes, but after we got married everything has remained civil between the two of us. She's just my secretary." He assures.

"Oh, she's civil, alright." I wasn't forgetting how close she seemed to get to him, and she definitely owned looser and less revealing clothes.

"Eloise, you can trust me. I'm sorry for being distant, this is all new to me. But, I promise that cheating will never be something that you have to fear." William spreads his fingers to the back of my hair massaging my scalp, relaxing me from my mind. This had been the closest we had gotten to one another since my panic attack.

"William, she practically flaunted her body at you right in front of me," I mutter, rolling my eyes at his ignorance. It didn't matter if I trusted him or not. Celeste had already gotten a piece of William and now she was motivated to take the whole thing.

"She didn't know you were my wife." As soon as the words leave William's mouth, I know he's already realized how much of an idiot he's being. For someone who went to MIT he sure as hell lacked comprehension.

"And that's supposed to make it better? That she respects that you're *my* husband when I'm around but throws herself at you when I'm back home wondering where you are?" William's jaw tightens as he stares down at me with that hypnotizing stare. A few seconds pass before William finally speaks.

"You're right," William says, extending himself over to the phone placed on the desk and dialing a number.

Was that all he had to say?

"Yes, Mr. Wren?" Calliope's voice echoes through the receiver, I shoot a look at William, arching up an eyebrow to question him. But William ignores my gesture as he speaks with Celeste.

"Would you mind coming in to speak with me for a

second?" William asks, but by his tone I was sure that Calliope understood that it was a demand. It doesn't take much time for her to saunter in.

"You wanted to see me, sir?" She asks as she enters the room to stand right in front of the desk. William's hand slides slightly up my leg and he gives my knee a firm squeeze.

"Calliope, you can pack your things up today and go." William's voice, along with his features are stern and intimidating, but even with that, Celeste still has the balls to question him.

"Is this because I didn't know she was your wife?" She questions, throwing a look of disgust my way.

"That and some, you can leave now." William waves a hand at her as she walks away, the anger dually noted by the clacking of her heels and the slamming of the door on her way out.

William's hand remains on my knee, but I don't miss the slight shift upward as he grasps onto my thigh. If this man thought I was going to give him anything at this moment, he was mistaken.

"I'm sorry, Eloise."

I clench my legs and take a deep breath before removing myself off his desk. But William is quick to get up and block me. I don't let a word escape my lips as I stare up at him. I had nothing else to say but I also didn't want to risk him hearing my words wobble or voice croak.

He had fired his secretary, I hadn't asked him to, but he did. It had been a battle my mother had lost with my father.

"Eloise?" William asks, forcing me to respond.

"Yes?" I say, managing not to croak.

"I should have done that a long while ago and I'm sorry it

took you having to come here hurt by my distance and actions for it to be done. For that I'm sorry and I promise I'll do better because Eloise you deserve better." William's face moves in closer to me, his lips hovering extremely close over mine. But right before either one of us could get any closer to touch William backs away, allowing me to leave.

I clear my throat and back away from the desk, not exactly sure of what to say or do.

"I'll see you at home." Is the only thing I could muster out of my brain before walking away.

Before the door closes behind me, I hear William chuckle as he replies, "I'll see you at home, blondie."

I walk past the secretary desk where Calliope's stare practically shoots daggers at me. Charlotte is precisely in the same spot that I left her in before, a proud smile etched on her face.

"I can't believe he fired her." She whispers, entangling her arm around mine. "Wait, does that mean he cheated on you?" The smile falling instantly from her face.

"No, not really." I say, pressing the button for the elevator. The doors open instantly as we enter. "They had a thing before William and I were married. He promised that nothing ever happened afterward."

And I was going to trust and believe him.

"Well he must definitely like you if it only took one visit from you for him to fire her." I take in Charlotte's words but can't help to feel uneasy about the thought of William liking me.

"I wouldn't say he likes me, I think he just respects me."

Charlotte gives me a shrug as we exit the elevator together.

"Whatever it is, our fathers could surely learn a thing or two from him." Charlotte mumbles.

A smile forms on my lips at the thought of William being a better husband than what I had grown up seeing.

William was truly nothing like my father.

And that meant I wouldn't end up like my mother.

Chapter Nine

Present

Work had been hectic with the rumors that were circling around. Eloise's father, Harold, was set to retire by the end of this year and news of his retirement would be announced soon. If anyone were to know first it would be me. Being that our contract stated that once I married Eloise I would take over as CEO once he retired.

Despite the agreement I knew that I was perfect for the position. I had worked my ass off to get to where I was. The only reason we had to merge our companies was because my father refused to listen to me when it came to making economic decisions which later caused us to begin drowning in debt.

Harold took his chance at offering us the merger plan, but he wouldn't agree to give his business to anyone after his retirement. I graduated from MIT and proceeded to get my MBA at NYU.

I had made a name for myself within corporate America, and I was going to make sure I maintained it.

The knocking at my door turned me away from the multitude of files on my desk that I had to work through. "Come in," I mutter, knowing the only person that would be bothering me during work hours would be Liam.

On cue the man walks in. His blonde hair tied in a bun, his tattoos covered by his suit. He takes a seat in front of my desk, sending me a cheeky smile that had most of the girls in the office in his bed in seconds.

He was notoriously known for being the office's playboy, but in the men's eyes, he was notoriously known for being a king with numbers, which made his position as CFO deserving.

"I don't have time for you today." Liam raises his brow at me and looks at the mess on my desk.

"Maybe if you were a tad bit organized you would have all the time in the world." I roll my eyes, leaning back in my chair, giving into his presence.

"What can I do for you?"

"Word around the office is that you're going up the ladder very soon." Liam leans back in his chair, his stare taunting me as if he knew something I didn't.

"Do you know something that I don't, Liam?" I highly doubted Harold would've told him before he had mentioned it to me.

"Harold's secretary or mistress, whichever you prefer to

see her as let it slip that he was leaving soon. He told her that it was over and that he would be focusing his time on his family." Liam gives me a smug smirk, knowing that if the words came out of Lizzie herself, then they were likely to be true.

"I don't even want to know what situation you were in with Lizzie for her to be spewing out this information." I mutter in disgust.

The last thing I wanted to know was that my close friend was fucking my father-in-law's mistress.

"Listen, her and Harold are finished. So, I took that opportunity to be there for my friend and figure out what the intel was." Liam sputes.

No matter what he said, it didn't matter. As long as he stayed away from Eloise I didn't care who Liam fucked. And whatever he spewed out was bullshit because he had been fucking Lizzie way before Harold ended their relationship. This time Lizzie just let some information slip.

But if the rumors were true that's probably why Eloise's parents had been so persistent on Eloise getting pregnant. Maybe Harold just wanted something that guaranteed his bloodline would still be a part of this company after he resigned.

But, if a grandchild was what he wanted, he was going to have to continue to wait.

Liam readjusts his suit as he gets up from the chair. He is obviously done with the conversation after saying what he came here to reveal.

"Also, would it kill you to have a female secretary? Victor's fine, but I miss Calliope." Liam mutters.

I fired Calliope after Eloise had found out about our

past. I then hired Victor who had worked in our mail room prior to taking up this position to remove any worry that Eloise might have about another woman taking the position as my new secretary. The last thing I wanted was to make Eloise feel like she wasn't worth more than my past flings. She was more important than any of them.

"I bet you still have her number, just call her when you're feeling lonely because Victor's staying." Liam only gives me a sly grin before getting up and walking away. But before he opens the door he looks back over at me with a knowing smirk.

"What is it? Spit it out."

"You know, I thought that you were whipped when you were with Jasmine. But now that you're married to Eloise, I think you're *really* whipped."

I let out a scoff as I turned back to my tasks, but the only two things running around in my mind are that I'm about to become CEO and my marriage might take a turn for the better.

"Vermont?" I offered this woman to go anywhere in the world for our one-year anniversary and she chose Vermont. I bring the glass of wine to my lips, the rim of the glass cutting off my view of her.

"Yeah, I've never been and I heard it's just as beautiful and fun in the summer as it is in the winter." Eloise's voice is soft and subtle, as if she needed to be in order for me to agree on this trip.

"If Vermont is what you want, then it's where we'll go." I reason. I didn't care where Eloise and I went as long as we were far away from her fucking parents. It had been awhile since I last had to talk Eloise down from a panic attack caused by them and I was going to make sure that I didn't have to do it again.

"Do you have an itinerary in mind?" I ask, curious as to what the hell she sees in Vermont. Eloise takes a bite of her fish, humming with satisfaction before speaking.

"Well, I know a plane is much quicker, but what if we drive there?" She pouts, looking at me with those crystal blue eyes that made you want to grant her all of her wishes.

"Like a road trip?" I ask for clarification.

Eloise's face beams with joyousness as she nods her head at me, "Yeah, I think I'd enjoy a road trip."

I let out a chuckle at her bubbly response. Eloise was a gem in the midst of all the piles of rocks. And I was forever grateful for whatever higher being granted her as my wife. I could have been stuck with a prissy heiress who only cared about having an heir and a birkin.

"Where would you have wanted to go on our honeymoon, if you had been given the chance to choose?" The question was out of my mouth before I could stop myself. I'm not sure why I cared to know. It's not like we could turn back time and choose a different destination.

Eloise tilts her head to the side in thought, "Hm, I haven't really thought about that." Her lips curl into a smile as she looks over at me, taking her bottom lip in between her teeth, which she often did when deep in thought.

But for some reason, this time around, it caused an uncomfortable tightening in my pants.

"You must've had something in mind at the time." I state, curious to pick at her mind.

Eloise lifts her brow up as if what I had said was an absurdity. "Far from it, not that you're a bad husband or anything. But at the time I wasn't really inclined to marry you. In fact I was hoping we wouldn't make it to the altar, let alone the honeymoon."

I can't help but let out a laugh at Eloise's bluntness, her own laugh joining in with mine. And something about our boisterous laughter colliding with one another felt melodious.

Once our laughs subside, the silence becomes comforting, or maybe that's just her stare from across the table.

"But I'm not upset that we did make it to the altar." Eloise says, so low that I could barely catch the words.

"Me too." I whisper back before continuing to eat my dinner.

"If a road trip is what you want, then it's what you'll get, and I promise this time around, our honeymoon will be much more enjoyable."

Eloise looks back down to her plate, in efforts of hiding her blushing cheeks from me. "I don't know." She says, clearing her throat before looking back at me. "Our last honeymoon wasn't non-enjoyable, in fact I can think of a couple, or at least *one* thing that I enjoyed from it." Eloise brings her lip in between her teeth and I would've given up all my assets to know what exactly she was thinking about at this moment.

"I think I can too, blondie." I tease.

This time, Eloise holds her stare as her cheeks turn into the most beautiful shade of pink. Eloise had made her first move in our game of chess, and I was more than willing to continue playing.

Regardless, I think both of us would come out winning.

Chapter Ten

Eloise

Nine Months Ago

I had tried my best to ignore Ulysses as much as possible. But ignoring Ulysses meant that I'd also be ignoring Charlotte. They weren't twins but they might as well have been because those two were always attached to the hip. We were all close in age which forced us into the same groups of friends when we would hangout. But even if it weren't for that, those two would still be inseparable.

I often wondered if Ulysses and I would've even dated if it weren't for Charlotte. We didn't have many common interests, and I doubt we'd run in the same circles if I didn't have Charlotte in my life.

Ulysses liked to say that he would've spotted me at a

restaurant or family function and that I would've caught his attention immediately.

"I don't have to like the same things as you to notice your beauty, babe." Is what he said when I asked him about the possibility of having never been together if it weren't for Charlotte and I's friendship.

Ulysses wasn't someone I was in love with, or maybe I was. I guess he would be the closest thing. But it was nothing like the romance books or poems that I'd read. If anything, Ulysses had been a comfort. He was someone I was friends with and cared deeply about. He was also someone my parents would agree to me being with.

That was until William submitted his resume to my father. And that resume must've looked phenomenal because it got my father's stamp of approval to marry me off. When my father had told me I would marry William I had rushed to Ulysses and ripped off the bandaid. Maybe that hadn't been fair to him. But, there was no reason in trailing him along, not when my father had already begun putting together dates for William and I.

He had been upset with me more than he was with my father. "You should've fought for us; you should've fought for me." He had screamed, and I still remembered the tears in his eyes as he said it. I hadn't realized that Ulysses had even cared for me like that. And even though his anger had hurt me, he was right to feel that way and shout at me because he was right.

I should've fought for him. If I had truly loved him I would've denied my parents. But, the yearning of wanting to satisfy my parents wishes had been more potent than wanting to continue a relationship with Ulysses.

No matter how much I think back to the day of our break up it won't change a thing. And it definitely won't change the fact that William and I are headed to Charlotte's birthday event. An event that I couldn't skip without Charlotte being royally pissed at me.

"I like the way you look in blue." I turn to face William, who is sitting beside me in the car. He usually drove himself everywhere, I on the other hand depended on our driver, Cory or William to take me from my place to place.

I was surprised that William had decided to allow Cory to drive us tonight. But it was probably the best option for parking, which was always horrendous for these events. Charlotte was known for putting together the most extravagant birthday parties for herself. She'd offered to throw me one but any chance I got where there was little attention on me I would take. So, birthday parties were out of the picture for me.

This year she rented out a whole rooftop of a club in the city. At first I was going to go alone but Dev rangled William into going.

"Thank you, you look nice," I reply, tugging at the ends of my dress, scared of it riding up too much.

William looked... sexy.

He was wearing a black dress shirt that was open around his chest. The silver chain he wore occasionally glimmered in the light. But his slicked-back hair and beard were what tied him together.

Of course, after the honeymoon, I craved William to be my husband.

Like an *actual* husband.

One that would...

Hold me.

Kiss me.

Fuck me.

"Just nice?" William teases, adjusting the collar of his shirt as the car comes to a stop.

A smirk plays on his lips as he looks down at me.

"Okay." I shrug, sending him a smirk of my own. "You look sexy."

William lifts his brows at my sudden courage to say what's on my mind rather than keeping it in. Before William can say anything, Cory opens his car door. I can instantly hear the loud music and the chatter coming from outside the place.

William steps out of the car and extends his hand out for me to take. I take his hand and exit the car. I move to the side while William takes a second to speak to Cory before coming back to my side.

"Bye, Cory." I wave as he makes his way back to the driver's seat.

"Bye, Miss Wren."

I chuckle, shaking my head at his reply.

"Is our last name not to your liking?" William asks. He brings his arm around my waist as we begin walking towards the entrance of the club.

"Just not used to it; I also don't think I like being called Miss all that much."

It made me feel older than I was. I also didn't want to be seen as just William's wife. I was more than Miss Wren. And even though Cory didn't mean to demote me into just being somebody's wife, in this society it seemed to catch on.

"You'll get used to it, but Eloise Wren sounds just as sexy as I look."

My cheeks blush at his reference to my compliment. William walks us to the security by the doors and lets him know our names. The security guy lets us in, pointing us towards the elevators that lead to the rooftop. William presses the elevators button before peering back down at me.

"You know, I think I like the way pink looks on you too."

I furrow my eyebrows at his statement before looking back down at my outfit.

"But I'm not wearing—"

William skims his knuckles against my cheek and immediately, I'm aware that he's referencing my beet red cheeks.

I groan and push his arm away, walking into the now-open elevator.

"So, what do these parties contain?" William presses the button to the rooftop and leans back onto the elevator wall, his eyes dragging up and down my body. This dress must've captivated him more than I thought.

"The same as any other party, I guess. Drinks, music, dancing, cake, and sometimes if you're lucky sex." The last one comes out as more of a joke, but the darkening in William's eyes sets me back a bit.

"And?"

"And, what?" I ask, unsure of what he is getting at.

"Am I lucky?" He asks, the doors of the elevator ding open and we're met with the loudness of the music. I almost freeze in my spot, but instead I follow William out the door before he turns to look at me.

"Well you're married to me, so I'd say you hit the jackpot." I joke. Hoping it would get me out of this flirtatious situation that I'd thrown myself into.

But William takes that as an opening to check me out again. His eyes moving up from my legs, stopping at my cleavage, before finally meeting my eyes.

"I'd say you're more than right, blondie." William takes a step closer to me, and I incline forward instinctively.

"You're here!" Charlotte pushes herself between William and I.

"Of course! I would never miss your birthday." Charlotte wraps her arms around me, bringing me into a hug. In front of me I see Dev walk up and talk to William, which distracts him from staring at me.

"I know you wouldn't miss it, but I know things have been awkward with Ulysses!" Charlotte shouts over the music and it was loud enough to get William's attention again.

"What do you mean? We're fine. There's no awkwardness here." I shift my eyes between her and William, hoping that she'd get the point and stop talking about her brother in front of my husband. Charlotte looks at me in a lost stare.

She was definitely drunk.

"I don't know. You guys just seem a bit off. You know he still asks about you. He really loved you." Dev brings his hands to Charlotte's shoulders, pulling her towards his chest.

"Hey, buttercup, why don't we go dance for a bit and let Eloise and William get a drink."

Thank you, Dev, for the drink.

Charlotte pouts at Dev before looking back at me. "But I wanted to dance with Eloise, like old times."

I know William and I had arrived a bit late, but not that late that she would already have been drunk. But Charlotte always had the time of her life at her parties.

"Let me get a drink, and I'll meet you on the floor," I tell her, scooting closer to William, who had an arm out for me already.

Charlotte lets out a sigh and lies against Dev's chest. "Fine Dev, let's go dance until Eloise comes and steals me from your arms."

"You better watch out, Dev." I tease. Dev turns and gives me a playful smile in return.

"What do you want to drink?" William asks, pulling me towards the bar.

"Anything with tequila." Just as the words leave my mouth a body bumps up against me, pushing me right into William.

William grabs my waist to steady me.

"Watch it, you dick." William barks at the very drunk blonde man that's just pushed me into him.

"Damn, sorry man." The overly drunk blond slurs before walking away.

"Who is that?" William asks, pulling me closer to the bar, away from all the drunk and high people surrounding us.

"I don't know, most of the people here aren't really people I socialize with." It's not like I socialized with many people besides Charlotte in the first place.

"Is that why you dated Ulysses?" My eyes practically bulge out at Willliam's upfront question.

What did Ulysses have to do with any of this?

"I dated Ulysses because he liked me and I liked him." I retort.

It had been easier to talk to him because we practically grew up together, but that didn't mean that I only dated him because of that. Ulysses was a good friend and an even better boyfriend. Maybe I wasn't in love with him, but most people in our society were almost never in love, rather just together for business purposes or to have children.

The way I saw it, Ulysses would be a better man to marry than an old man looking to have kids or grab at my father's money.

"And now?" William asks, grabbing ahold of our drinks that he had ordered from the bartender and passing me one.

"And now I'm married, so those feelings are irrelevant." I utter in annoyance.

"You know William, you don't get to ask me these questions. Not when just a couple weeks before our wedding you were still pining over your ex. And only a few weeks ago did you just fire the secretary that you had been sleeping with prior to our marriage. I know my position and requirements in this marriage. So, if you're trying to question my relationship with Ulysses the only thing I can say is that we are friends. And you'll just have to deal with it." I shoot back the drink in hand before slamming it down on the counter and walking away.

I came here to celebrate Charlotte's birthday, not to have an argument with my husband. I move through the crowd, bumping into a few people before making my way towards the huddle in the booth.

"Eloise!" Charlotte practically jumps off her chair and

wraps her arms around me once again. I bring her into a tight hug before pulling away and encouraging her to take a seat back down in the booth, even though she's in the mood to dance.

"I'm so happy you're here." She slurs.

"So you said before." I tease.

"I'm happy you're here too." A deep voice murmurs from behind me. I turn around to face Ulysses, who's taken a seat right beside me. Probably a little too close than exes should be. Dev sits on the other side of Charlotte handing her more water each chance he can get.

"Hi," is all I manage to say.

"Hi," he mimics, a sly grin appearing on his face.

I open my mouth to say something, but nothing seems to come out.

What do you say to your ex, who you broke things off with to marry someone else?

"How's married life?" Ulysses asks, but the pain in his eyes doesn't go unnoticed. My chest tightens and I force myself to reach for a deep breath. This was precisely what I had been trying to prevent. I knew things needed to go back to normal, but that didn't mean that it would make this interaction any less awkward and painful.

"It's alright, William's a good man."

And despite his caveman tendencies, he was a good husband. Maybe there was little affection in our relationship, but that type of connection had to develop over time rather than being a product of tequila shots.

"Better husband than I would've been?" Ulysses questions, bringing himself closer to me.

"Ulysses." Dev's voice sounds different than what I'm used to hearing. It sounds stern and authoritative like William's does when he's speaking to his workers... or when he's making me come.

"It's just a question," Ulysses mutters, holding up his hands in defense. His eyes move away from Dev, back to me.

"Come dance with me." It's not a question, but rather a statement.

"I don't think that's a good idea." I bite my lip nervously and look around the crowd, trying to spot William. But he's nowhere to be seen.

"I don't—"

"Yes! Let's dance! The four of us like old times!" Charlotte pushes Ulysses and I out of the booth and walks us over to the crowd of dancing people that are probably too intoxicated to remember this party tomorrow.

I pull Charlotte to the side to avoid having to be cornered by Ulysses, though it becomes a little challenging when Dev obviously wants to have his turn dancing with his girlfriend. But I'm able to dance through a couple of songs with her before feeling Ulysses up against me.

"Are you ignoring me?" He asks, this time, I can smell the liquor on his breath. I turn around to face him, his hands finding themselves around my waist. But I'm quick to tug them off.

"I'm married," I mutter, making sure that if he can't tell by my voice he can definitely tell by my face that I'm annoyed with his invasiveness.

"But you're not in love." He remarks.

He had me at that one.

But respect had nothing to do with love.

"Love doesn't develop overnight."

Ulysses raises a brow, shocked by my words.

"You can't possibly believe that this marriage will end in a love story."

I take a step back at the harshness of his voice, a tone that felt odd coming out of Ulysses.

"You don't know anything," I utter.

I turn to walk away but his hand grabs ahold of my wrist, pulling me back to him. My body slamming into his hardened chest.

"Did you sleep with him?" The question comes out meek and his eyes hold hope for my answer. That wasn't a question he should be asking, but if roles were reversed I'd be more than curious to know if he had moved on. Ulysses's hand gently caresses my cheek, awaiting my response.

"I don't think this is appropriate." I manage to say, removing his hands from my body. This wasn't a conversation to be had in a club in the middle of a dance floor. It actually wasn't a conversation we should be having at all.

God, I hope no one had taken a picture of us.

This would look terrible for William and I. And I don't even want to know what my parents would begin to think or say. That would be a lecture of a lifetime. I turn away, leaving Ulysses alone in the crowd. I had to find William and apologize for my outburst earlier. He had been right and I was just upset because... because why?

Because he had every right to question my relationship with Ulysses?

I walk around the perimeter of the rooftop, searching for William but he's nowhere to be seen. I stop by the opened elevator doors before turning my head to see him staring at me from the elevator. The doors begin to close and before I can mutter a word he beats me to it.

"You're married now, huh? Doesn't quite look like it."

Those words hit like a punch in the face, but I couldn't say that I didn't deserve them. And just like that, somehow our step forward took a million steps back.

Chapter Eleven

Eloise

After William had left last night I only stayed until Charlotte received her cake and left right after. And as mad as William looked he still managed to send me a text to let me know that Cory would be waiting downstairs for me. When I got home I saw the light peek from under the door that led into his study. I had contemplated knocking on the door to speak with him. But ultimately decided that the last thing William wanted to do was talk to me.

But that didn't stop me from knocking on the door this morning, but no response came from the other side.

Was he the type to give the silent treatment when upset?

As much as it would sting to be ignored by an angry William for days, I was used to that sort of treatment from my father. I would just have to wait until he got over it.

Despite not getting a response I open the door to his study and walk in. But William wasn't there. I look over at the working antique clock his father had gifted him in the corner of the room to read the time.

I was right; it was ten in the morning, and by this time, William was already in here working.

Had he even slept at home last night? Maybe he had gotten so upset by my antics at the club that I basically pushed him into someone else's bed. Without even thinking, I stomp over to his bedroom, preparing my mind to find the unslept in bed.

My chest begins to tighten with every step I take towards his bedroom.

Fuck, not a panic attack, not now.

I swing the bedroom door open, revealing an unmade bed. I step in and examine the bed. Only one side had been slept in, the other side was completely neat and untouched. The tightness in my chest begins to diminish as the lingering thoughts of William being in bed with someone else last night leave my mind.

"I didn't hear you knock." William's voice sounds from behind me, turning me away from his bed to look straight at him. He walks out of the bathroom, a towel held dangerously low around his waist. He brings a hand across his wet hair, sliding it back completely, away from his face.

"I thought..." I linger on the second unsure of what to say.

What did I think?

That he had gone out and been with someone else? That he realized that this marriage wasn't worth it, that I wasn't worth it?

"You thought what?" William asks, his voice low and his face stoic.

"It's ten, and you weren't in your study; I was worried that something had happened." I manage to say, trying to play it off as a worried wife rather than a jealous one.

"Worried that something had happened or someone?" He questions, not taking a single step closer to me like he usually would when conversing.

"The latter," I admit.

"Doesn't feel too good does it?" He mutters, this time finally letting the pain show on his face.

"William, last night, nothing happened." I take a couple steps closer trying to reach out to him. I just wanted him to hear me out.

"Oh no? Because it sure looked like a great reunion between the two of you. He sure didn't understand that the ring on your finger meant you were taken, despite having been at our wedding to see it for himself." William's voice heightens, but it doesn't scare me, arguments tend to make me a bit anxious. But, I was just going to have to learn how to bottle up these emotions because arguing sometimes came with marriage and this was an argument we were going to have to have.

"I told him he needed to stop, I told him I was married," I explained, taking a step closer to him. I needed him to reach for me or at least let me touch him. I needed the guarantee that even though he was upset he was still my husband, he was still loyal to me.

Instead, William takes a step back and rubs his hands across his face, scratching the stubble that was already beginning to come in.

"Eloise, what you said doesn't matter. It's what you allowed to happen. It's the fact that after I had asked if you still cared for him you refused to respond." He barks.

"That's not fair, if Jasmine had agreed to take you back sooner, you would have left me." William had pined after his ex right before our wedding, and I couldn't blame him. He had been madly in love with her, and the only reason they had broken up was because of this marriage.

"But I didn't choose Jasmine, I chose you!" William shouts, finally taking a step closer to me. But this time I take a step back.

"You didn't choose me, you chose money! You chose a company!" William could be upset with last night's situation. But he didn't get to make me feel like shit for something that wasn't true. This marriage wasn't real and no matter how good we got along, nothing about our relationship would be genuine. This was something of convenience and the only thing we had to do was make it bearable.

William takes a step back at my words, as we continue staring at each other in silence. It takes a few moments, but William finally lets out a sigh before walking over to sit on his bed.

"I don't know what you want me to say, Eloise. I'm trying here." He finally utters.

"And I'm not?" My voice comes out in a whisper but I know he heard.

"Eloise, I want this to be as real as it can be between us, but not if he's still in the picture."

"William, he's Charlotte's brother. They're basically attached to the hip." I groan, trying to get him to reason with me.

William lets out a sardonic laugh and shakes his head, looking around the room as he gathers his thoughts."Eloise, I've seen them separated on various occasions, I think he's only attached to you."

"And what would you like me to do about that, William? I can't control the man." I lift my hands up in desperation, wanting to be done with this argument already.

"I want you to tell him it's done, I want you to set boundaries."

"I have." I groan.

"You haven't, not the way he needs to hear it because trust me, once those words are said, he'll back the fuck off." William stares me down, and at this point, I'm ready to wave my white flag in surrender.

Apparently, I needed to figure out other ways to tell Ulysses that I was married because, obviously, the ring, wedding, and marriage papers weren't enough for him to understand.

William gets up from the bed and walks past me straight to the door, holding it wide open for me.

"Until you set those boundaries, then this will be nothing more than what it has been." William's voice becomes emotionless again. Once again we were back to step one in this marriage.

I walk over to the door, stopping right in front of him, refusing to allow any sort of emotion to show.

"And what has it been?" I manage to ask clearly and concisely despite the hurt daring to show through.

"A respectful relationship, a friendship at most." William's face didn't break, unlike mine, which I'm sure was already turning red from the pain I was feeling within my chest. I manage out an "okay" before heading towards my room to fall apart in peace.

Chapter Twelve

A week had passed since Eloise and I's first actual argument. That wasn't how I had pictured our first argument going, but then again, I've never pictured Eloise getting as mad and frustrated as she did. For the most part, since the argument we've done a great job at ignoring one another. I wake up early every morning to get out of the house before she's awake, and then I stay at the office for longer than I'd like, just to prevent running into her in our own home.

Most nights, she was either tucked away in the home library or in her bedroom. I only knew this because even after our argument, I still cared enough to know where she was and what she was doing.

I had even begun driving myself to work and having

Cory stay around the penthouse in case Eloise wanted to step out for a bit. And maybe I also wanted to make sure Ulysses was nowhere near her. And if he was, then I wanted to make sure that no boundaries were being crossed.

I let out a frustrated groan, running my hands through my hair as I made my way down towards the living room where I knew Eloise would be waiting. I hated this feeling that was bubbling up inside my chest.

What was it?

Jealousy?

Distrust?

It's not that I didn't trust Eloise, I just didn't trust that dick of her ex who somehow found a way to slither his way to her every chance he got. But I couldn't just blame him, not when Eloise obviously had some lingering feelings for him as well. Whether it was love or not, it was real. And that was more than enough to have me take a step back and reevaluate this relationship of ours, or lack thereof.

Eloise stood in the living room in an overly tight dress, pacing back and forth. That seemed to be something she always did out of habit when she was anxious.

"Is everything alright?" I ask, keeping my tone low and stoic. I didn't want her to think that we were over our argument. It would only lead her to believe she's forgiven and continue her relationship with Ulysses. Truthfully, I didn't see any issue with what I had asked of her. It's not like I wanted him gone completely; I knew that wouldn't be possible with Charlotte being her best friend. But I just wanted her to set clear boundaries, ones that he would actually understand.

Eloise stops right in front of me, her breasts practically bursting out of her dress.

Could she even breathe in that thing?

"I've gained weight." Her voice wobbles as she stands still in front of me.

"And the issue is?" I ask, not quite sure what she was trying to get at. If the dress was too small, just throw it out or burn it for all I care.

"No, William, my mother bought me this dress. She wants me to wear it today." I take a step closer to her, my eyes landing back towards her chest. The dress was stunning on her; it was too bad it was doing more bad to her than good. I fit my hands in between the tiny space that the dress had against her breasts; Eloise's eyes look up at me in shock, obviously not entirely sure as to what I'm up to.

"William, what are you—"

I pull at the thin fabric, ripping it apart.

"William!" Eloise shrieks, covering her stunning body away from me.

"Now, you can wear whatever you want. You could have done so before because no one tells my wife what to wear. Understood, Eloise?" I ask, the tone in my voice sounded more annoyed and pissed than it should be towards her. But I hated how her parents somehow managed to control her like a puppet.

Eloise remains silent, her arm blocking her breasts from view even though she has a bra on. It wasn't like I hadn't seen her in a bikini.

It wasn't like I hadn't seen her naked.

And I most definitely had because that night had been

the only image that appeared in my head anytime I had my hand wrapped around my cock at night.

"Eloise, I asked a question," I say, this time changing my tone. I didn't want her to think I was annoyed with her, I'd show her parents my distaste for them later today.

"I don't know what to wear, now." Eloise's voice is small and meek, and it makes me want to break the boundaries I set up for us and just bring her in my arms.

"Come, I bet we can find something in your closet." I put my hand out for her to take, but Eloise just looked at me, those sky-blue eyes holding back tears.

"William," she murmurs.

"What is it?" I ask, taking a step closer to her, brushing my hand across her face to comfort her. Nothing felt worse than seeing Eloise cry. I was trying my best to make this marriage work, but seeing her like this made me feel like a fucking failure.

"None of my clothes are fitting me." She replies, looking anywhere but at me.

None of her clothes fit her?

Not even any of the new ones that she had bought a week ago?

"Are you pregnant?" The question leaves my mouth before I can even think it through.

Eloise's eyes snap back to mine, a look of horror on her face.

Well, that was my answer.

"No, I'm not pregnant, why do I look pregnant?" Eloise drops her arms away from her chest to walk over to the nearest mirror. I grab ahold of her quickly before I cause her to develop body dysmorphia even though I'm sure her mother had already caused it. She struggles against my hold, my arms wrapped tightly around her waist, holding her back from going to any mirror.

"No, not at all, blondie. I was just trying to understand how a woman who went shopping last week for clothes could have such trouble fitting into them this week." I explain, bringing over my shoulder and carrying her up the stairs toward her bedroom to take a look inside her closet. Surely, there had to be something there that she could wear.

"It doesn't fit because I don't buy my clothes, my mother does. Which means she picks out my size. Now put me down!" Eloise shrieks, smacking her hand against the back of my thigh. The slapping does nothing to me, though. Instead, I make my way into her bedroom and towards the closet where I finally put her down.

"You didn't have to do that." She mutters, fixing her now tousled hair. Her golden hair looked beautifully loose like that. Lately she had it clipped up or in a bun. But I much preferred it down like this.

"I did. Now, why is your mother buying you all your clothes? And why don't you tell her it's not your size?" I ask.

"You want me to tell my mother that I don't fit into the clothes? Do you want to know what her response will be? Because I already know, and it involves me on a treadmill with five almonds in my stomach and a pack of gum to get me through the day."

The thought of Eloise being forced into an eating disorder by her own mother makes me stick to my stomach, but it also infuriates me enough to grab all the clothes off the rack and throw them on the floor of her room.

"William, what are you doing?!" She shrieks, her hands wrapping around my arm to hold me back.

"I want all these clothes thrown out," I growl, stacking them all into a pile.

"William, they're expensive."

"Then donate them, Eloise. But I don't want you wearing them or even thinking about having to diet to get into them." I utter angrily, throwing more of her outfits onto the floor of her bedroom. I would have someone come and get them as soon as they could and donate them. But I didn't want them here as a reminder to Eloise of how thin she used to be or needed to be.

"What will I wear? I don't have money, I get all my clothes from my mother." I drop the last of the clothes onto the floor and pull out my wallet, handing over my black card.

"Use this and buy yourself the clothing that you like and the clothing that fits you comfortably." I gestured my card toward her, but she hesitates to take it.

"I don't—"

"Eloise, you're my wife, what's mine is yours. Take the damn card." I mutter.

Eloise hesitates again before finally grabbing the card from me. A sigh escapes my mouth as I look at the amount of clothes that remains scattered across the floor.

"William, it's really okay. I can try—"

One glance from me shuts her right up, "Get dressed with anything that fits right now. We'll have to stop somewhere to get you something different to wear." I stomp right out of the room back to the living room where I wait for Eloise to come back down.

She was getting a whole new wardrobe today whether she liked it or not.

"WILLIAM, THIS IS REALLY NOT NECESSARY," ELOISE whispers beside me as the lady assisting us continues to add more clothes on the rack for Eloise to try. I ignore Eloise's comment and point toward the blue dress on one of the racks.

"How about this one? I think it'll bring out the blue in her eyes."

"Of course, sir." The sales lady looks through the sizes before taking the dress out to put on the side for Eloise to try on.

"William." Eloise's tone comes out stern, which is not something I'm used to hearing from her, but it's definitely something I like.

I finally peer down to look at my annoyed wife, whose cheeks are now pink from my comment about her eyes.

"Yes, blondie?" I play along.

I was still angry with her about the other night, but right now, she didn't need an irate husband. She needed a supportive one, and despite our own arguments, we would always be on the same team.

"We're going to be late; let's just pick a dress and go." Eloise pleads.

I was aware that her tardiness would probably fall on her, which meant she'd have to listen to her parents nagging.

"Okay, try on the blue dress. Everything else we'll take, and whatever you don't like or doesn't fit, we'll return."

"Will—"

"Stella, would you mind helping Eloise out of this dress and into the blue one?" I ask the attendant.

"Of course, you can follow me to the back."

Eloise and I follow Stella to the changing rooms. I sit on the couch as Eloise enters the changing room with Stella. Sudden grunts and chattering begin to come from the changing room, and I can't help but get up and move toward the door, giving it a knock.

"Is everything alright in there?"

The door creaks open, and Stella pops her head out, "actually, we are having a bit of a rough time taking off the dress, I think the zipper is caught on the material of the dress, would you mind giving it a try?" Stella opens up the door wider revealing a flushed Eloise, with the zipper of her dress barely halfway down.

"I'll take it over from here, Stella," I murmur, pushing past her and shutting the door behind us. Eloise stands right in front of the mirror, her gaze remaining on me.

"May I?" I ask, holding her stare through the mirror's reflection. Eloise gives a slight nod, my fingers immediately trailing down her back instantly, stopping at the zipper.

The revealing skin on her back lifts into goosebumps, and I can't help but think about how good she'd feel and how good she'd look if I just took her in front of the mirror.

"William?" Her voice comes out in a hush. I look back towards the mirror, her bright blue eyes meeting mine.

"Yes?" A knowing smirk appears on her face, letting me know she's caught me red-handed in my fantasies. And the confidence that she exudes with that knowing smirk makes me want to follow through with said fantasies.

"The zipper."

I cleared my throat and looked right back down at the reasoning behind this interaction. I grasp the zipper and hold onto the fabric of the dress, trying to bring it down, but it was no use, the zipper just wouldn't budge.

"Have you got it?" Stella's voice trails from the other side of the door.

"Almost," I lie.

Eloise lets out a snort and quickly covers her face to hide the laugh that just escaped her lips.

"What is it, blondie? Don't think I can unzip the dress?" I challenge.

"I mean, you haven't even moved it a bit." She replies, her stare challenging me right back.

"Oh, what the hell. It's not like you care about the dress, right?"

Before Eloise can even respond, I bring my hand under both sides of the dress where the zipper keeps them fastened together and rip the dress apart.

Eloise lets out a gasp as the dress falls down to the floor, leaving her in her laced bra and thong. She reaches her hands up to cover the nipples, peeking their way through the thin fabric, and even though I should walk out and let her get on to trying the dress, I don't. Instead, I bring my lips towards her ear, our gaze never leaving the other's.

"It's nothing I haven't seen or enjoyed before, blondie." Her eyes widened at my words, and I send her back a wink before making my way out so that Stella could help her with the new dress. As I take a seat on the couch, I try to control my hard-on as much as I can, but the image of Eloise just won't make its way out of my head.

I had torn two dresses off of my wife's body today and all it resulted in was an annoying hard on.

As Eloise steps out of the fitting room with the sky blue dress pressed to her subtle curves, I realize that it won't be going away anytime soon.

Chapter Thirteen

Eloise

The fitting room had become a sauna. *His stare, his touch, his words.* They had my heart beating right out of my chest.

Was he no longer mad at me?

Was he into me?

I was relieved to finally choose the dress for tonight's dinner and get out of there. Of course, William didn't let me leave without having picked out a few more dresses and outfits that I liked.

How could someone be so upset with me and so loving at the same time?

Even as we sit right next to each other in the car, I want to gather the courage to ask him straightforwardly. But instead I keep quiet as I peer out the window, waiting to appear in front of my parent's building. They didn't live too far from where we did so they must be questioning our tardiness by now. But, maybe they wouldn't say a single thing. They hadn't even called to question what was taking us so long so that was already a good sign.

But I wouldn't put it past my mother to corner me later on and question me about our lateness and my sudden change of style.

William's sudden grip on my leg pulls me away from my thoughts. I look up to meet his eyes, the car coming to a complete stop in front of my parent's building.

"Stop shaking; everything will be alright," William assures me, squeezing the leg that I nervously shook up and down subconsciously when I got nervous.

"Sorry, I can't help it sometimes." My parents hated how unable I was to control my panic attacks at times. Especially when the media was constantly down our throats, trying to find issues within our perfect family.

"It's okay, blondie. I'm always on your side." William assures his eyes peering into my soul.

Why did he have to look at me like that? It's like the man had x-ray vision or something.

"Come, let's get this dinner over with." William utters, getting out of the car.

I hold my breath as we ride the elevator up to my parents home. I could just picture my mother's stance in front of the elevator doors right now. Her arms crossed over her chest, and the obnoxious noise that came from tapping her Louis Vuitton's on the tiled floor showed her frustration.

"Breathe, blondie," William murmurs.

I let out a huff of air, and William brings his arm around my waist, placing his hand firmly on my hip.

"You're a married woman, Eloise. You don't have to listen to them anymore." William's reminder soothes me a bit. But he just wouldn't understand that no matter how long we were married, my parents would still expect a certain image and respect from their daughter.

The door of the elevator dings open, and just as I pictured, my mother stands there with her arms crossed over her dress and that damn heel tapping on the floor.

"Oh, how nice of you to show up, Eloise." My mother's cold tone makes my body stiffen; the only thing that brings me some sort of comfort is William's thumb, which moves up and down on my hip, reminding me that he's there... for me.

"I'm sorry we're late, Clarice." William mutters stepping out of the elevator, "we had something come up."

"Not a problem, William. The chef was running a bit behind anyway. Harold is in his study if you'd like to meet with him." My mother chirps, wiping away that grimace that had met me the minute I stepped foot inside the penthouse.

William shifts his gaze to me, raising an eyebrow in concern. I give him a nod, letting him know that I could handle my mother.

"Then I guess I'll head over to the study and make my presence known." William jokes before leaving the foyer and walking towards my father's office.

My mother's stare follows William out the door and turns back to me the moment he's gone. Those eyes practically dig into me like daggers.

"Really, Eloise? Tardiness? And what on earth are you wearing?" Mother's face shrivels in disgust as she takes in the dress that William got me.

"Why aren't you wearing the dresses I bought you?" My

mother interrogates, casting her gaze down at my outfit of choice.

"William preferred that I wear this instead."

My mother lets out an exasperated sigh before heading to the dining room. "You better not be gaining any weight Eloise, your cheeks are rounding up. And you know what your weight gain could do for William's image."

My mother continues to rant about my weight, the perfect diet, and perfect measurements. I don't even realize I've been biting my lip to hold back from spewing something hurtful her way until I feel the coppery taste on my tastebuds.

"You aren't pregnant, are you?" She asks, peering over the table to look down at my stomach. I wrap my hands around my waist, trying to block her stare.

"No, mother, I'm not pregnant," I mumble.

"It's a shame, really, that's the only excuse for weight gain, and even then, you should still be watching that you don't gain more than necessary." Mom lectures, readjusting the centerpieces on the table.

"Evelyn, can you tell the men that dinner is ready to be served?" My mother calls out to her maid of the month. They never really last long enough. Either my mother fires them for no fault of their own or they just realize that the job and pay isn't worth dealing with my mother.

"Yes, ma'am." She calls back.

"I can't stand her." My mother groans, shaking her head in disbelief.

I doubt Evelyn could stand my mother.

"Anyhow, what was it that we were discussing?" My mother asks, turning to me as she ponders in thought.

"We weren't dis—"

"That's right, you're weight."

I squeeze my knees, holding the panic and anger building up within me.

It's okay, Eloise. Just take a deep breath and count to ten.

Breathe in, one, *breathe out*.

"Have you been going to the gym?"

Breathe in, two, *breathe out*.

"How about pilates?"

Breathe in, three, *breathe out*.

"What's with this breathing, Eloise? Is this some sort of yoga routine?"

Breathe in, four, *breathe out*.

"Yoga! Have you tried that?"

Breathe in—

Fuck it.

"Shut up!" I shout, the words slipping through my mouth before I can stop them. My mother's eyes practically bulge out of her eyes, not having expected me to lash out in that manner.

"Eloise, what has gotten into you?" My mother rests her hand against her chest as if I'd physically hurt her.

"You have, mother. There must be some other topic other than my weight," I shout. My mother's face remains in shock, but she doesn't respond; she only looks at me with disappointment.

It's not until I hear someone clear their voice that I see William and my father looking right over at us. Both men look stunned, and it's evident that neither of them knows what to say.

My hands continue to shake from under the table, and

their stares at me don't do much to make it stop. I excuse myself away from the table and walk past my father and William right into the bathroom at the end of the hall.

I tightened my grip on the vanity and try to control my breathing, this time without my mother's voice in my ear. Tears stream down my eyes, but I try to focus on my breathing rather than what my makeup must look like right now.

Two strong hands on my shoulders have me lift my gaze up to the mirror. William stands over me, our eyes meeting in the mirror.

"It's alright. I'm here, blondie." I turn around to hide my face against his shirt, letting the tears and sobs out.

"I'm so proud of you, Eloise," William says, comforting me with his touch.

"Why are you here?" I ask, unsure as to why he's comforting me, when he's still angry with me.

"Why wouldn't I come and comfort my upset wife?" He asks.

I lift my head up to look at him, "but aren't you upset with me?" I wasn't used to comfort when I was upset, especially not when others were angry at me.

William's brows furrow as he looks at me with confusion.

"Listen to me, blondie" He says, holding my face in his hands so that I continue to face him. "I don't care how many arguments we have or how mad we are with one another. When it comes to your parents or anyone for that matter disrespecting you like that I won't allow it and neither will you. If you don't want to speak up, I understand, but you don't let them get away with that. You come to me and I'll set them straight. You are my wife and you should be respected.

Am I understood?" William's gaze looks determined but loving at the same time. I'd be completely stupid to confuse his kindness for anything but that. But I can't help but pretend that William may love me.

"Understood," I say, bringing my head back onto his chest.

I think I'm delusional when I feel William press a light kiss to my forehead, but as soon as I feel his hand move down to my back and move in soothing circles, I realize that William is comforting me again. Somehow, William is always there when I need him, but I'm too smart to believe that this will last.

Eventually he'll get tired.

They all do.

Chapter Fourteen

Eloise

Eight Months Ago

Unless interrupted, my days for the most part always stayed the same. I was used to the schedule, but at times it could get boring. I'd wake up around six every morning, where I'd meet William in our kitchen. Both of us having our breakfast, sometimes sharing a word or two, other times in silence.

Afterward, I'd get dressed and go to my pilates class, and right after that, I usually received a call from my mother, who always seemed interested in making sure I was maintaining my exact weight and that a jog here and there or one less meal a day wouldn't kill me.

Even after our last conversation a month ago, she didn't

care to keep pestering me about my weight. Regardless, I'd barely give her much attention on the phone.

After our conversation, I'd go back home to shower and change before heading out to my classes, which I had no interest in. I did well in them, but it wasn't what I wanted.

When I told my father that I wanted to pursue a career in education, he laughed in my face and let me know I was better off working as their maid instead.

"Eloise, we are meant to pay the service, not be the service." Is what he engraved in my head every time my aspirations were brought up. My father left me with few choices, which is why I ended up majoring in pre-law. However, I had zero interest in pursuing that career, and I wasn't sure how William would take the news of me not being interested in pursuing it.

I tried to ignore the topic as much as possible, which is why the minute I'd get home from classes, I'd crawl into the shell that is my library, reading a new book on my list or re-reading Metamorphosis until it was time for dinner, which I bring into the library with me.

It's a reclusive lifestyle compared to other socialites in the city. Even though Charlotte is much more outgoing than me, sometimes I feel that I'm holding her back from new experiences and having fun with other people who share more common interests with her than I do.

Even now, here I was like a hermit in the comfort of its shelf, while Charlotte is out at their family's gala. William and I were invited, but the last thing I wanted to do was see Ulysses. William usually worked late at the office anyway. Something that had worried me before, but I doubted

William found any sort of interest in his new secretary, Victor.

My heart tightens in my chest at the thought of William hiring a male secretary for my comfort. But I was sure it was because Victor had the qualifications that were needed. Unlike Calliope, he even resorted to sending me messages when William would be coming home late. Not that it mattered, it's not like we ever had dinner together.

Speaking of which, there was no message of the sort today. I take a bite of my salmon as I peer down at my phone, just in case I had missed the message. But my messages had remained vacant.

That was odd, maybe Victor had just forgotten.

A knock on the door of the library startles me and I immediately peer over at the clock that reads seven o'clock.

Who the hell would be here right now?

All the staff had gone home by now. The door creaks open and William steps out from behind it, a sigh of relief escapes my lips as I take a seat back down in my chair.

"You scared me." I mutter, taking another bite of my food. "What are you doing home so early?" I ask, surprised at his sudden presence not only in our house but also in the library. He never came in here; he was usually in his home office, which had his own book collection separated from the library. I wasn't sure if he had ever actually read any of the books or if he just had them propped up on the shelves for show.

"I'm sorry about that," William walks over to my table, peering down at my plate of food and the stack of books to my right.

"You read all that?" He asks, taking the first book off the

stack to read the synopsis. For the most part, I'd have no issue with him touching any of my books but that one happened to be an erotica that I had planned to read next.

I burst out of my chair reaching for the book, but William raises his arm so it's out of my reach. His head peering up at the synopsis, a wide smile appearing on his lips as he continues to read it.

"William, give me back my book," I demand, crossing my arms over my chest, hoping to look somewhat intimidating.

"I had no clue that this genre was of your interest." William teases, handing me back my book, my cheeks flushing red, giving away my embarrassment.

"That of many," I mutter, putting the book under the stack of others before sitting back down.

"So, do you?" William asks.

"Huh?"

"Do you read all those books?" He repeats the question I had completely forgotten he had asked.

"Oh, yeah I do. These are the books I want to get done by this month." I chirp, excited to talk about something I enjoyed.

"You read all those? In a span of a month?" He asks, looking back at the stack of books that were now only eight, rather than the fifteen I had started with.

"It's not like I have much to do," I shrug.

Maybe it was stubborn of me to say that,but it was the truth. My only focus was school. And although I was practically a housewife, I had no duties to perform. We had maids, chauffeurs, and a chef. I had no chores or liabilities to fulfill

"I wish I had more time for reading. Come to think of it, I haven't read a good book in awhile, any recommendations?"

William asks, taking a seat across from me, removing his suit jacket and shoes to make himself comfortable.

"What do you like to read?" I ask, pushing my plate towards him as an offer. I push my seat out and walk towards the shelves trailing my fingers across the books, awaiting his response.

William brings the plate of food closer to him, taking a piece of salmon into his mouth. "I'm open to anything. I wouldn't say I'm a big fan of romance but I wouldn't mind reading one if that's what you're into." My fingers halt against the spine of a Lovecraft novel.

He wasn't asking me for a reference, he was asking me for my interest. He's trying to enjoy something that I like as well. "I wouldn't say romance is the only thing I read or like." I say, walking towards the section where I keep my romance books. I pull out a few of my favorites and bring them over to the table where William continues to enjoy the food and helping himself to my glass of water.

"I'm still interested in seeing what you like." William says, bringing the books towards him to read the synopsis.

His black hair looked a bit disheveled, probably from him running his hands through it. Something I had fantasized about doing since that one night. I clench my legs as I watch the veins in his hands bulge out as he turns the pages of the books. His blue eyes followed the writing in the book before raising back up to meet mine, a smirk appearing on his lips, having caught me staring.

"I'll take this one," William says, shoving the rest of the books my way. I clear my throat and bring them to the side to put away later.

"How come you aren't at work or the gala?" I ask. Maybe

that wasn't something I should have asked. But I wanted to know why he was here... with me. William gives me a shrug, leaning back in his chair, his unbuttoned shirt spreading open, showing me a glimpse of his defined chest.

"How come you aren't at the gala?" He retorts in a playful tone.

"Not really my thing and I wasn't entirely ready to go out yet." Acknowledgment shines in William's eyes, which lets me know that he's aware of what I'm trying to say. I'm not ready to present ourselves to everyone. I'm not ready to shove it down Ulysses's throat, even though at some point he'll have to get used to it.

"Well, if my wife doesn't want to attend a gala then I don't see why I should. Besides I had my fair share of those throughout the years, now that I'm heading towards my thirties it's becoming tiring." He sighs as if just thinking about the gala was exhausting.

"And work?" I straighten my posture, aware of the slouching that my mother would have commented on if she were here. William had probably caught up on a lot of work which is why he had decided to call it a night. That and many of his friends were probably at said gala at the moment.

Since my parents were in attendance tonight it made no difference if we showed up or not, but next year we would be expected to show up, especially if my father planned to retire by then. William would be the new CEO and since I'm his wife, I'd have no choice but to go. It was part of the contractual obligations not only within our marriage but this society.

"I decided to call it a day a little earlier today, I'm sorry I scared you. I thought that since Victor hadn't messaged you today that you'd assume I'd be home soon. Next time I'll have him text you if I'm on my way home." William assures.

I frown, surprised by his revelation.

He had been texting me through Victor?

I suppose that made sense, but it wasn't something I had expected.

"Why do you tell Victor to text me?" I ask.

It wasn't a big deal for Victor to text me, but I was curious as to why William didn't just text me himself.

Besides today and our shared mornings, we barely ever spoke to one another. Tonight felt like something out of the twilight zone.

"I don't know, I just want you to feel comfortable." William shrugs, ignoring my stare as he picks the book back up, skimming through the pages.

"Comfortable?" I question, wanting a better excuse than the one he had used. William snaps the book close before meeting my eyes again.

"I didn't want you feeling uncomfortable or having doubts. That way you know where I am and what I'm doing." William's voice lowers, but not in annoyance or anger. The silence in the room thickens, as we stare at one another.

I wasn't exactly sure how to respond. I knew what he meant to say was that he didn't want me worrying about cheating anymore.

"Eloise—"

William's throat bobbed as he opened his mouth to continue his sentence. But nothing comes out. Instead, his stare intensifies, and I can't stop my mind from imagining how good it would feel for him to take me on this table right now.

"Yes?" I manage to croak, tightening my grip to the bottom of my chair.

William clears his throat before standing back up, collecting the borrowed book into his hand.

"Thank you for the meal and book. I'll make sure to let you know if I like it. If you don't mind, I think I'm going to call it a night and head over to bed."

I clear my own throat this time and get back up to put the rest of the books away.

"Have a good night," I say, but just before I can turn towards the shelves, William blocks my path, making me look right back up at him.

"Yes?" I ask, my voice comes out so low that I'm not even sure if he's heard me. But whether he did or not, it really didn't matter. William lowers his lips onto my forehead, gives me a kiss.

He steps back, whispering a "goodnight" before leaving.

I stay in the same position, books in hand, feet frozen in place.

My lips finally spread into a genuine smile.

Chapter Fifteen

Present Day

"You did not say that." Charlotte squeals, laying back on the lounge chair. I cover my face, mortified at the recollection of my attempted flirting with my husband.

"Sadly, I did, but he obviously didn't seem to mind it," I say, in hopes of making myself feel a bit better. I had gone to bed that night hoping that my flirting would have William knocking on my bedroom door late at night. But, instead I was met with a restless night and a vacant bed. But, he had flirted back so that must mean he was interested. Besides the bar, the only other thing that William had experienced in our time in Fiji was me.

And if the bar was his only enjoyment in our honeymoon then this marriage was more of a lost cause than I thought.

"Of course he didn't mind it. He probably hid away in his room with his hand in his pants the whole night." Charlotte teases, applying sunscreen on her arms before passing me the bottle to do the same.

"Oh god, I doubt that." But, despite my reply I was hoping that there was some sliver of truth.

I wanted to further my relationship with William, but had no idea what else to do. If I asked Charlotte what she would do she would encourage her plan of seduction.

But what if that didn't work? What if William turned me down? We had been together for a year and nothing had ever occurred between us, not even a kiss. If he really wanted something with me he would've done so already.

"Stop overthinking it. It's all very new, it's going to take time." Charlotte encourages, trying to bring me some form of comfort.

"New? We're literally leaving on vacation to celebrate our one year anniversary." I sigh, laying back onto the lounge chair. Dev and Charlotte's penthouse was glorious and came with its own rooftop pool. Occasionally when the New York weather was breathable rather than humid and sticky Charlotte and I would enjoy our day by the pool.

"I know that, but I mean between you two it's still very new. I think William is just taking it slow and doing what he should have done before marrying you, which was to actually get to know you." I shrug, lowering my sunglasses from my head to cover my eyes. Maybe Charlotte was right and William was trying his best to not rush our relationship.

Our marriage was unconventional which unfortunately meant that no matter how much I hoped for a realistic marital relationship we were probably never going to be like that. Just good friends that sleep together when it comes to having children. But other than that we would be nothing more.

"And I can't believe he's taking you away from me on your birthday again." Charlotte groans, turning her head to face me rather than up at the sky.

"I know, but maybe we can do something when I come back," I reassured her, hating that I'd be breaking my birthday tradition for the second year in a row.

"Maybe? The answer is definitely." Charlotte corrects and I can't help but giggle at her feistiness. Charlotte had always been a great friend. She made living in this society easy. We didn't care about fitting in with people that didn't care about us as people.

That was the reason why I dated Ulysses; he loved me for me. He didn't care that I was a social pariah who used any excuse she could to not have to speak with anyone or to attend our family's lavish parties. He didn't care that I wasn't part of a clique or that I didn't always dress in designer clothes.

Maybe I wasn't in love with Ulysses but he was the only man that wasn't after my father's company. And as good of a man that William is, that doesn't erase the convenience that our marriage is for him.

"What are you two gossiping about? Leonora's new nose job?" Ulysses's voice captures my attention as he walks towards us.

"That's her second rhinoplasty. If she keeps it up, she'll barely have a nose to look at," Charlotte answers.

"Leonora has a nose job? But her nose was perfect." I say, subconsciously sitting up and bringing my legs closer to my chest to cover myself in front of Ulysses. Even though a bikini was standard, it still felt a bit uncomfortable to wear around my ex-boyfriend. Especially while being married to William.

"Of course, you would say that you think everyone is perfect," Ulysses mutters, rolling his eyes at me. He pulls the lounge chair closer to me but stops halfway. That was something he had always done when we were a couple so that we could lay and cuddle together on the lounge chairs. Now, it was just a muscle memory he'd have to break.

"I just didn't see an issue with her nose," I say.

"You know, neither did I." Charlotte seconds.

Ulysses gives us a shrug, obviously not wanting to start a debate.

"What's up with the dry skin? You usually make a jump in the water before sunbathing." Ulysses runs his fingers down my back and looks at them as if I were some old wooden furniture that had been collecting dust. I scoot to the side, trying my best to ignore his presence and touch.

Why did he have to do things like that?

I could understand muscle memory but the touching, the closeness, and the teasing.

"I just haven't felt like taking a swim yet," I reply, not exactly lying but not telling the truth either. William had said he would come by with Dev after their meeting and that we could possibly go out for dinner if I was feeling up to it so I didn't want to get my hair wet. And no matter how many times I entered the pool with the intentions of keeping my hair dry it just never worked out. A pool was no fun if I wasn't embedding myself within the water.

"Your back is getting a little red, here let me rub sunscreen on it." Ulysses stretches over to grab the sunscreen that I had placed on the floor earlier. I move my legs away from my chest and move to the side to face Ulysses.

"No, that's fine, Charlotte can do it." I offer my hand out so that he can pass over the sunscreen, but instead he looks between my hand and my face, looking at me as if what I had said was absurd.

"What are you talking about, Eloise? I've always rubbed sunscreen on your back, it's no big deal." Ulysses gestures his hand toward him in a spinning motion to have me turn around. But instead I just grip the lounge chair and begin counting my breaths in my head. He was beginning to make me uncomfortable and anxious and unlike Charlotte and I, he never had to learn how to take 'no' for an answer.

"Ulysses, she said no. The quicker you come to understand that she's a married woman the less awkward you'll make our group interactions." Charlotte mutters, grabbing the sunscreen away from Ulysses's hand.

His eyes search my own almost as if he were waiting for me to jump to his defense. But instead I look away and focus on the crystal clear water of the pool. It looked enticing but regardless of if I wanted to take a dip, I didn't want to be alone in there with Ulysses.

"Whatever, you two are bores anyway. I'm going to use the pool for what it's meant for, which is for swimming, not gazing." Ulysses remarks, getting up and heading towards the pool. His comment hitting me in the chest harder than I thought it would have.

At some point I knew Ulysses would begin to get upset at our deteriorated relationship. The only reason I continued to be his friend was because of Charlotte. I tried to exclude him from my life as much as possible but even when it was just Charlotte and I, Ulysses would find a way to slither his way into our plans.

William was quite understanding, more understanding than I had been with his secretary. But he understood that Charlotte was my only friend and sadly that meant that sometimes Ulysses came with that friendship. The least I could do was set boundaries, even though Ulysses had trouble respecting even that at times.

"Don't mind him. I think he's finally realizing that things just can't be the same as they once were between the two of you," Charlotte whispers, squeezing the sunscreen onto her hand before applying it to my back.

"I know, but things will only continue to be uncomfortable between us if he doesn't respect my boundaries and realize that I'm married." I look back towards the pool, watching as Ulysses swims laps back and forth, not bothering to stop for a break.

He was upset.

And as much as I'd like to walk over there and apologize for setting boundaries, I couldn't. It was just something he was going to have to learn to respect.

"I can take over, Charlotte." That deep voice brought my eyes away from Ulysses instantly. I peer up to see a shirtless William standing over me. My eyes trail up his exquisitely sculpted body before landing on his own peering down at me. The smirk playing on his lips told me he had caught me checking him out.

"You don't have to tell me twice, here you go." Charlotte hands William the bottle of sunscreen before walking over to Dev, who stands by the pool, waiting for Ulysses to finish his laps.

"You don't have—"

"I know what I can and can't do, Eloise," William says, his voice deep and husky near my ear. "But I also know what I want to do."

I feel the cold sensation of the sunscreen on my skin, more than I had with Charlotte. William rubs the sunscreen onto my back, making sure to apply pressure into any knots he finds.

"You were looking at him," William murmurs, obviously not wanting the others to pick up on our conversation.

"We got into a bit of an argument." I admit, not wanting to keep any secrets between us, not when we were just starting to get somewhere.

"About?" William presses further into a knot, a moan escaping my mouth in response. I can feel William tense behind me for a bit before continuing. I look over towards the pool, afraid of having been heard. But the three seemed to be in their own little world, laughing at whatever Dev had said.

A slight tug on the braid that Charlotte had made for me tugs my view away from the pool.

"About what, Eloise?" William's voice sounds more stern and intimidating. But, unlike my father's, it doesn't rile up any nerves.

"Boundaries. He had wanted to rub sunscreen on my

back, but I let him know that it wasn't necessary." William's hands move down my spine, snaking around my waist, pulling me towards him. The sudden move has a gasp escaping my lips.

William lets out a low chuckle and brings his lips onto the crevice of my neck. He leaves a kiss but doesn't move away, instead he stays there as his breath sends shivers down my skin.

"You're a good girl, aren't you?" He asks.

I gasp at his words, but as I turn around to look over at him, I see that he's already gotten up. He brings his hand down to me and nods his head over to the pool.

"Come on, it's nice out today, blondie. Let's enjoy the pool."

"I thought you said we would be heading out for dinner after your meeting? That's if you still want to." I say, taking his hand anyway to have him help me up. And if William was going to take advantage of the beautiful pool day then I should too.

"We can still do that, but that pool seems to be calling my name." A giggle escapes my lips as we walk over to the pool; Ulysses sends me an occasional side eye as I continue to stick close to William.

If the boundaries hadn't painted the picture well enough before, being near William sure had. And though it stung to see Ulysses so upset with me, it had to be done.

Ulysses and I were over.

I SLAP AWAY WILLIAM'S HAND AS HE CONTINUES TO PICK off a piece of chicken from my plate. "Stop it, it's mine." I push my chinese take out away from him and hover over it in protection.

"Who knew my wife was greedy when it came to orange chicken." William tisks, taking a seat back down in his chair and taking a bite of the chicken and broccoli.

After the pool, William and I had decided to grab some takeout and head home. Now we were plopped in the library together eating out chinese takeout and discussing a recent book I had let him borrow.

A routine we had inhabited in our unconventional marriage. The last time we had been here together like this was actually the first time he agreed to read a romance book I liked.

"I'm a fiend when it comes to chinese food." I say, stuffing my face with another piece of chicken. I could never get enough of eating this. If my mother saw me now she'd probably break into a panic attack.

"Don't doubt it; by the way you're refusing to give me a piece."

"You're the one who decided to get chicken and broccoli, the most boring thing on the menu." I point out, looking down at his steamed plate of vegetables and grilled chicken.

"I like my chicken and broccoli, but your meal looks exceptional, and I just wanted to see if it tasted as good as it looked." A sigh slips my lips as I stab the orange chicken and slide it over to his container. "Here," I mutter before getting back to my meal.

"See, was that so hard, blondie?" He teases, taking the piece of chicken into his mouth.

"I'm an only child, and it's very hard."

"I'm an only child too, I don't find sharing to be hard." He retorts.

I roll my eyes and give into his teasing, "but then again look at your parents and then look at mine."

William clears his throat and sets down his fork, "I used to think my parents were the worst, but once you put them next to your parents, they look like saints."

I didn't need to convince William that my parents were terrible, he knew that from experience. William's parents had brought up our marriage to him as a choice that he could make. William was selfless and of course saw it as a way to help his father out of some bad business deals.

My father sat me down in his office and told me what decisions he had already made for my life. And I sat there and nodded.

"Hey, you still there," William asks, shoving my shoulder lightly.

"Yeah, sorry, I was just thinking about this whole situation," I say, waving my hands in the air to insinuate our relationship.

"It's not too bad, is it?" William asks, but by the look in his eyes I could see he desperately wanted me to say no.

"It could've been worse, that's for sure," I reply with a slight smile.

And it really could have. We weren't the only ones to have married out of contractual duties in our society, and we certainly weren't one of the bad pairs. At least we were loyal to one another .

"So, you're saying it could be better," William states,

looking up at the ceiling as if trying to wrap his mind around the problematic equation that is our pair-up.

"I think we're getting there, don't you?" I ask.

We were finally making progress. Our dinners felt like... dates. Even if we stayed home, it still felt like we were getting to really know each other. For god's sake he was revamping our whole honeymoon experience.

William looks back at me, a hint of a smile playing on his lips. "I think so too, blondie."

His eyes stare deep into my own and I don't know how somehow we always end up in this same position with his eyes looking into my own, reaching for my soul. His face tilts towards mine, the tips of our nose a millimeter away from touching. But my anxiety gets the best of me when I clear my throat and look away, causing William to do the same.

"So, our anniversary." I chirp.

"It's right around the corner." He completes.

"Will we be doing anniversary gifts?" I ask.

William turns his body towards me once again to face me.

"Of course, did you have something in mind?" He asks.

The heat rushes to my face at the thought of my stupid anniversary gift idea.

"Kind of," I mumble.

"Let me hear it, blondie," William says, flexing his hand in a come here motion.

"Paper."

"Paper?" William asks, "like printer paper?"

A sudden giggle erupts from me as I lean into his shoulder to compose myself.

"No, it's the traditional gift for one year of marriage.

We're supposed to give each other something related to paper." I explain.

William gives me a slow nod, his eyes telling me his mind is already running around with ideas.

"Sounds fun, blondie. Paper it is." He assures before taking a bite of his food.

"Paper it is," I repeat.

Chapter Sixteen

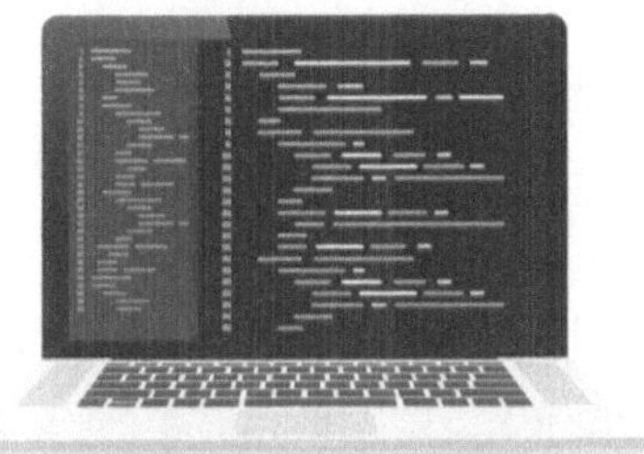

William

I wasn't against driving, in fact I really liked it. But driving out of the city always gave me some sort of headache. But this would all be worth it for Eloise.

"What did you bring in that bag of yours?" I ask, referring to the large knitted bag that sat by her feet.

"Oh, I brought snacks for us, a blanket, and four books, one of them being for you." She chirps as she pulls out the fuzzy gray blanket from the bag and covers herself.

"Which books did you bring?" I ask.

I knew one of the books had to be The Metamorphosis because she never went anywhere without it. I had seen her read it a couple of times, but even if she wasn't reading it, she always brought it around everywhere.

Recently, Eloise had finally built up the courage to share some of her favorite romance books, which took some time to get to. The first time I had asked her for her favorite romance book, she gave me something she called a closed-door romance. I was not as interested in those books as much as I was in the current books she had been giving me. Eloise had finally become comfortable with sharing these smut-filled books with me and my mind couldn't help but think of Eloise and I in the characters' positions.

Just knowing that she read these books turned me on way more than it should. It was just a book, but somehow I'd end up fisting my cock with the thought of my wife riding it.

"I brought a thriller that I haven't gotten around to finishing, a romance book I've been wanting to read, and I brought you the third book to that BDSM club series that you've been enjoying," Eloise says, clearing her throat before shoving the books that she had taken out to show me back into her bag.

"And what about that fourth book? It wouldn't be Kafkaesque, would it?" I tease, knowing she had the book somewhere within that bag.

Eloise turns her head over to me, her lips spreading into a lovely smile.

"The one and only." She giggles, sliding the overused book out of the bag and presenting it out in the open. I let out a long whistle at the beaten up book. It looked like it had been through war, which was odd being that Eloise seemed to always take care of her belongings. All her other books she had let me borrow were pristine and barely looked read.

"I know, the poor book has been through a lot. But it's my favorite and my first-ever copy. So, I plan to keep re-reading it until I can't any longer." Eloise skims the pages of the book and takes a whiff.

"Somehow it smells like my childhood." She states, bringing the book back into her bag.

I'm pretty sure the book smelt like mildew, but I wasn't going to be the one to break it to her. Her book didn't smell like her childhood, but it was her childhood.

"Can we listen to some music?" Eloise asks, clicking on the car's touchscreen stereo. She skims through its application, trying to locate an app but ultimately finding nothing.

"Why don't you have any music platform?" Eloise asks, still sliding through the small list of apps, probably to make sure that she hadn't missed it by mistake.

"I don't really listen to music," I admit.

Eloise snaps her neck back to look at me. Her jaw and eyes are wide open in shock. "What do you mean you don't listen to music? That's impossible."

It wasn't that impossible. Sure, there was music all around us, but I didn't really like to subscribe to music platforms. I also hated listening to the ads that would pop up, so I decided not to bother with it at all.

"William, you have to say something. I'm starting to get worried that I married a psychopath."

"I just don't like paying for subscriptions." I keep my eyes on the road but can see her distaste for my response through my peripheral vision.

"Oh great, I married a cheapskate instead." Eloise groans dramatically.

"You know you're a millionaire, right? Fourteen dollars a month won't kill your wealth."

"Billionaire, blondie." I correct.

"Huh?"

"I'm a billionaire." I clarify, not trying to sound too obnoxious while saying it.

Eloise lets out a sigh, shaking her head at me in disbelief. "That's even more of a reason as to why you should pay for a subscription."

I roll my eyes and hand her my phone, "Fine, go ahead and subscribe me to your favorite platform."

Eloise takes the phone that is already unlocked from my hand, downloads the necessary app for the music, and sets up an account for me.

"Great. What are some music genres that you're into or artists that you like?" Eloise asks.

I hum in thought as I switch onto the left lane to go a bit faster. "I don't know, I guess I've always listened to everything." I never was picky and I had a few favorite artists here and there, but I didn't really mind what we listened to at the moment.

"Great, so you like country?" She chirps, immediately putting on a song that right from the start made my ears bleed.

"Absolutely not." I stretch my hand over and turn the volume knob down until the music's completely gone.

"Hey, what do you have against country music?" She whines, trying to turn the music back up. But I keep my hand over the knob to prevent her from putting that monstrosity back on.

"I just don't like it. I don't like the beat, I don't like the lyrics, and I don't like the singing." Eloise lets out a sigh in shock at my declaration.

"My question is, how can someone with such impeccable taste like country music?" I ask, taking a moment to steer my eyes off the road and over at Eloise who's body language though annoyed was juxtaposed by her white dress and loose tendrils of blonde hair made her look angelic.

"I like it because it's good, and I think you'd like it if you just gave it a chance, please." I look away from her puppy dog eyes and pouty lips, which only make my pants feel tighter, and focus on the road.

"I'm telling you I won't like it. Not even the lyrics gratify me, it's always the same thing. Guys drunk on beer, he did something stupid that he can't remember and the girl is now mad. So now, he's writing a song about it to apologize."

I bring my eyes back towards Eloise, whose pursed lips and empty stare at the car window make me want to stop the car on the side of the road and get her on top of me.

God, what the fuck was wrong with me?

What was this woman doing to me?

I spent a year trying to distance myself as much as possible so that she wouldn't feel pressured to do anything with me. And now everytime we're together I can't help but think of having her.

"I'm not entirely sure what country music you're listening to, but not all of them are like that." She rebuttals, "Plus, it's probably a very common occurrence amongst people to have drunken regrets, right?"

Why was she asking me like I had some experience in that myself? Was this a hint at our honeymoon? I had no regrets of that night, not in the sense of having had sex with my wife but rather feeling guilty that maybe she had only agreed to it to fulfill her *wifely duties*.

I found Eloise attractive and in these past months I've grown to care for her and developed a need to protect her.

But I had never found her unattractive to the eye. I wasn't blind. I could see her beauty even if she didn't and our honeymoon was not something I had regretted, it was just something that felt rushed. Our first time shouldn't have been like that and Eloise deserved better.

"Can't relate," I mutter, gripping the steering wheel, looking back at her for a split second for our eyes to meet. "I've never had any drunken regrets." Eloise scoffs at my statement, shaking her head in denial.

"You've never had any drunken regrets? Not a single one?" She urges.

"Eloise, I can confidently say that I have never regretted a single thing that I've done while drunk. And I can promise you that if I did something while drunk, I was definitely thinking of doing it while sober."

I don't look at Eloise, but instead listen to the hitch in her breath. Which tells me that she's gotten the answer she was digging for. Eloise clears her throat, shuffling in the seat next to me.

"Are today's top hits, alright?" She asks, flicking through what I assume must be a playlist on my phone.

I can't help but let my lips rise into the knowing smile that Eloise just might not have had any regrets of that night.

"That's perfectly fine."

I HAD NEVER EXPERIENCED A BED AND BREAKFAST before but this had been a part of the Vermont experience that Eloise was looking forward to. I would've been fine in a hotel suite but this trip wasn't about me. I wanted Eloise to experience the honeymoon she should've had. Not the one that was forced upon her and ultimately a disaster, thanks to my sulking.

"Hello, welcome to the Montville Farms Bed and Breakfast, I'm the innkeeper, Jane. You must be the Wrens, is that correct?" I look over to my right, where a chirpy young woman who can't be more than twenty-three years old looks up at me with a bright smile. Her auburn hair tied in two separate braids that went along with her overalls and converse.

I wasn't sure if this was her regular style or some sort of stereotypical farmer uniform.

"Yes, that would be us." I greet, waving my hand at her.

"Great, I'm so glad you guys made it. You guys actually booked the cozy corner, which means we have to make our way out of the house and towards the newly renovated barn shed we have out in the yard." Jane grabs ahold of Eloise's suitcase and leads the way through the house and out the backdoor as she explains the layout of the area.

Cozy corner?

Barn shed?

This was the last time I put Victor in charge of choosing Eloise and I's vacation stays.

As soon we walk out of the house, we're met with the mesmerizing beauty of the greenery that surrounds us.

"Even the air here feels lighter and less contaminated than the city," Eloise says, pushing her shoulder jokingly against my arm.

The worst decision that I could've possibly made was to

look down at her in that second. Eloise looked enchanting, but even that wasn't the right word to describe how much her beauty stood out against the greenery behind her. Eloise looked like the very first flower that bloomed in the beginning of spring, the same flower that you choose to take home to keep.

"What is it?" She asks, looking behind her in confusion. Probably having thought that I was staring at anything but her.

"Nothing." I brush off.

Jane leads us to what looks like a miniature white barn with black accents.

"Here is where you will be staying for the remainder of the week. In here you have your own little private home, away from the house so that you can still have your bed and breakfast experience while having a bit more privacy."

The interior was cozy and had what looked like a California king bed right in the center of the room, up against the wooden panel walls.

"One bed?" Eloise squeaks.

"What was that?" Jane asks, moving a bit closer to hear Eloise. But, Eloise had spoken low for either me to hear or no one at all.

"I was sure I had asked for two rooms."

Translation: I told Victor we wanted two rooms.

"Oh, I'm sorry about that. The description for the couple's cozy corner must've not been clear enough on our website, I'll mention it to our social media manager. I was pretty sure that she'd fix that the last time we had siblings show up here with the same issues." Jane tisks, taking a look around the area, as if she could come up with some sort of solution to the one bedroom fiasco.

Wait, did she say siblings?

"We aren't—" Both Eloise and I say in unison, cutting off at the sound of our voice.

"Siblings." We finish.

"Not siblings? But two separate bedrooms?" Jane's eyebrow rises with her question, obviously confused about our sleeping arrangement, which was none of her business.

Why did she even care about our sleeping arrangements? We would be paying for two rooms. Isn't that better for her?

"Yeah, we prefer to sleep separately. We like our own space."

"You New Yorkers just get weirder and weirder. But, sadly, I don't have any rooms available at the moment. Not until Monday, if you'd like, we can reserve it for you; until then, I hope you won't mind dealing with these new sleeping arrangements." Jane leans back and forth awaiting our response so she could get out of this awkward situation.

I'm about to agree to her offer, but Eloise beats me to it.

"No, it's okay. We can deal with it for the remainder of our stay. It was our fault anyway. I'm sorry about that."

Jane stops her pacing and blows out a shaky breath, thanking and apologizing to Eloise.

So, this is what it looks like when two anxious women meet in the wild. It's just a conversation full of thank yous' and sorries.

"Let me show you two the bathroom." Jane gestures for us to follow her towards a door in the corner of the room, opening it up to reveal a toilet and sink.

"Uh, where's the shower?" Eloise asks, sending me a look of concern.

Translation: Victor is a dead man.

"This is the best part! You're going to love it, follow me." Jane squeals, grabbing ahold of Eloise's hand and pulling her to the glass patio door on the side of the room, to the right of the bed. We walk onto the side of the barn, where we're met with a wide wooden outdoor shower. Made with wood paneling.

"It's a nice private outdoor shower!" Jane exclaims, "well as private as the outdoors can get, I guess. There's no roof, but the door is obviously lockable, but no one is allowed to walk on this path for privacy reasons of course. So, you don't really have to worry about any onlookers roaming around."

I give Jane a polite smile before looking over at Eloise, expecting a look of annoyance.

But instead Eloise lets out a giggle, entering the shower in excitement.

"This is so cute!" She squeals, looking up at me. I lean against the frame of the shower and take in her excitement.

"I'll leave you guys to it, the farm here has some fun activities if you guys are interested in signing up for it. We also serve breakfast between eight and ten in the morning. If you need anything, just let me know." Jane chirps before walking back to the house. I turn back to Eloise once Jane is out of sight.

Eloise jumps into my arms, surprising me with a hug. My arms immediately slide around her waist, holding her close to me. A feeling that felt right and odd at the same time.

"Thank you for this, William. I can already tell this trip is going to be amazing."

"It's my pleasure, blondie."

I settle her back onto the ground and follow her back into the cozy barn, watching her as she plops onto the large bed, her dress camouflaging into the sheets, making it look like she's floating on a cloud.

This trip was just a minuscule of many things that Eloise deserved, and I couldn't wait to continue giving each and every little thing she desired to her.

Chapter Seventeen

Eloise

This trip was going to be so much fun we decided to use the rest of our day to walk around the farm for a bit and take a look at the interior of the bed and breakfast. I was so excited when I found their living room filled with books. Surprisingly, many of the books were quite modern.

I had also taken that time to hunt down Jane and asked her where I could sign up for the activities that the farm had. I signed William and I up for their horseback riding lessons. I remember being a child and begging my father to let me take lessons but like most of the activities that I was interested in he always denied me of that enjoyment.

"Penny for your thoughts?" William asks as he walks past the patio doors with a towel hanging dangerously around his waist, another towel in his hand, drying off his hair. The drops of water trailed down his abdomen, all the way down to his v-line. I clear my throat and look away, pretending to be looking at something on my phone.

"Nothing really, I'm just thinking about the horseback riding I signed us up for. I've never been, have you?" I was curious about what William had experienced. Though we both grew up wealthy and within the same social groups, we lived completely different lives.

"Yeah, a couple of times growing up." William goes to the dresser where I had stored our clothes before.

Was he going to change right here, in front of me?

Before he could decide that for me, I headed into the half-bath, locking myself in there.

How long would he need to change?

Was two minutes enough?

Crap, and to top it all off I left my phone on top of the bed. I take a seat on the toilet, looking around in the small confined area. There wasn't much else I could do but wait, my eyes make their way to the bottle of hand soap that's sitting on top of the sink.

I sigh and each over for it, taking a look at the ingredients. Not that I knew what any of the ingredients were, but I had to pass the time somehow. Maybe if I read it three times, he'd be ready and dressed by then.

After reading the label three times I place it back on the sink. I flush the toilet and wash my hands so that it doesn't look like I just ran in here to hide. I open the door and standing right in front of me is William. His skin was now dry, but the towel still hangs around his waist.

"Sorry, I was just waiting to get changed in there."

William murmurs, and the smirk that plays on his lips tells me he knows exactly why I was quick to run into the bathroom.

"Not a problem, the bathroom is all yours." I move past him and towards the bed, getting under the covers. The only light in the room was the lamp on William's side of the bed and the minute that light turned off it would just be William and I in the darkness. My heart begins picking up its space at the thought of being alone in a bed with William again, the last time we shared a bed was during our honeymoon and that wasn't the best experience either.

The bathroom door opens again and William walks out in only his briefs. He slept in only his briefs during our honeymoon but I had just assumed that it was because he was too drunk to get anything else on him.

"Is this okay?" William asks, gesturing towards himself.

"Um, no, yeah, that's fine."

William shakes his head and lets out a chuckle, sliding into the bed and stretching over to turn off the lights. He settles himself beside me, letting out a sigh before stopping his movement.

I wasn't sure what about this situation was making me panic. I tried closing my eyes to relax, but all I could think about was the last time we shared a bed and how the outcome of our actions had become uncomfortable.

Breathe in, "one," *breathe out.*

"Eloise?" I hear his voice whisper to me.

Breathe in, "two," *breathe out.*

"Eloise?" He says again, this time I feel movement on his side of the bed.

Breathe in, "three," *breathe out.*

The lights turn on and I open my eyes to see William hovering over me.

"What's going on, why are you anxious?" William's face turns soft as he asks the question, his hand moving up to wipe a tear away. I hadn't even realized I had begun to cry.

"I'm not sure." I managed to croak.

It was our first night on this trip and I was already ruining it. The last thing I wanted to do was talk about why I was panicking about sharing a bed with my husband.

William turns over to his night stands and pulls out the remote for the television that's hanging on the wall, across from our bed. I wasn't sure what he was up to but William turns it on and scans through an assortment of wildlife documentaries, before choosing one on marine life. William continues his silence as he adjusts his pillows and shits off the light.

"Come here." He finally whispers.

I turn my head over to face him as he lays on the bed, the pillows giving him enough leverage and comfort to look at the TV. I hesitated to move closer, I wasn't exactly sure what William wanted me to do.

But he doesn't give me a moment to think it through, instead he moves his arm around my waist and brings me towards him. My head is now pressing against his warm chest. The television's light lit up the room with hues of blue.

William runs his hand down my hair, and the voice of the narrator, along with the clashing of the waves and the sounds of the aquatic animals within the documentary, begin relaxing me.

"I don't know what it is about these documentaries, especially the ones about marine life. They always make me relax when I'm stressed or nervous. I used to watch them as a kid and they'd make me fall asleep every time."

William moves his other hand up and down my back, soothing my speeding heart and calming down my breath.

"Thank you," I murmur, barely able to say another word. William just holds me tighter, continuing to stroke my back.

"You don't have to thank me, I'm your husband, Eloise."

"Not all husband's would be this understanding of panic attacks. You probably feel deceived by my parents for locking you in a loveless marriage with a faulty wife."

A single tear drops from my eye and down onto William's bare chest. William's hand freezes on my back, but only for a few seconds before he continues his movements. I can feel him shift from under me, probably to get a better look at my face. I close my eyes and bury my face within his chest. I didn't want him to see me crying, even if he already knew I was. My parent's barely noticed my panic attacks and growing up with them meant that I got them frequently. But, when it came to William he always had a knack for finding me during an episode or just being around during one.

He probably hated having to deal with it, just like my parents had. But, despite his possible hatred for it he was always there to calm me down, even when he didn't even know it.

"Eloise, how can you even think that?" William's hand brushes my chin, his fingertips grasping it lightly to have my eyes meet his.

I try to move my face away from him so that he doesn't see the redness of my eyes from crying but he holds it in place.

"Eloise, I don't think you understand how easy I have it.

I could be married to a loudmouth, egocentric, greedy heiress. Instead I got a quiet, caring, selfless woman for a wife."

I take my bottom lip between my teeth nervously and William's gaze follows the movement.

"Who could be upset to be married to a beautiful woman with an even more beautiful heart?" William's eyes darken and I swear for a moment he looks just like he did the night of our honeymoon. I move in closer, my nose now hovering over his. William lifts his hand to my cheek, his feather-like touch sending a shiver down my spine.

"I think we should go to sleep, we have to wake up early tomorrow if you want to make it to the botanical gardens on time."

I clear my throat and pull back from William, trying not to take his rejection to heart. But the ache in my chest wasn't making it easy.

"Right," I clear my throat and turn away from William. "Goodnight," I mumble into the pillow. I wasn't sure if he had even heard me, but after what seemed like a minute, William's arm found its way around my waist, bringing me into his chest. His hot breath on my neck sends shivers throughout my body, my nipples perking up at the thought of him kissing that sensitive area.

But despite my yearning, William does not advance any more than he already has. I close my eyes and settle into his embrace while trying to calm my mind from fantasizing about him taking me on this bed, at this very moment. After a while, my mind begins to relax its racing thoughts, and I fall into a peaceful slumber, but right before I fall asleep, I feel William's lips against the sweet spot of my neck, leaving me the kiss I had been yearning for.

"Goodnight, blondie," William whispers, leaving another kiss on my bare shoulder before finally falling asleep beside me.

Chapter Eighteen

William

Last night I wanted to kiss Eloise. Well, actually, I had wanted to do more than just kissing. I had wanted to take her into my arms and fuck her in as many positions as she could take before she collapsed on top of me from exhaustion. She had wanted to kiss me, Eloise was making a move and showing me what it was that she wanted. But I couldn't make the move, not when I'd only want more than just a kiss and I wasn't sure if she was ready for that just yet.

I look up from my phone just as Eloise slides into the chair next to me with her breakfast plate and a bowl of fruit. "I brought us some fruit." She chirped, placing the bowl between us and digging into her breakfast.

"Thanks, blondie." I stab the honeydew with my fork and look right back down to my phone to go over the itinerary for today. Eloise had wanted to go check out the botanical gardens today which were a bit farther away than where we were currently staying.

But it wasn't like that mattered. If Eloise wanted me to drive us to Florida right now I'd do it just for her. Tomorrow we'd go horseback riding and I'd also planned to take us into town so she could enjoy the local shops. I wasn't too keen on horseback riding, but maybe that's because I had done it plenty of times before. I wasn't going to take Eloise's first time away from her.

"I can't wait to see the botanical gardens. Today is going to be so relaxing and beautiful." Eloise takes a sip of the coffee I had gotten for her and lets out a moan at the taste of the fresh brew that Jane had made for us. If she moaned like that over a cup of coffee I wonder what other sweet sounds I could make escape those lips just with a touch.

I shift awkwardly in my chair, annoyed by the sudden tightening in my pants.

"Did you like the fruit?" Eloise stabs the pineapple with her fork and takes a bite out of it rather than putting the whole thing in her mouth. Her lips pucker around the fruit, the pineapple juice dripping down her chin.

Fuck me.

I needed to stop acting like a horny teen, I'm twenty-eight and married to her. Her eating food should not turn me on.

"Do you want some?" Eloise raises a brow and extends her fork with pineapple over to me. She obviously interpreted my staring being for the pineapple rather than her. I'd be lying if I didn't want to grab ahold of her wrist and pull her closer to me so I could get a taste of the pineapple on her lips. But instead I stretch my neck to fork and bring the fruit to my mouth.

"It's sweet, just like I like them." Is all I say, but by the flush in her cheeks I know she understood that I wasn't talking about just the fruit.

Eloise clears her throat and takes another sip of her coffee. She pulls her phone out between us and sifts through her apps until she finds the one she's looking for.

"So, while you were getting dressed this morning I compiled a playlist for us. All of different country songs that I think you may like. You know, ones that don't talk about drinking, hooking up, and breaking up."

A deep chuckle leaves my lips at Eloise's quirkiness. "You can try all you want, blondie." I push myself closer to her, our noses practically touching.

"I. Don't. Like. Country."

A devious smile plays on her lips, and it takes all the strength I had to hold myself back from pressing our lips together.

"We'll see about that." She says, pushing me away to eat the remainder of her breakfast.

"I KNEW I'D GET YOU TO SING ALONG WITH ME!" ELOISE giggles; if the seatbelt wasn't strapped in, I knew she'd be jumping out of her seat.

"I'm not singing." I tease, knowing I was definitely getting used to the lyrics now and actually enjoying them.

"Yes, you are, and you've hummed to the other Kacey Musgraves and Noah Kahan songs, so you must like them.

"I wouldn't say Noah Kahan is—"

"I refuse to hear you finish that sentence. He is as much a country music artist as any other country singer. And that doesn't take away that you were humming to the songs of other artists."

I rolled my eyes and peered over at Eloise, and I couldn't help but smile at my boisterous wife, who looked more than ready to jump out of her seat.

"Fine, I liked the songs you chose even though you did say that none of them would involve drinking, hooking up, and breaking up. Which was a lie." I tease, just to see her get riled up again.

"I had to do what was necessary to have you give the music a chance. If I told you exactly what you didn't want to hear then you wouldn't give my playlist a chance." She rationalizes.

"That's still morally incorrect, you lied to me." I try to reason, even though I couldn't care less about her little white lie.

Eloise shrugs and leans back in her seat. "Morality can't justify a wrong."

"If it's morally incorrect then it's wrong," I argue.

"Hm, but not everyone has the same morals. Therefore, your morals don't justify a wrong." Eloise retorts, opening the book she had lying on her lap.

"You'll be a good lawyer someday."

And that was the truth. Eloise was intelligent, she hadn't gotten into Columbia because of her father's money but because she had the grades to prove it.

Despite my compliment Eloise seems to stiffen next to me.

"Did I say something wrong?" I ask.

I knew that Eloise had decided to take a break from pursuing law school, which was understandable after having to deal with many changes in her life this year. But she never said not returning was an idea she had. If that was the case I didn't care. I was going to support Eloise. Besides, many women in our circles stopped working once they got married.

My mother certainly had and so had Eloises' mom.

"No, you didn't say anything wrong." Eloise's voice is soft and mellow, and though I don't mind it, it's still a complete change from how she was acting a few seconds ago.

"Do you not want to continue an education in law?" I didn't want to pester her with questions like her parents would, but we were a team now. If she didn't want to pursue her career that was fine, but as her husband I felt like this was something that she should be comfortable sharing with me.

"I don't think so," Eloise responds meekly.

"Blondie, I don't really care if it's not something you care to pursue anymore. I just want to know these things, that's all." I look over at her for a second just to show her that I wasn't upset.

"Did you have something else in mind?" I ask, trying to turn the conversation back to something she likes.

"I've always wanted to be an elementary school teacher."

Always? I thought she had always wanted to be a lawyer. I remembered the galas and events where Eloise's parents bragged about how Eloise wanted to study law. And when she had gotten into Columbia that had been the talk amongst all the socialites.

"How come you didn't choose to major in education?" I asked the question, but I knew the answer. No one who came from a wealthy background demoted themselves to a career that barely paid a living wage. But if teaching was something that Eloise had wanted then I couldn't see a reason for her not to go ahead and study that career.

"It wasn't one of the options." She mumbles, turning to the next page in her book.

"What do you mean?"

I wasn't quite sure what she was trying to say with her statement. I knew she was a couple years younger than me but from what I can remember. There are a plethora of options when choosing a major.

"My father said he'd only help me pay for school if I chose law or business, and so I chose law." She states matter-of-factly.

"What?" I tighten my grip on the wheel.

I don't know why I'm surprised by what Eloise is telling me, it's not like she was raised by the best parents. I grew up privileged but my parents were the best that they could be. And despite our issues they were still my most significant support throughout college and career. I chose my field not because I was pressured to follow in my father's footsteps but because I enjoyed being a software engineer. It was some-thing that came easily for me and my dad having his own tech company made it easier for me to climb my way up the rank.

That and marrying Eloise.

"Blondie, if you want to be a teacher I'll support you all the way. I don't give a fuck what other people say about us. I want you to do what makes you happy. I'll fund your education completely, you just worry about getting that degree." I say.

Eloise turns away, hiding her smile away from me. If I weren't driving I'd grab ahold of her chin and have her face me. There were very few times I got to see Eloise's genuine smile, so every time it made an appearance I wanted to see it.

"Thank you, I'll keep that in mind."

I turn the car into a dirt path leading to the gardens' entrance. Eloise squeals next to me, stomping her feet on the floor of the vehicle like a giddy child.

The minute I park up the car she practically jumps out the door and waits for me by the garden entrance.

"Never been to a botanical garden?" I ask, unsure as to why she's so excited to see plants.

"Actually, I've seen many. Which is why I'm excited to see what they have in this garden." Eloise looks back down towards her phone to look at the catalog of plant species that are listed in the botanical garden's website.

"If you like plants so much, how come we don't have any in our home?" I ask.

Eloise faces back up to look at me and gives me a shrug before stepping forward down the trail.

"I do have some plants, they're all just in my bedroom. I didn't want to disrupt your interior design."

What she was trying to say is that *I don't feel comfortable living in our house.*

I grab onto her wrist, turning her around to face me. A

gasp slips her lips, but she doesn't say a single thing as she looks up at me with those sky-blue eyes.

"Eloise, that penthouse is *your* home just as much as it is *mine*. It's *ours*. And I better see that whole house covered in plants when we get back home, understood?"

My voice comes out authoritative. It's the same voice I tend to use at work but never around Eloise. But I wanted her to understand that she was allowed to do whatever the fuck she wanted in our home and with her life.

I was not her father.

"Understood, thank you," Eloise says, turning back around and walking down the path once again. I follow a few steps behind as she looks around and occasionally stops to speak out about some of her favorite plants and any well-known facts that she knows about them. I enjoyed seeing her speak about her interests, I wish it was something I saw often.

Eloise comes to a sudden halt, gasping at whatever caught her eye. She runs in the direction of what she sees, and I quickly pick up my speed to catch up and see where she's gone.

"William, look!" Eloise spins around in the field of flowers, standing out in the light blue sundress she chose to wear today.

"Isn't it beautiful?" She gestures to the flowers surrounding her.

"Yes it is." I sigh, watching her dance around the field of flowers.

She looked beautiful, she looked free.

Eloise sends me back one of those genuine smiles again.

Eloise was an intelligent woman, but at this very moment, she was utterly oblivious to the fact that in the midst of all the flowers, she was, without a doubt, the prettiest one in the field.

Chapter Nineteen

etting into bed after dinner was less awkward than it had been last night. Both William and I had found our place on either side of the bed. I opened up my over-used copy of The Metamorphosis and William began the beginning chapters of the romance book I had let him borrow.

"What's the reason for the obsession with that book?" William asks, turning the page in his own book before looking at me.

I shove my bookmark between the pages before closing the book to look over at William, who has now done the same to his own book.

"I've never felt as connected with a story as I have with this one," I say, giving him a shrug as if my response had been more than enough of an explanation.

"How so?" William props himself up against the pillows and reaches over to his nightstand to leave the book on it.

My grip tightens around the book in my hand. I wasn't entirely sure if I was ready to admit my emotional connection to the worn down book in my hands. But even if I did, it's not like it would come up as a shock to William. He, like Charlotte and even Ulysses, knew how my parents treated me.

William's hand grasps my own, rubbing gentle circles with his thumb. "You don't have to share if you don't want to. I was just curious."

"It's not a secret or anything." I shrug and lean back into pillows I had set behind me for comfort.

"I guess I've always resonated with the main character. He's used by his parents all throughout his life and once he turns into a hideous bug his family is quick to neglect him. Because even though that's their son, what good is he to them if he cannot provide what they need?"

William remains stoic to my response.

"You're not a bug, Eloise."

"No, I am not. If I were, my parents would have no use for me."

"You aren't a pawn," William mutters as he grips my hand in his.

"Aren't I, though?" I ask, my annoyance seeping through my tone.

"I'm even a pawn to you. I am just a bridge between you and my father's company. It's my marriage to you that keeps you next in line as CEO." I dispute, removing my hand away from his and tugging the sheets up towards my chest before setting my book down onto the nightstand.

"Eloise, maybe it started that way, but I don't see you as a pawn. I see you as my wife." William scoots closer, carefully bringing his hand back to my own.

"William, just because you no longer see me as a pawn doesn't mean that I wasn't used as one before. And I hate to remind you, but my parents still plan to use me as a pawn in hopes of me getting pregnant. And that still sounds like a crappy game of chess to me." If my tone didn't share my annoyance with him, then my face surely did. William softens his gaze and moves his hand down from my hand and to the curve of my hip.

"Eloise, I can't turn back time. We're married now." His voice comes out in a whisper, maybe he's worried that if he uses any other tone I'll break into a panic attack.

"I am very much aware of that," I mutter, flicking the ring of promise around my finger nervously.

"What I'm saying is that you are no longer a pawn to either me or your parents. I don't give a fuck what they want from us. We won't be having a child until we are ready." His hand reaches down to the crevice to my lower back.

"You got that, blondie?" He asks, using his hand's position to bring me closer to him.

"Yeah, I got it."

"You're not a bug at all, not to me." He reassures me.

Though William's words are beautiful and something I've been craving to hear for years. They aren't coming from the mouths of the people that should be saying that.

"Look at me, Eloise." I shift my eyes to William's dark gaze.

"You can depend on me. We are family. It's you and me against the world, blondie. You got that?" His hot breath grazes my lips and just like last night I'm tempted to kiss him.

William's grip on my waist tightens and for a second I think he may even travel it down to my ass. "Do you understand?" He murmurs once again. His eyes shift from eyes to my lips. I instinctively lick them, self-conscious of them being chapped.

"Eloise." He says sternly.

"Yes, I understand." I finally whisper.

"Good," William brings himself closer, grazing his nose against my cheek and down towards my neck.

This felt new, it felt different.

We hadn't been this close, this intimate, since the honeymoon. William's grip loosens around my waist, and he gives my neck a chaste kiss. After waiting there for a few seconds, he finally pools back, lifting his hand to bring a strand of my hair to the back of my ear.

"Goodnight, Eloise." He whispers, laying back down on his side of the bed. This time there were no warm embraces. We stayed on our own side peering up at the ceiling before sleep finally took over.

I woke up to an empty bed and a soundless room. William must've gotten a head start on his breakfast. I reach for my phone on the nightstand to check the time. We had horseback riding scheduled for this afternoon.

It was only eleven, so we still had a little over two hours

before the activity. This gave me enough time to shower and get dressed. Maybe we could even head over to town and try out a cafe down there before coming back and continuing today's agenda.

I went to the shower with a towel in hand. The heat of the summer's sun was intense but the air was breathable compared to that of the city, which I had grown used to after years of living there.

I take my time in the shower, knowing I still have plenty of time before we have to leave for the cafe, that is, if William is interested in going.

I make my way back into the room after my shower and there's still no sign of William. I go to the dresser and take out my outfit for the day. Dropping the towel on the floor I pick out my underwear and bra and begin putting them on. As I adjust my bra from behind I hear the creaking of the door. I grab a hold of my shorts and top to cover my chest as I turn to look over. William walks in shirtless, his shorts hanging low on his torso and a tray of food in his hands.

He closes the door behind him and turns to face away from me.

"Sorry, I went on a run and stopped to get us some breakfast. I wasn't sure if you were up yet." William explains.

I rush to get the clothes on my body before giving him the clear to turn around. William turns and heads towards the bed, placing the tray of food on top of it.

"I got you some fruit and coffee, I was thinking I could take a quick shower and we could head downtown to get something to eat and just look around." William, grabs a fork and takes a strawberry into his mouth. He runs his hand through his damp hair, slicking it back, the sun's light shines through the window and onto his skin. His sweaty skin glistened and taunted me to touch him.

"What do you think?" Williams asks, breaking me away from whatever dirty thoughts were beginning to arise in my mind.

"Huh?" I ask.

"Heading downtown for lunch." William restates, the smirk on his lips taunting me.

I clear my throat and reach for the coffee he brought me, taking a sip. "That's perfectly fine." I manage to squeak out.

"Perfect, I'll just take a shower and then we can go," William says, bringing another strawberry into his mouth and walking past me to head out towards the shower. I take a bite of banana, but stop mid-chew when I feel a hot breath on the back of my neck.

"You're welcome to continue your gazing while I'm in the shower, I'll even let you touch if you're a good girl." William's voice is hot and heavy in my ear, and I want so badly to turn around and take him up on his offer as he walks away. But I'm too scared to make that move, too scared to take what's probably a joke literally.

Riding horses had been my idea, but I already regretted it. We could've just taken the day to enjoy walking around downtown, rather than standing right in front of a horse I'm too scared to get up on.

"You scared?" Jason, our instructor, asks as he approaches me.

"I hadn't realized how intimidating it could be to get on a horse." I duck my face, embarrassed to look him in the eye. In my defense I hadn't realized how tall the horse was. And now here I was on a stepping stool, trying to figure out how to get on the saddle.

"It's not too bad, princess. Plus, Cherry here is sweet and kind. One of the best horses that we have out here for beginners." I hold back a smile from the pet name he gives me. I didn't want him thinking I was wanting anything but help from him. It was also a pet name Ulysses had for me and hearing it again after a while didn't feel right.

"Why Cherry?"

"She was born under a cherry tree and ironically they're her favorite snack." Jason's bright smile widens as he pets the black mare. His light brown hair was longer than I was used to seeing on a man. He kept the strands of hair tucked behind his ear while the over used cap kept it in place.

Jason had a rugged look to him, but it went well with his personality. At least from the tiny bits of interaction I had with him .

"Never been on a horse before?" He asks, taking a step closer to tighten the strap on the saddle that he had instructed everyone how to put on.

"That obvious?" I ask, tilting my head over to the saddle he was fixing up for me.

"Not too obvious, princess." He looks away from the saddle and allows his eyes to linger down my body, which instinctively makes me cross my arms over my chest as a barrier.

"Her name is Eloise and don't worry, I got it from here." William's voice rises from behind me, his chest pressing against my back. I uncross my arms and let my arms fall at my side. Now that William was here, Jason would get that I wasn't interested.

But despite the death glare that I know William has to be sending him, Jason still gives me a flirty smile before looking back up at William, "she's all yours." Jason takes a step back before turning around and heading back to his horse.

William walks around to face me, my hand now rising towards the horse's saddle. His face doesn't show any anger or discontent. On the contrary, he's staring down at me with a playful smirk displayed on his lips.

"Flirting with the instructor, are we, blondie?"

I suck my teeth and hold back my smile, pondering over whether I should defend myself or play along with the idea.

I bring my hand up onto his chest and gather the courage to take a step closer. "Jealous?" My eyes lock with his, and though the coward in me wants to hop on this horse and ride far away, I manage to hold his piercing stare.

William moves in closer, leaving little space between us. We had been playing this game since our first night here. The touches, the stares, and the teasing. I was more than tempted to collide my lips with his. But he had been the one to keep pushing back and I think he had more than enough time to figure out what he wanted.

"Don't play this game with me, Eloise." His voice comes out in a dominant growl. He had never spoken to me in that tone before.

Well, actually, that was a lie.

The last time he spoke to me in that tone, he had me grasping our bed sheets.

I swallow the last bit of moisture I had in my mouth before bringing myself closer to him. Any closer, our lips would finally touch.

"What game am I playing exactly?" My voice comes out silky and seductive without even meaning for it to. But I had had enough of the teasing.

"If you want something, say it blondie." He eggs on, bringing himself closer, his eyes daring me to make the next to move. But, I had shown my interest in him and showed him where I stood. The ball was now in his court.

I stretch up on my toes, my lips now only a couple of centimeters away from his.

"No William, if *you* want something, take it." I challenge, managing to stand still on my toes for just a bit longer, in hopes of finally getting the reaction I want from him. But, my lips remain bare as he moves his arm across from me to steady the straddle and help me onto Cherry.

"Come on, don't want to keep our instructor waiting." Is all he says as he straddles me in and then gets on his own horse, right beside me.

JASON TAKES US THROUGH THE FARM'S TRAIL AT A steady pace. There are only a few other people along with us but all I can feel is William's gaze on me from behind. He could continue to glare all he wanted. The ball was in his court and it was his move.

"Okay, I think we've gotten used to being on the horses enough to speed up just a bit, am I right?" Jason blurts as he walks us out into a beautiful meadow.

"Just a reminder that our horses are very well trained. If you want to speed up or stop, the answer is all in the rein." Jason reminds us.

Everyone around spreads out in their own groups, some speeding up while others like me keep to the same pace.

"I'd thought you'd be having a fun ride on your horse there." William says, bringing his horse beside mine.

"I might be a bit nervous," I admit.

"Of riding? That's a shame." William bites back a smile.

If William wanted to continue this little game, I was more than happy to play along, better yet, I was more than happy to play dirty.

"It is, I've been told I look hot while riding." I raise my eyebrow, challenging him to make his next move. But I don't expect William's face to darken completely.

"I don't doubt it." He replies, his jaw tightening as he continues to look at me with that deadly glare. "Let me guess, was it Ulysses?"

My mouth gaped open at his sudden question about Ulysses, and I didn't think the teasing would turn to jealousy so quickly.

"Ulysses," William snarls. "How does someone even say his name in bed?"

I shouldn't have felt offended by his dig at Ulysses' name, but for some reason, I did, and before I could even think twice about my reply, the words left my mouth before I could stop them.

"How does someone moan the name William in bed?" I snap back.

William's stupid smirk makes an appearance again as he raises his eyebrows at me in astonishment at my sudden comeback. He lets a chuckle escape his lips as he peers down at me, and suddenly, I'm not with the lovely man I've been happy with these past few weeks. I'm with the man who had my knees weak, begging to come during our honeymoon.

"I don't know baby, but you did a phenomenal job."

With that William hikes up the rein of the horse and trots away at a faster pace, leaving both Cherry and I frozen in place.

WE SPEND ABOUT AN HOUR IN THE MEADOW BEFORE Jason has us all trot back to the horse stables. I did end up picking up my pace and riding Cherry like one should and I hate myself for not doing it sooner. William joined along and no other words were said, instead we enjoyed the rest of the time we had in the meadow and the rest of the trail back to the stables.

William gives me a hand when it comes to getting off of Cherry and putting everything back where it belongs. The fellow riders finish much quicker and head out before us while William begins to put everything away for his own horse.

"You guys can head out, I'll take care of the rest." Jason says, walking to our stall.

"You sure?" William asks.

"Yeah, you two lovebirds, go enjoy the rest of the day."

Huh, William and I were lovebirds now? A few hours ago I was his princess. Guess William's comment put him in his place.

William thanks Jason before swinging his arm around my waist and leading me out of the barn. I couldn't help feeling a bit tense, especially after what went down earlier. Maybe it would've been best if I hadn't made that comment, but it isn't fair for him to constantly be teasing me. He either wanted something between us or he didn't and he had to make up his mind and decide. Or maybe I just had to be the bigger person and say what I felt, rather than just thinking it.

"Willi—"

My body is suddenly turned and pressed up against the barn's door as William's lips collide with mine. And Jesus Christ, I had been yearning for those lips to be pressed against my own for months. William's hands glide across my back and make their way down towards my ass, gripping them firmly. A gasp escapes my mouth from his tightening grip, and William's tongue slips in, colliding with my own.

I wasn't sure how a kiss could feel so erotic, but this one did. William pulls away, resting his forehead on my own. Those blue eyes look deeply into my own before he speaks.

"It took me a whole fucking year to kiss you again. And I'm hoping you don't regret this because I don't ever want to stop." His breathy whisper hits my lips and intensifies their swolleness. I bring my lips back up to his, kissing him firmly, his lips once again dancing with my own. I break away and look back up at him again, his smile awakening the butterflies in my stomach.

"If that kiss wasn't a good answer enough, I want to let you know that I'd really, really, really like to continue kissing you again." I say, giving his lips another peck.

"Good, because I'll only be getting more creative from here, blondie." William steps away and tugs on my arm to bring me over to his side.

"Let's go get changed and then we can find a place to eat." He says, holding me close to him as we walk towards our barn.

William opens the door and I step in right behind him, walking over to my nightstand where I had left my phone while we went on our ride. William does the same and lets out a sigh before excusing himself to take a call from work. I immediately open up my messages to text Charlotte but get sidetracked by an unknown number.

I read the message and send a quick reply back, not liking the joke one bit. This had to be someone messing with me.

UNKNOWN

Hello, Eloise. I think you owe me something.

ELOISE

I'm sorry, who is this?

I get a reply back instantly, and as eerie and bothersome as the message was, I wasn't going to give the person the time of day to keep on wasting my time.

UNKNOWN

Who I am is not important, but what you owe is. I want the money that was promised, Eloise.

ELOISE

I think you've got the wrong person.

I send a reply back before deleting and blocking the number instantly. The last thing I needed was a freak trying to harass me for money. This must've been some idiot who had nothing better to do. Well he wasn't ruining my day or my week.

William makes his way back in and brings himself down over to me and doesn't stop until my back is laid down on the mattress. He presses his lips to mine once again, his body hovering over mine, his arms closing me in.

He pulls away from the kiss and begins caressing my cheek, his eyes flickering between my eyes and lips.

"Eloise, I'm going to make the rest of this week the honeymoon you deserve and after this week is over I'm going to make this the marriage you deserve. I promise you that." William's voice is low but stern, his vow to our future sounding like a proper business agreement.

But I knew that the business aspect between us was gone now, we were going to make this work.

Chapter Twenty

After dinner William and I walked around a park that was near the restaurant. He had also managed to sneak a few kisses here and there. From time to time I would check my phone worried I'd get another message from an unknown number. Maybe it had all been a misunderstanding or just a sick prank.

"What's got you so deep in thought?" William asks, bringing me closer to him as we walk towards our car from the park.

I shake my head and lean into him, "Nothing, just enjoying the moment, that's all."

William snakes his hand right above my ass, taking a moment to contemplate his next move before committing to lowering it completely and grasping it.

"I can't wait to see you in one of those tiny bikinis you like to tease me with, tomorrow." He whispers in my ear.

Heat rushes to my cheeks from his admission, but it feels good to know that I held such an effect on William to have him fantasizing about me in my bikinis.

Tomorrow we'll be going to Warren Falls. I hope it'll be as lovely as the pictures and videos I've seen. But even if it wasn't I'd still enjoy my time with William. This trip had already been much better than our honeymoon had been and that was already more than I could've asked for.

"I can't wait either." I confess joyfully, reaching up to give William a peck on the lips.

"Come, let's go home." William says, nodding his head towards the car that was now in view.

Home.

I guess that made sense. Wherever we were was home.

ONCE WE GOT BACK, WE IMMEDIATELY GOT READY FOR bed and followed our nightly routine. Both of us slid into our own side of the bed, a book in hand, the space on the bed between us seemed much farther away than usual or maybe that's just because I craved to be closer tonight.

Maybe it was because I wanted something more than just a kiss. The romance book in my hand hadn't improved the thought. I tighten my legs together, trying to calm the arousal between them. But as I continue to read the steamy pages the more I want to throw the book to the side and get on top of William.

"How's your book?" I tilt my head over to the sound of William's voice beside me, his eyes glued to the page in front of him.

"Good." I manage to squeak out.

The book was indeed so fucking good that I was imagining jumping his bones this very second.

"Yours?" I asked, curious to see if he was on a spicy chapter himself. I had begun giving him romance books for him to read and he was currently reading an erotica that I had given him after having him ask me consistently for books with more than just vanilla sex.

"I'm on a very intriguing chapter." He responds, adjusting himself up against the bed frame.

"Good, me too." I managed to say, but the stupid response immediately made me want to slap myself in the face.

Good, me too?

What the hell was wrong with me?

William clears his throat before he begins speaking to me, no, not speaking— reading.

"*Micah grabs ahold of my hair, tightening his grip. My scalp burns but the pool of wetness dripping in between my legs craves for more pain, more of him.*" William reads, his voice stable and low.

I tighten my hands around my book, pretending to ignore him, but fail completely. I can only imagine my own pool of wetness that was currently building up between my own legs.

"*He tightens the restraints on my arms and brings the*

head of his cock to my lips. 'Open wide Imogen, I'm going to fuck your mouth until you're crying and gagging all over my cock and then if I see fit I'll bend you over and fuck your tight, pretty, little cunt. Understood?' He growls, pulling my hair. My mouth opens in a gasp and Micah thrusts his cock in my mouth." William's voice becomes shakier as he continues to read. He's becoming just as aroused as I am. Suddenly his voice comes to a stop and I can feel his eyes on me.

"Does that sound intriguing?" He asks.

"I— uh— yes." I managed to speak.

William's lips form into a smile, and I can tell he's trying to hold back a laugh at my coyness.

"Should I continue, or would you like to read your own intriguing chapter?" He asks, his hand moving across the bed and up my spine, the hairs of my skin raising my nipples pebbling beneath my nightgown

"You can continue if you like."

William smirks before peering back down to his book and continuing to read.

"Micah bends me over, my ass up in the air, his tip taunting my throbbing entrance. I needed to feel his cock stretching me out. Without warning he slams himself into me, a moan escaping my now swollen lips and my pussy tightens around his large member. Fuck, it didn't matter how many times we'd fucked, my pussy somehow always remains tight for him. 'Please, sir.' I beg."

Sir.

That had been what I called William that one night together, that one word had made him feral. Fuck, and I wanted him to go feral now.

His fingers remained trailing up and down my spine and

I desperately needed more. William continued to read but I just continued my fantasy of him. Continued my fantasy of having William's hands over me and his cock deep inside of me.

My breathing picked up its pace as William continued to read how the characters reached their climax, and just as he was about to finish, I got up from the bed and walked over to the dresser.

"I think I'm going to take a shower," I say rather quickly as I grab a towel.

"But you just took one." He counteracts.

"Right— yes, I did." I manage to spew. "But, I'm getting a bit hot and we— sweaty, right, I'm getting sweaty and it's hot. So, I'm going to take a shower... now."

William only looks at me with an astonished gaze as I continue to babble like an idiot. I open the door to the outside and make my way to the shower. I turn on the shower and hang my towel on the hook right outside. I remove my nightgown, the night's chilled air grazing my skin. I shimmy out of my panties and enter the shower, closing the door behind me. I try to let the water cool me down as best as possible. But the need for William was too strong.

I close my eyes and trail my fingers down from my neck towards my nipples, giving them a pinch before moving down towards my aching pussy. My fingers find my clit immediately, moving them in a circular motion. Picturing William's strong hands on me and his hard cock teasing my entrance, just like in that fucking book that he had read to me.

The sudden sound of the door swinging open startles me into opening my eyes. William stands in front of me, completely naked. His dark gaze glides down my body, taking me in.

My nipples harden and goosebumps rise from the caress of the light breeze. For a moment William and I continue to stare and right before I can utter a word about his presence, my body is pushed back onto the wooden wall and his lips are on mine. His hands roam down my spine and cup my ass, bringing me closer to him. His thick member pushing against my abdomen.

William separates from our kiss, one of his hands still holding me firm to him. His other rises up to cup my cheek.

God, that dark blue gaze of his was going to kill me. I

"You told me to take what I want, correct?" He growls.

William runs his dark gaze down my body once more, almost as if he were taking a picture in his mind. And I wanted to do the very same. My gaze trails down his body, taking in every inch of him. from his eyes, to those sculpted arms, and that beautifully developed V line that led all the way down to his thick length that was ready to be inside of me.

Fingers grasp my chin, pulling me up to meet William again.

"Answer me, blondie. You said I should take what I want, does that offer still stand?" He says, his voice, just as much as his eyes filled with want and need.

And fuck, I needed him just as much.

"Yes, tak—"

Before I can finish my sentence William rises me up into his hold. His hands tighten around the globes of my ass, pushing us back under the shower-head. William's lips crash onto mine, biting and sucking the moans right out of me.

"I love hearing your sweet moans, Eloise." He whispers, trailing his lips down my neck, sucking on that sweet spot that has me grinding into him for more than just mere kisses.

"Don't worry beautiful, we'll get there soon. Just let me enjoy what I've been so fucking patiently waiting for." He growls, taking my nipple into his mouth.

"Oh, fuck." I cradle his head in my hands, encouraging his motion to continue.

"Do you know how many times you've fucking taunted me with your dresses?" He growls moving onto the other nipple who was craving the same attention.

I rub my clit onto his hard abs, needing some sort of release.

"William, please." I beg.

William releases my nipple with a loud pop. He brings his face back up to mine, our lips a millimeter away from one another and our eyes staring at each other with deep yearning.

"Do you know how many times I've wanted to come home from one of those fucking boring events and saunter right after you just so that I could rip the fucking dress off of you. Fuck, blondie the only thing I could think about any time I needed a release was that night together." William admits.

"Me too," I reply, letting myself be vulnerable once again.

"Eloise?" He says.

"Yes?"

"I'm going to fuck you rough against this shower until you come so hard that you squeeze every last drop of cum out of me, and then I'm going to go bring you back inside onto our bed and eat it all out of you until your thighs are shaking, understood blondie?" He growls, his breath hot on my lips.

"Yes."

Fuck yes. I needed him inside me now.

"Yes, what?" He teases, a devilish smirk playing on his lips as he brings his hand to his cock and aligns it with my entrance.

A smile plays on my own as I recall the memory of our honeymoon.

"Yes, sir."

William thrusts himself deep inside, and my pussy instinctively tightens around his thick cock, trying to get used to his size once again.

"God, you feel so fucking tight." He groans, thrusting his hips upward, deep into my cunt. His lips find my nipples once again, sucking and tucking on the sensitive nubs.

"William, I need more." I beg, needing him deeper, rougher, and faster.

"Fuck, I love how much of a dirty whore you are when it comes to my cock, baby." William groans, speeding his thrusts and fucking me harder.

"But that's okay isn't it, blondie? Because you're my good little whore." He pounds deeper into me, my pussy becoming wetter and tighter with every stroke inside me.

"Yes sir, I'm your..."

Thrust.

"Little."

Thrust.

"Needy."

Thrust.

"Whore."

William tightens his hold on my waist and brings his hand to my hair, gripping it tightly and pulling my head back.

"Remember what I want from you, blondie. I need to feel that pussy tighten around my cock. Right now it's not tight enough, understood?" He groans before biting and licking that same sweet spot on my neck that had me grinding up against him earlier.

"Oh fuck, yes, sir." I moan, my hips automatically moving in sync with his own thrusts as my clit rubs onto his abs, stimulating me enough to tighten my hold around his cock.

"That's it, baby, you're doing such a good job."

God, why does his praise feel so good? No one else's ever felt as good as his did.

A whimper escapes my lips as I feel my climax begin to rise.

"Oh fuck."

"You better hold it, blondie. Ask for it like a good girl." He growls, pounding deeper and deeper, I clench my abs, holding onto my climax that I so desperately needed to release.

"Please, sir, please."

"Hold it like a good girl, blondie. That's right, tighten that grip."

"I c-can't." I stutter, holding onto the orgasm for as long as I can before finally releasing it despite his refusal.

The orgasm flows throughout my body, and my pussy spasms around William's dick. A groan escapes his lips before he holds me tighter and shoots his load deep within me.

William doesn't remove himself from me, but instead, he removes the grip he has on my hair to turn off the shower and then brings it back to my ass to hold me up.

"Fuck blondie, that was amazing." He murmurs in my ear as he carries me back inside.

"William, we'll get the bed wet!" I shriek as he removes himself from inside of me and settles me on the bed.

William only shrugs and brings himself over to me, giving my forehead a kiss.

"That was the plan anyway." He murmurs as he continues trailing kisses down my body. A giggle slips past my lips and William moves back to hover over my face.

"I love hearing that sound. Do it again for me, baby." He demands.

"I can't just laugh on demand, William."

William raises an eyebrow in challenge, and before I can stop him, he's tickling me, my giggles and pleads spilling out immediately.

"So my beautiful wife is ticklish." He muses.

William's eyes rise to look above me before he finally looks down at me, his eyes finding mine again.

He pulls away the wet strands off my face before setting a light kiss on my lips.

"Happy Anniversary, Eloise." I look over at the clock he was looking at on the nightstand before turning back to him.

"Happy Anniversary, William."

"It will be." He replies, moving himself back down to the heat between my legs.

Chapter Twenty-One

William

My cock was beginning to harden at just the thought of being able to be inside Eloise again. I hadn't expected to fuck her against the shower or fuck her at all tonight. But knowing that my reading had gotten her all hot and bothered enough to take a shower had me stiff in my pants. And now I had her here sprawled on the bed, and she looked like an angel.

I move down towards her glistening pussy, which had my cum dripping out of it. Fuck, I have to know how good we taste together. I kiss the sensitive bundle of nerves before suckling it. Not too much, but enough to have her arching her back for me and trailing her fingers through my hair.

"Wait, Will, it's sensitive." She hisses.

Fuck, I loved when she called me Will.

Not many people did, only those I was close with, and

Eloise was as close as they came. I let go of her swollen clit and lap my tongue up and down her folds, teasing her entrance. But just a swipe and the taste of our mixture has me ready to bury myself deep within her and fill her up with my cum once again.

I plunge my tongue into her and bring all my cum into my mouth. I lift myself up and hover my lips over her mouth. It only takes a second for Eloise to look into my eyes and know exactly what I want from her. She opens her mouth and I drip our mixture right into it. I watch as she swallows all of it like the good girl she is and kiss her plump lips.

"Don't we taste so good together, baby?" I growl into her lips and move down towards her neck, sucking on that sweet spot she loves so much.

"Yes, sir." She moans, arching her back for more.

"You want more, blondie?" I trail my tongue down her perky tits, bringing her hard nipple into my mouth.

"Yes, fuck. You promised, shaking legs." She groans, pushing my head further down back to her pussy.

A chuckle escapes my lips at her urgency. But, right now, I wanted to tease her more than I wanted to make her cum.

I grab a hold of her wrists and bring them down to either side of her. "I'll keep my promise, blondie. But, first, you'll have to learn to be patient." I tease, kissing her perky little breasts again, leaving behind my marks. Seeing them bruise up gave me extreme satisfaction.

I wanted to claim her in every way I could. And I didn't care if it made me some kind of possessive asshole.

I give each of her nipples attention, her nails clawing at my wrists for release. But her moans and lustful eyes let me know that what she really wanted was more.

"William, please." She moans.

I let go of her nipple with a loud pop and hovered back over just to take in her beauty again.

"Don't fuck with me, Will." She snaps, becoming even more upset about our prolonged situation. But, fuck I loved seeing her get snarky with me. I remove my hands from her wrist and flip her over by her hips.

"Ass up, baby." I growl, moving her ass closer to my face.

"What are you doing?" Eloise asks, turning her head back to look at me.

A smirk plays on my lips as I spread her ass cheeks.

"Don't worry, blondie. I'm just going to keep my promise. Make sure your back stays arched because if it doesn't we're just going to have to start over." I spit on the ring of nerves that I'm sure she's never even tried to play with before. But then again Eloise has a habit of surprising me. Maybe my beautiful heiress of a wife likes anal play.

I run my thumb over the tight entrance, tracing it in circles. Eloise remains stiff in her position. Determined to stick through my demands like a good girl.

But that wouldn't last too long.

Eloise's creamy skin lacked any type of blemish or scar. But fuck it just made you want to leave your mark on her. She was my wife, the ring on her finger proved itself. But for some reason I wanted there to be even more proof. Even if it would only be for my eyes.

I bring my face down towards her dripping cunt and swipe my tongue up from her clit up to her entrance, my thumb still on her tight little hole. I insert the tip of my thumb into her tight ass and bring my lips back to her clit. I suck on the bundle of nerves and inch my thumb deeper into her ass.

"Oh fuck, yes, more." Eloise moans. Her fingers grasp onto the sheets tightly but her position remains intact.

"You're a good girl, Eloise. You're doing such a good job, keep that back arched, and I'll continue to give you more, baby." I finish pushing the remainder of my thumb into her ass and bring my other hand up to her pussy. I insert two fingers into her wet pussy, earning a few hushed words from Eloise.

I push my fingers out of her pussy and slam them right back in, curving them into her g-spot. Eloise cries out as I do the same with my thumb, moving them in sync.

I insert another finger in her pussy and fuck her hard, her moans and pleas growing louder. I know she doesn't know whether to focus on the tightness of her ass or the pleasure in her pussy and I fucking love seeing her like this.

Eloise cries out for more as she clenches her pussy around my fingers. I remove them instantly and rub her clit with enough pressure to have her pull back out of her stance.

"Did you just move, baby?" I tease, pushing my thumb in deeper into her ass, a hiss escaping her fucking lips, but that's not the response I need. I smack my hand against her pale ass, a yelp escaping her lips. But despite the slight amount of pain she puts herself back into position and I remove my thumb away from her ass.

"What did I say would happen if you move, Eloise?" I ask, rubbing her already pink ass.

"That we'd start over." She answers.

"That's right, baby, right from the start." I spit on her ass and repeat the same steps as before. Teasing her ass, sucking her clit, and fingering her pussy.

I insert a third finger and fuck her pussy with them harder than last time. "I love hearing how wet your pussy gets for me, Eloise. Come for me like a good girl in the position that I want and then I'll fuck this pretty cunt of yours." I remove my fingers and rub her clit hard and fast, Eloise lets out a strangled moan and clenches the sheets, her back arched perfectly and her head held high like a good girl.

"That's it baby, scream for me. Come for me, Eloise." I growl.

"Oh fuck," Eloise's legs begin to tremble as I press harder on her clit.

"Fuck me, I can't take it." Eloise falls onto the sheets, and I smack that pretty little ass of hers before hoisting her back up by the hips, her thighs still spasming from the orgasm.

"No, wait. I can't anymore." Eloise says in between heaving breaths.

"I think you can, blondie."

I align my cock with her entrance and take her hard and fast. I watch as my wife moans for more as she milks my cock of every drop of cum I have.

This was just the start of our honeymoon, I was going to catch up to a year's worth of sex with my wife.

Chapter Twenty-Two

"You've got to be kidding me." William's cold gaze trails along my body as I finish adjusting my bikini top. A devious giggle slips my lips as I look at him through the mirror. I grab the dress I'm supposed to be wearing and pull it over my body.

"Eloise, everything is out." William growls, standing up from the bed to stand right behind me.

"You didn't mind on our honeymoon." I fire back. Just because we were officially together now didn't mean he could take over my parents position as puppeteers.

William wraps his arm around my waist and pushes my back towards him. He leans down to my ear and whispers, "I was drunk and out of your way for most of it. In fact, when I finally saw you in one of these skimpy things, it finally led to us christening the hotel bed."

Shivers run across my body and I wanted to so desperately turn around and get on my knees for this man. But if we started now we would never get around to going to the falls. "I cease to see the problem." I tease, unwrapping his arms from my waist and walk away towards my nightstand to pick up my phone.

"The problem is, blondie, that I'll have to try very fucking hard not have a complete hard-on all day," William growls, giving my ass a smack.

I let out a yelp and turn around to reprimand him jokingly only to be met with a rectangular object, wrapped in yellow wrapping paper.

"Happy Anniversary, blondie." William says for what seems like the millionth time today already. But it's not something I want him to stop saying. I take the gift from his hand, curious as to what William got me for our anniversary. We had both agreed on sticking to a paper theme for our anniversary. It had been difficult trying to find something for William. But after some research I found the perfect gift on an etsy shop. It wasn't something extravagant or expensive. But how expensive could a paper gift be?

"You want to open the gifts now?" I ask, taking the wrapped box from his hands to mine. "I thought you'd want to do it during dinner."

William shrugs his shoulders and nods down to the gift in my hand. "I'd rather see your reaction to the gift now." He says, taking a step closer.

"Come on, blondie. I'm usually a shitty gift giver, but I think I actually got it right this time." His grin rises as I give into his persistence. I unwrap the pastel yellow paper, unsure to what it is I'm uncovering. I toss all of the paper onto the floor and look down at a book sealed within a plastic bag.

"William what is–" A gasp slips my lips and my fingers tighten on the book as I look up to meet William's gaze. The man is sporting a bright smile.

"There's no way this is real." My eyes begin to water as I look back at the book in my hands.

"Die Verwandlung." I manage to whisper, taking in the book closely.

"The Metamorphosis, yes it is. A first edition." He clarifies.

"What? How? Can I remove it from the plastic?" I ask, my fingers gripping the plastic wrapped book in my hand.

"It's your book now, blondie. You can do whatever you'd like with it. Though I do hope you take much better care of this version than your original copy."

I roll my eyes at William's jab. My copy may be hanging on by a string of tape, but that's because it's my first and favorite copy. This one was different. This copy was an original and I couldn't even read in German so there would be no point in me stuffing it into my bag everywhere I go.

I open the bag and remove the book from the plastic. I bring it to my nose and take a whiff of the pages before turning it over to the first page. It even had the scent of an old library book which for some reason always made me happy.

I look back up to William's eyes; his blue gaze holds a calm and gentleness that I've begun to find comfort in. Somehow, this man who was barely a friend is turning out to be a safe haven.

"William, this must've been so expensive. I don't even

know what to say because not even a thank you would be enough." William cups my face with his hands and lowers himself to press a delicate kiss to my lips.

"Eloise, you deserve this and more. I don't need a thank you because I don't even deserve it. I don't even deserve you." His thumbs brush against my cheek, his gaze peering right into my soul as he whispers, "but now that I have you, Eloise, I'm not giving you back."

His lips meet mine again, his tongue begging my lips for entrance. I'm quick to further the kiss, my arms reaching over his neck to bring him in closer. I moan into the kiss. Despite his amazing kissing that was bound to end with me naked on our bed again I wanted to give him my own gift. I pull away from William's grasp, a groan escaping his lips instantly.

"Oh, hush, it's my turn." I walk over to the drawer where I had been keeping the gift wrapped up in. "I do have to say that it's not as extravagant as your gift. But I'd thought you might like it anyway." I raise the box towards him and William quickly grasps the blue-covered present and begins unwrapping it. The look on his face is precious, like a child opening up his first christmas present of the day.

William pulls out the wooden frame and looks back at me. I can't really tell if he likes it or not, which makes me nervous as he continues to stare at me.

"You don't like it?" I finally manage to ask.

William furrows his eyebrows as he looks between me and the gift.

"Eloise, of course I like it, it's us blondie. I've just never seen something like this before." I look down at our origami artwork of us at our wedding. I had sent the artist the exact image to match it to and the color theme of our wedding which she matched perfectly with the origami flowers she added to the art piece.

"Is this replicating the wedding picture that we have in our living room?" William asks, taking in every detail of the piece.

"Yes, actually, it is." It was one of my favorite pictures from the wedding. We almost looked like a real couple, we almost looked happy. I didn't even realize that William had taken notice of the pictures framed in our living room.

William takes my hand and places a kiss on it. "I wish I had gotten to take that dress off of you. You deserved a better honeymoon than what I gave you. I'm sorry for that, baby."

I shake my head, kissing the inside of his wrists. "It doesn't matter anymore, William. We can do things right now."

"I will, blondie." He assures.

"I will, too, no more hiding away."

Chapter Twenty-Three

Eloise

"William, are you sure we should be rearing off the path?" I ask as I trail close behind him through the trees and green foliage. William looks at me with a grin.

"Scared I'll lose us?"

"Yes." I say without hesitation.

"You don't really give off the boyscouts look. In fact, you don't even give off a man of the wild vibe." William lets out a chuckle as he offers me his hand to trail down towards him.

"Do you hear that?" William asks as I step closer to get right in front of him.

I stay silent and try to pick up on any noise around us but hear nothing. At least nothing but the rustling of the trees and from the slight breeze that comes through very few times. "I don't hear anything, honey." I whisper.

"Then I need to make sure I take you to the Doctor as soon as we get back home because that noise, blondie, is the sound of water." William grabs hold of my legs and carries me bridal style, bringing us out from the trees and in front of a beautiful waterfall. "Oh my god, this is even more stunning in person." I take in the rushing of the falls as it lands onto the still water, bringing the area to life.

"I'm glad you like looking at it, blondie. But you're going to like being in it way more." William puts me down and removes his shirt. I take off my own clothes as William watches me pull off my dress, revealing my bikini.

William's gaze darkens, and he looks around at our surroundings. "Get in," Is all he says as his eyes glue themselves back onto my body.

I look around, looking for anyone that could be watching. William has something planned and I'm sure he'd rather not have any peeping Toms trying to take a look at what we're doing.

I take a step into the water and begin walking further, but I can hear William on my trail as he walks through the water. I make it far enough where the water hits my abdomen and William presses himself up against me. And by the feel of his hard on my ass I know he's completely naked right now.

"I didn't know we were skinny dipping, sir, if I had, I would've taken everything off before entering." I reach over to the strings on my back that are holding my bikini top, but William's hands grasp my wrists.

"That's because I have a different plan for you, my lovely wife." William whispers into my ear. "You see those rocks over there to your right?"

I look over to the side that seems to be blocked out from most of our surroundings and give a slight nod.

"You're going to swim over there and take off these bottoms and lay them out on the rock but keep the top on, understood?"

"Yes, sir."

"Good, now swim." He says, letting go of his grip on my wrists.

I swim to the rock and pull on the strings of my bottoms. I pull them up with one hand, dangling them in the air a bit before tossing it on the flat rock.

I peer over my shoulder and watch as William's back muscles flex with every stroke toward me. As he nears me, he raises himself from the water and shakes the water off his hair. I hold myself back from dragging my tongue up his chest to catch the water droplets that are currently sliding down his perfect body.

"What are you looking at, blondie?" William comes and stands right behind me. His cock rubbed up against me.

I lean over the rocks and arch my ass, letting them peek up from the water. "I think you know exactly what I'm thinking of." I tease, peering back over my shoulder to look at him.

William's hand slaps against my ass; he tightens his grip and pushes himself closer to me. "Bring that ass down to me, beautiful." He growls, pushing me back down towards his hard-on.

"You're such a fucking tease, you know that, blondie?" William growls in my ear.

"I've been told on occasion."

William tugs at my hair, and a gasp escapes my lips. His

grip tightens. The burning of my scalp only makes me further my ass onto his cock.

"The only occasions I care to hear about are the ones involving you and I, blondie. So, I'd be very careful with how you respond next time."

"I will, sir." I moan, biting back a smile that stops me from spewing out anything that would have him punishing me rather than providing me the pleasure that I'm craving.

"Good girl."

He lets go of my hair and instead trails his hand down my spine, stopping at the strings holding onto my top. He pulls at the string slowly and untangles them. My breasts dropping free, my nipples hardening even more.

I raise my hand up to the knot on my neck, to pull the whole thing off already. But William's hands are quick to stop me again.

"Did I say you could take it off yet?" He growls.

God I loved when he spoke to me in that tone. If he opened up an application for a new secretary I wouldn't mind applying and taking over the position. I'd piss him off on purpose just to hear him speak to me in that assertive tone that has me wet.

"No, sir."

"Good, so be a good girl and wait for instructions."

I move my hands back down to my sides and let William continue his trail back down my body. His hands stop at my waist for a moment and then finally he brings a hand between my legs.

I open them wider, giving him the access he needs to please my greedy pussy. "William, please., I beg as he runs a finger up and down my folds. What I really need is his cock inside me.

"You want my cock, baby?" He asks, circling my clit.

"Fuck, yes, please." I whimper.

William inserts a finger into my wetness, his rough palm rubbing against my clit.

"There's something about seeing you in a bikini that has me go feral for you, Eloise." He brings my earlobe in between his teeth and gives it a gentle suck before moving down towards my neck.

And there's something about fucking outdoors where anyone could hear and see us that made me go feral.

"Please, sir. I need to feel your cock inside me." I beg.

William brings a hand up to my hair and grasps my hair back, tugging on it enough for me to let out a yelp. William uses that opportunity to bring his fingers into my pussy, hitting that sweet spot that makes me scream.

Fuck this felt euphoric.

I wasn't sure if I was focusing on the burning pain of my scalp, the hard pebbling of my nipples, or the build-up of my release.

"Yes, just like that. I'm almost there." I beg, clenching down onto his fingers, feeling the orgasm building up within me.

"You better be fucking quiet when you come all over my fingers, you greedy little whore." And I did just that, biting down on my lip. I hold back my screeching release as the orgasm trails through my body. The slightest noise escaping my lips..

"What a good fucking girl. I think your greedy cunt

deserves my cock now." He growls in my ear. Pushing me down onto the flat rock, William stands behind me aligning his length to my entrance. But right about when he's about to push in I hear voices of a group of people coming our way. I try standing up in a hurry but William pushes me down onto the rock.

"William people are–"

"I don't care if you don't, blondie. I'm sure they'll get the picture." William's cock continues to tease my entrance as I ponder on the idea of being seen like this.

Fuck was I really considering this?

I must be because before I can overthink it, I slip the words "I don't mind" right out of my mouth.

William thrusts into my pussy, his cock filling me up completely. I bite down on my lip, trying my best to hold onto my moans. Afraid of having any incomers listening to us.

"Don't get shy on me now, blondie." William pulls me back by my hair, my back arching so that his lips can meet my ear.

"Let them hear, let them see who owns this greedy cunt." He growls, smacking my ass and thrusting into me harder and faster. I grip the rock as much as I can, letting my moans escape without a care. I hear the voices slowly fading away, and obviously, no one feels the need to stay and watch.

"That's it, blondie, squeeze my cock. Show me how much you crave to be filled with my cum." His hands land on my ass, and I'm sure they're going to be sore tonight. But I don't care. I need more; I need William to control me.

"William, please. I need you to be rougher. I need–" William pulls on my bikini top and stops me from uttering a single word. The cloth tightens around my fucking throat, my back arching as much as possible to be able to catch some breath but to still feel the grip of the fabric on my throat.

"Just like that, baby. Keep your ass up for me." William tightens his hold on the fabric as he rams his cock deeper and deeper. I feel my senses highten as he squeezes the fabric tighter, cutting off my airway.

"That's right baby come for me, just like this." I release the hold on my orgasm, and William releases the bikini top from his hands. I fall forward, too weak to hold myself up. William is quick to catch me as he continues to move gently inside of me, releasing his load deep inside of me.

"Was that rough enough for you, blondie?" He whispers near my ear.

I lay there on the rock, catching my breath and trying my best to control the shakiness of my thighs. I peer up at William and give him a smirk, "not even close."

William raises his eyebrows in surprise and pulls out to lie next to me on the rock.

"Then I'll just have to try a few more things back at the barn."

"I'll hold you to that." I tease.

William hums, his eyes still remaining on mine.

"What is it?" I ask.

"It's our anniversary." He whispers, moving in a bit closer.

"It is."

"Let's make some vows." He states, bringing his hand up to play with the strands of my hair.

"Didn't we do that on our wedding day?"

"Yeah, but I think now that we're actually together, we deserve new ones, better ones." He declares.

I can't help but giggle. I didn't think there was anything wrong with our previous vows. But, if William wanted to make a vow. Who was I to stop him?

"What do you want to vow, my dearest husband?"

William brings his hand up to cup my cheek and gives me a sigh as he ponders for a second. His eyes never once leave mine.

"Eloise, this time, it's all going to be different. I vow to be a better man for you. I vow to be a better husband. Someone you can depend on. Someone who's going to fix all your problems and never cause them. Eloise, I vow to be a husband you can depend on and trust. I'm all yours, and you are all mine, my beautiful Eloise."

A tear slides down my cheek, but William brushes it away with his thumb.

"See, I already fixed that tear." He teases.

"Oh shut up and kiss me." I say, trying my best to suppress an oncoming sob.

William brings me close into his arms and gives me a long, passionate kiss.

As I kissed him back, taking in his vow and passion, I just hoped he really meant it because a heartbreak from William would destroy me.

Chapter Twenty-Four

The last few days in Vermont had been exciting and even passionate. Something I didn't think our marriage would ever bring, let alone in Vermont. To be clear, I had nothing against Vermont, but it wasn't Paris. But I guess that love didn't need to be in a special place for it to be passionate.

Love.

I guess that's what I would call this, wasn't it?

By all means, I wasn't ready to express my feelings just yet. I wasn't prepared to be so vulnerable. This was all so very new. And maybe even just the heat of the moment. The truth is that when we go home tomorrow, this might all end. This all might just be something that's happened in the heat of the moment, here on vacation. And just because we were trying to make this marriage work didn't mean it would end up fixed.

I look at the vacancy on William's side of the bed. He had stepped out to get us some breakfast. I told him I didn't mind going with him to have breakfast, but he was insistent on having it in bed.

My phone rings on the nightstand, and I reach over to pick up the call, Charlotte's voice bursts through my phone's speaker as she begins singing Happy Birthday to me. I let her finish her offkey rendition of the song before speaking.

"Thank you for blessing me with those beautiful vocal chords of yours."

Charlotte laughs, and I guess Dev must give her a snarky comment because she tells him to shut up.

"Happy Birthday, Eloise." Dev hollers.

"Thank you!"

"Sooo..." Charlotte speaks.

"Yes, Charlotte?" I tease.

"Come on, don't do this to me. I haven't even gotten a single text from you this week, which is unlike your honeymoon, so that must mean things are going well."

Charlotte had wanted this to work out for me. Above all, she wanted me to feel what she felt for Dev. She had said that her heart practically stopped when their eyes met. And I'm not sure I could relate to that feeling exactly. But if everyone's love story was the same exact way, there would be no uniqueness in anyone's story. Hell, that's why I read any of those romance novels. Something about them just gave me hope of love coming to me in some way. And even if what William and I had wasn't yet love, it could someday be just that.

He obviously cared for me; he wouldn't defend and protect me from my own family if he didn't.

"I think that this trip was what we needed." I finally say, trying not to give too many details away. I trusted that Dev wouldn't say anything, and I was pretty sure that Charlotte would spill the beans to him regardless. But talking about my intimate relationship with William, knowing that Dev could possibly pick up on it, was weird.

"Dev left so you can spill the beans." Charlotte says rapidly, obviously on the edge of her seat, wondering about William and I's trip.

"Charlotte, it's all been so nice. The trip, the time we spent together, and don't even let me get started on the sex." I rub my hands over my face, trying to calm my excitement as I think of just how well he took me last night. I had fallen asleep after round three, wholly exhausted.

"Oh my fucking god, I knew it. I mean, after your honeymoon, it was obvious he was good. But alcohol makes many things better than they are sometimes. But now that you were sober... you were sober, right?"

I burst into a fit of laughter, and Charlotte does soon after, too.

"Of course I was, Charlotte." I assure. "And all of it has been amazing."

"What I would give to be a fly on the wall at this very moment." She whines.

"To see me have sex? A bit voyeuristic of you, isn't it?"

"And so what if I am?" She laughs.

"Nothing at all, but I would say that you should probably wish to be more of an outdoor fly. I think you'd see more action that way."

"Eloise! No, you have not!" She practically shrieks over the phone.

"I have, and somehow it feels even better, maybe even sexier. Hell, if you're a voyeur, I think I'm an exhibitionist."

Charlotte lets out a squeal on the other end of the line. I can't help but join her, excited for this new change in my life.

"Charlotte, I think this may work." I sigh into the receiver, feeling relieved that, for once, this marriage isn't a burden or something I have to worry about.

"I knew it would, Eloise. You just needed time to grow." Her voice sounds wobbly, and I know she has to be crying.

"Charlotte, are you crying? Please don't cry; you'll make me cry." As soon as I say the words, my voice begins to wobble, and I hold back tears.

"Oh, Eloise, I can't help it. I'm just so happy for you." She says, stopping to blow her nose. "You just deserve something good in your life. And even I can admit that not even my brother was that for you. And when William came into your life, I just knew that maybe if he got his head out of his ass that it could actually work." Charlotte sighs into the phone, and I'm sure that she was trying to calm herself down. Even I've allowed for a few tears to escape my eyes.

"I can't wait for you to come back home so we can sit and talk about everything. And even though he might share a piece of birthday cake with you, don't forget who you started that tradition with because I expect to share one the minute you get back." She says, toughening her voice to sound more assertive.

"I would never miss the chance to share a chocolate cake with you." I promise.

Charlotte and I give our goodbyes. and shortly after hanging up, William steps in with a basket in hand.

"Were they out of breakfast trays?" I ask, reaching my hand out to see what was in the basket. William slaps my hand away and pulls the basket behind him.

"No, this is a special request from me. Get ready for me, blondie. We're going to enjoy a nice birthday picnic." I break into an immediate smile. This would be the first time I've ever done anything for my birthday. Even when I shared a piece of cake with Charlotte, that was all we ever did. I was always too upset about being alone for the event anyway. Ulysses got annoyed a couple of times because I refused any extravagant parties he wanted to throw me, but the truth was that they were never for me. He loved the parties and the crowds, and I liked... something more intimate and something like a... picnic.

"Come on, blondie, go get ready. We have a picnic to dig into."

I CLING MY ARM AROUND WILLIAM'S AS HE WALKS US over to a field of flowers that are located on the farm and settles the blanket onto the grass in front of it. Behind us is a tiny pond with a small trickling waterfall. "I remember how beautiful you looked so happy in the field of flowers at the botanical garden and thought that maybe you'd enjoy the picnic here." William says, taking a seat on top of the blanket and patting the spot right next to him for me to sit.

I take a seat beside him as he begins pulling out the food from the basket. "Did you ask Jane to help you with this?" I ask, taking the tupperware from his hands.

"I did; she was more than willing to help me out." William finishes adjusting the platters of food on the blanket and then wraps his arm around me.

"I know we're celebrating your birthday here, just us, today. But, if you want, we can always throw a party when we get back." I scrunch my nose up at his suggestion and quickly shake my head.

William laughs and gives me a shrug, "I assumed you wouldn't want to but thought I should suggest it anyway." William shrugs and passes me a cheese and cracker from the charcuterie board. Besides the buzzing bees that made a stop once in a while, the picnic was really nice. "You looked so beautiful in that field of flowers." He murmurs beside me.

"How did I look?"

William grabs my thighs, and pulls me over to him so that I'm straddling him. "You looked angelic." William says, brushing a strand of hair behind my ear.

"I brought something else." William says, reaching for the basket. "But you have to close your eyes."

I do just that as he rummages through the basket and pulls out whatever he has hidden in there. I hear the flicking of a lighter, and soon after, William instructs me to open my eyes. In front of me is a chocolate lava cake with a lit candle right on top.

"Make a wish, blondie." William brings the cake closer as I think of anything I could wish for. But my mind draws me to a complete blank. Right now, I had everything and more. There was nothing that I didn't already have. I think for the first time in my life, I actually felt happy. There was no anxiety, no panicking, no loneliness, and no more fucking sadness. William had somehow found a way to make me feel secure and happy. The only thing I wanted was for this to last. And that's precisely what went through my mind as I blew out the candle, sending out a wish for William and me to be happy forever.

"Was it a good wish?" He asks, setting down the cake and taking out two forks for us to enjoy. I'm still straddling William, but he doesn't seem to mind the position.

"I think it was." I say, grabbing the fork that he offers from his hand and digging into the cake. "This cake is so good." I moan.

I take another piece of the cake into my mouth and try to hold back from dancing in excitement over a piece of cake. But really, it was more than just this cake. It was my life and, most importantly, my marriage not being as terrible as I thought it would be.

"I wasn't sure how much fun Vermont could really be, but I think you proved me wrong, blondie. I'll let you handle all of our trips from now on." William grabs my waist and brings me even closer, settling his face in the crook of my neck.

"I knew you would like it; it must be so pretty out here during autumn and winter." William lays sweet, delicate kisses on my neck, and I bury my hand in his head of hair, pulling him closer to me.

"I'm sure we can make a trip up here again." William murmurs into my neck before sucking on that little sweet spot. I roll my hips onto him, and I'm sure that we would've escalated into a steamy sex session if my phone hadn't chimed.

"Do you mind getting that for me?" I ask.

William pulls away and reaches over to the other side of the blanket, grabbing my phone to bring over to me. He freezes, and his grip tightens as he looks down at the message.

"What is it? I ask, reaching my palm out for him to hand over the phone.

"Not a what but a who." His jaw tightened as he hands the phone over to me. I look down at my phone and instinctively roll my eyes.

ULYSSES

Happy Birthday! Wish we were celebrating together.

"This guy has some fucking nerve." William's eyes darken as he takes back the phone to reread the message.

"He's just trying to get to you." I pull the phone away from his grasp and throw it on the grass.

William doesn't seem too impressed by my actions, though. I cup his face and make him look back at me.

"William, I'm your wife."

William's frown turns up into a smirk as he wraps his hands back around me, holding my ass tightly and pulling me in closer.

"Repeat it, blondie." His lips are near mine as he whispers the words.

"I'm." I pull the strap of my dress down and look back at his darkening gaze.

"Your." I pull down the other strap and tease the hem,

finally feeling brave enough to pull it down completely, freeing my breasts from the dress's hold.

"Wife."

William's demeanor finally relaxes as he looks down at my bare chest.

He reaches his right hand up to cup my breast and leaves the other one grasping my ass.

"If I fucking see him, I'm beating the fuck out of him." He snarls before bringing his lips to mine.

"Just make sure he doesn't land a hit on that face of yours." I manage to say between kisses.

"Not a fucking chance, blondie." He replies, lifting up the skirt of my dress and slipping his fingers past my underwear and straight to my slick folds.

"Somethings missing, my beautiful Eloise." He growls in my ear as he presses a finger deep inside me.

"What's that?" I ask, riding up and down to match the rhythm of his fingers entering in and out of me. William removes his fingers from my sopping pussy and brings them over to his mouth, sucking my juices off his fingers.

"Your gift, Eloise."

"What is it?"

William brings his hand into the picnic basket and pulls out a square velvet jewelry box. I look down at his gift and back up at him before taking it from him.

"Open it, blondie."

I opened the box to a golden peridot and diamond choker necklace that I knew cost over twenty thousand dollars because Charlotte and I had seen it on one of our shopping sprees, and I felt too guilty to spend such an absurd amount on a necklace.

"How did you–"

"I asked Dev to ask Charlotte, who answered immediately. Do you like it?" William asks, his eyes moving between me and the expensive jewelry in my hand.

"Of course I do, it's just so expensive–"

"It's not even close to what you're worth, Eloise," William says, cutting me off and bringing his hand up to comfort my cheek.

"Will you put it on me?" I finally ask.

William removes the choker from its case, and brings it around my neck, fastening the clip without even having to look.

"Impressive." I tease.

"Not as impressive as the way you look with that necklace wrapped around your neck."

"I think your hands look much nicer." I bite my lips and look down at his hands that had moments ago been deep within my pussy, and I wanted nothing more for them to be back in there, making me come.

William races his brows and glides his hands back up my thighs, pulling my dress down even more before grabbing me and pulling me towards the ground and hovering over me.

"Are you teasing me, Eloise?" He murmurs, pulling my dress past my hips and down towards my feet, pulling them off so I lay naked against the picnic blanket.

"I think it's called initiating."

William lets out a deep chuckle, and his eyes darken as they take in my nakedness.

"I guess I'll have to follow through then." William comes down and brings his lips to mine, his tongue fighting against my own and his fingers playing with my hard nipples. He breaks away to look back down at me.

"I'm going to fuck my beautiful wife with nothing but that ring and this necklace on your body." He growls.

I lift myself up to meet his face again and near my lips to his and mutter the words, "Then be a good boy and fuck your wife, Will."

THE MINUTE WE GET TO THE ROOM, WILLIAM excuses himself to take a shower. The picnic sex seemed to relax him and possibly even made him forget about Ulysses's stupid text. And that's really all it was. Just a silly text.

Ulysses got the point across last time when I told him that I wasn't and would never be interested in him again. It's not like him to continue chasing after someone who doesn't want anything to do with him.

I let out a groan as soon as I hear the chime of my phone once again. Hopefully, he hadn't tried texting me again. The simple thanks I sent on our way here should've let him know that I had no intentions of being with him again, but just trying to be polite. But the message wasn't from Ulysses at all. It was from a new unknown number.

UNKNOWN

I don't like to be ignored, Eloise. But maybe this will catch your attention.

A video pops up right underneath the text, and as soon

as I click on it, I feel the color immediately drain from my face. There I was in a hotel room, naked. Ulyssess's body hovering over mine.

What the fuck?

Who the fuck was this?

And how the hell did they have this video?

I didn't even have this video, and I wasn't sure how this person could've gotten their hands on it. The only other person who could've had this video was Ulysses. But what reasoning would he have for blackmailing me? And why would he ever put out a video that would affect him in some way as well?

The anonymous number messages again, this time with a request.

UNKNOWN

I hope this video motivates you a bit more, Eloise. I want $150,000 In cash delivered to me by the end of this week. I'll wait for your message telling me you have the money to give you the following instructions. I'll be waiting, Eloise.

This couldn't be happening.

Now that things were finally working out, I was now falling on my face. If I didn't give this person the money they wanted, that video would surface on the internet, and I'd have to endure the repercussions that would come with it. I didn't even want to think about how William would take seeing my naked body spread out through the internet for everyone to see. Not to mention it was a fucking sex tape with Ulysses, a man he couldn't fucking stand. I could hear my parent's disapproval already.

This time around, I think that William would be on their side of the argument. I look at the message and think of the only person who could be affected by this as much as me and hope they have a way out of this or at least some fucking answers. Before I can overthink it, I send the message over to Ulysses, letting him know that we needed to talk.

"You all packed up for tomorrow, blondie?" William asks as he steps into the room from his shower. I shut off my phone and look up at him.

"Um, yeah, just a few things I need to pack up, and then we'll be all set for tomorrow." William comes closer and steadies himself on the bed. Each of his arms on either side of me, closing me in.

"Good, then we can spend our last night here, under the sheets, with your naked body underneath mine." William presses a kiss on my neck and trails down.

I feel the knot in my stomach tighten at this secret that I'm now withholding from him. But it would be for the better, right? All I had to do was give this person some money, and then it would all be over.

I clear my throat as William plays with the buttons of my pajama shirt, and that catches his attention.

"What's wrong?" He asks, immediately moving his hands away from my shirt.

"Nothing, I'm just not feeling too well. Would you mind if maybe we just slept tonight instead?" I ask. William moves to lay beside me and presses a kiss to the side of my forehead. "Of course, I don't mind. Is everything okay?" He asks, running his fingers through my hair to soothe me. But it somehow just made me feel guiltier. Here, this man was trying to make me feel better, and I was lying straight to his face.

"I'm just tired." I squeak, trying my best to stop my panic attack from arising.

"Hey, look at me, blondie." He raises my chin so that our eyes meet, but the comforting smile he gives me isn't one I deserve.

"This is real. What we have is real, blondie. And we're taking it back home with us, okay?" William whispers reassuring words to me, each one tightening the knot in my stomach.

"I'm actually going to use the bathroom, and then we can go to bed if you don't mind." William presses a kiss to my forehead and gets up from the bed, handing me his hand to help me up. I take his hand and snatch my phone with the other to bring to the bathroom with me.

"I'll set up the bed for us, blondie. Take your time, and let me know if you need anything. If you want, I can even put up one of those ocean documentaries again."

God, I didn't deserve him.

"That'd be nice," I say, slipping past him and into the bathroom.

I close the bathroom door and immediately let my body settle on the hard surface of the door, and let out a breath of air. I needed to gather my thoughts. My phone's chime brings a wave of anxiety. God, please don't let it be the blackmailer. I look down at the phone and Ulysses's reply.

ELOISE

Hey, we need to talk.

ULYSSES

I was just thinking the same thing,
princess.

ULYSSES DIDN'T HAVE A CLUE WHAT WAS COMING TO
him. But he was the only person who had a copy of that
video. So whoever's bright idea it was to blackmail me with it
had to be someone that was close to Ulysses. Close enough to
enter his phone and send themselves the video or to know
about the video in general.

Fuck me, who could've done this?

And why would they do it?

Worst of all, I didn't know how I was going to get away
with giving that large amount of money away without getting
caught. This whole mess was going to end up blowing up in
my face, and I have no clue how the hell I'm going to be able
to fix it all after.

My marriage with William had just started, and now I
feared it would end soon.

Chapter Twenty-Five

William

"How was your little week getaway with the wife?" Liam asks, giving me a light shove as he syncs up with my step. I roll my eyes at Liam, earning me a smirk.

"You dirty dog, I knew you were having a good time with the wife when I hadn't gotten a single reply back." Liam gives me a pat on the back and shakes his head in disbelief. I hadn't realized that my nonexistent sex life hadn't gone unnoticed by the people in my life. I also hadn't realized that they gave a fuck.

I mean, it's not like I was concerned by who the fuck Liam was getting with, as long as it didn't break HR protocol or get me into a mess. So far, he knew how to play his cards. Anyone who got with Liam knew that it wasn't out of commitment, let alone exclusivity.

"I didn't respond because your comments on the new hires aren't important, especially when they're comments based on their fuckability rather than their actual work ethic." I slap the folder I have in my hand on his chest. Liam holds his hand to his chest and fakes a pained expression.

"Not going to lie, that one hurt, buddy."

"I'm sure it did." I chuckle, and stop at the elevator, and press the up button.

"Got a meeting with the boss?" Liam asks, lifting his brows in surprise.

Despite Harold being my father-in-law and the CEO of the company I would be taking over after his retirement, I barely talked to the man. Most of the time, I just stuck to my life with Eloise and my work assignments. The dick always tried to run things in my marriage anyway. The last thing I needed was for him to come to bed with us, too. The fucker could barely hold his own marriage together, and now he wanted to give me advice and suggestions.

Fuck that.

Besides acing a married life, I would also do a fantastic job building this company. For fucksake, I already was. Despite Harold still being named the CEO of the company, I was running things around here, and everyone knew it. Rumors of Harold finally retiring were starting to spread like wildfire, and I was more than ready to take on this new position.

"Yeah, I'll have to listen to the fucker talk about anything but actual work." To top it all off, Eloise and I had dinner with my father tonight. And I'd have to hear my father repeat the same shit Harold would.

"At least you're not stuck playing golf with these fucking

investors this weekend. That's the last fucking thing I want to do on my weekend." He grumbles.

"You've got me there." I step out of the elevator and wave Liam a final goodbye as I walk towards Harold's office doors. I stop by his secretary's desk out of respect and so that she wouldn't have to deal with the fucker's anger of me walking in unannounced.

"Go right ahead, Mr. Wren. He's waiting for you." I take a look at her messy hair and disheveled blouse before walking away.

"Your blouse is inside out." I say before pushing the door to Harold's office and making my presence known.

"Good morning, Harold." I walk over to his desk and take a seat in front of it.

"Morning William, how was your little getaway with Eloise?" The dickhead leans back in his chair and gives me a smug look. Like he's ready to dangle something over my head, and I don't fucking like it.

"It was fine, but that's not why you had me come speak to you today." And if I didn't speak to Liam about my trip and time with Eloise, why the fuck would I ever talk about it with her perv of a father who couldn't even keep his hands off his young secretary.

Fuck he was a married man, for Christ sake. And his new secretary had to be thirty-five years younger than him.

"You know, I'm trying to be respectful with you, Will. You're practically like my son now." Harold inclines himself closer to his desk, trying to look as stern and powerful as his old ass can.

But It's hard to take him seriously when I know that with just a flick of my fingers, I could send this man down in pain.

There's a reason he agreed to merge our companies. He wants to retire. And he wasn't going to hand his corporation over to just anyone. He had interviews, for Christ's sake. And I was the lucky bastard who passed his tests with flying colors.

"Except I'm not because if I was, it would make Eloise and I's marriage fucking weird."

The smug face returns as he lets out a deep laugh.

"Is she pregnant?" Harold asks, finally beating around the fucking bush.

"I don't see how that's any of your business," I mutter, trying to keep our conversation as civil as possible. Even though by asking that question, I had every fucking right to sock him right in the nose.

"So that's a no, or possibly an early pregnancy, so maybe a yes? You know her mother had the same issues when falling preg—"

"I don't give a fuck about you or your wife." I finally spit out. I stand up and bring myself closer to his desk to make sure that might height towered over him enough to show him he had no fucking power when it came to my marriage.

"Watch your fucking mouth when you talk to me, William. Don't forget that I'm the reason you're here." Harold stands up, but even on his own two feet, he has to look up at me.

"I don't have to do shit. I'm here because I married your daughter. And I married your daughter because you liked me enough to give me your business after you retire." Harold smirks, and in that moment I know the fucker has something up his sleeve. Of course, he wasn't going to play fair.

"You're right; I did agree to all that. However, a man just

wants the confirmation that once he retires and gives away his business, his daughter will still remain married. And that his bloodline will at some point once again hold the name of the company again."

Fuck, there was no way I could get away with murder if I killed this man right now.

"Which is why you're so inclined to know about your daughter's uterus," I add.

Fuck, I just assumed that the pressure that Eloise had been getting from her mother was just because Clarice was a fucking nutjob. Not because Harold wanted to add something as absurd as having a contractual child.

Don't get me wrong, I wouldn't mind having children with Eloise. I'd have them right now if that's what she wanted. But if Eloise didn't want children right now, neither did I. And now more than ever, I definitely don't want to have a kid; it'd only make Harold come out on top. This baby would be just another pawn, and by conceiving it right now, Eloise and I would be no better than our own parents.

"Well, Harold, I encourage you to lay down your hope because it's not fucking happening." I make sure my tone is stern and clear.

Harold sighs and sits back in his chair. He shrugs his shoulders and clasps his fingers together.

"Such a shame you feel that way, William. I guess I'll just have to wait until time takes its course. Or I can do what I've always done best and break Eloise in a way that always gets her to do what her parents need of her."

I tighten my grip on the desk, nodding at his threat as I try to control myself from ripping this man to pieces.

"Eloise won't be doing shit for you." I snarl.

And before he can test my patience any longer, I walk away because if I stayed a minute longer, I'd be walking out the door in cuffs.

"Are you mad at me or something?" Eloise asks, her voice soft and mellow as if trying to make sure that she wasn't bothering me with her question. I look down at her and raise a brow in confusion, her hands tightening around the hold of her bag.

"No, why would I be?"

Eloise shrugs and looks back at the elevator's screen to view what floor we are currently on.

"You just seem off, is all." She murmurs.

I sigh and take a step behind her, bringing my arms around her to Pull her closer to me. Harold's words had left a raging fire burning within me. And all I could think of was finding a way to break Eloise and me away from him.

I knew Eloise wouldn't give a crap if she had to turn her back on her family. They were never good parents to her. But agreements had been signed, and I had to find a way to leave this contract.

"I'm sorry, blondie. But work has just been hectic. I'll try not to bring it into our relationship." I press a kiss to her neck, where she tends to be shy because of how ticklish she is. Eloise shrugs her shoulders to block me from the sensitive area.

"All is forgiven. I'll try my best not to overthink every

single little thing." She says, turning around to face me and peck me on the lips.

God, she looked beautiful.

By all means, she always looked extravagant. Especially when she first wakes up in the mornings, with no foundation hiding those perfect freckles and no mascara darkening her very light but long lashes that accompanied her blue eyes so perfectly.

But there was something about seeing her in these pristine white dresses that made her look even more beautiful. And that necklace I had bought for her birthday had looked even more gorgeous around her neck.

"I like the necklace on you." I had been so caught up in my thoughts I hadn't even noticed that she was wearing it.

Eloise reaches up to her neck to touch the green stone.

"I thought tonight's dinner was a perfect event to wear it. That and I just wanted to wear it anyway, and since there aren't any galas in the near future, this was better than wearing it on an errand run."

I chuckle at her sincerity and bring my arm around her waist as I lead her out of the elevator.

"I will try to get you something a little less gala-like next year. I just saw the necklace and couldn't help thinking about how beautiful it would look around your neck." I whisper into her ear as we make our way toward my parent's dining room.

Eloise comes to a halt right before entering the dining room and turns to look up at me. Her hands grip my tie, and she pulls on it, gently bringing me closer to her.

"I think that next time, you better get me a collar and a nice little leash to go with it. I find that maybe that'll satisfy your true want and reasoning for buying me the choker in the first place, baby." With those words, she gives me one last kiss on the lips and sashays her way into the dining room to greet my parents.

I can hear my mother's cheers as she greets Eloise.

I adjusted the hard-on that threatened to tear at my slacks and to calm the image of a naked Eloise on her knees with a collar around her neck and her tongue out, begging for my cum to touch her tongue.

"Where's William?" My mother's voice breaks away from the fantasy, and it immediately feels like a bucket of ice-cold water has been thrown over me.

Thanks, mom.

I round the corner and enter the dining room, where my mother still holds Eloise in an embrace, and my father stands right beside her. His eyes meet mine, and I can tell he's already pissed.

"Eloise, honey, please take a seat." My mother insists, bringing out a seat for Eloise to sit.

Eloise obliges and takes a seat. My mother quickly makes her way over to me to give me a hug.

"When are you going to shave off that beard of yours? It looks distasteful, doesn't it, Eloise?" My mother tisks.

I roll my eyes and chuckle at Mom's distaste for my beard. She's always hated any type of scruff. She'd constantly berate my father when it came to him not maintaining a strict shaving schedule. The woman barely let him grow an inch of hair.

Dad rolls his eyes and gives me a pat on the back tells me he knows exactly how it feels.

"I don't know, Lisa. I love William's scruff."

My mother sits across from Eloise and scoffs.

"I don't understand how it doesn't bother you." My mother mutters.

Eloise shrugs and ducks her head to look down at her palms, but I don't miss the blush of her cheeks, and I'm sure my little minx is thinking of how good my scruff feels between her milky thighs.

"It's because Eloise understands how important a beard is to a man." My father teases, and my mother just dismisses his comment with a wave of her hand.

"Please, we should dig in before the food gets colder."

We eat in peace for the most part. My parents ask questions about our trip. They hadn't questioned why we hadn't gone to a more luxurious location. Most socialites made their way to Paris on a regular weekend. Vermont wasn't really on the top of anyone's list—at least not anyone but my Eloise.

"The pictures look absolutely beautiful and romantic. You must've enjoyed your time together. I can't believe it's been a whole year since your wedding." Mom swipes through the photos on Eloise's screen in adoration.

"You two look so in love." My mother chirps.

Heat rises up Eloise's face, and she looks over at me. I raise my eyes over the glass of whiskey and take a sip.

"Well, Eloise, I hear your father is heading into retirement very soon." My father announces.

There it is.

The big reason for the invitations.

"Oh Donovan, hush, no work talk at the dinner table." My mother scolds and hands Eloise back her phone.

My father rolls his eyes and lays back in his chair, taking a sip of his own whiskey.

"It's not work talk, my dearest Lisa. It's family talk. Harold is our family now." My father tries to reason.

But there was no reasoning needed. He was going to get his way regardless. The man wanted to know if I would be getting what he so desperately wanted. From my conversation with Harold today, the man had some balls, bringing them up in front of Eloise.

"Well, it's news to me," Eloise replies.

"Well, then again, he's just waiting on an announcement before doing so." My dad states, nudging at the truth of why Harold refuses to retire yet.

"Not now, Father," I grumble.

He was being a real dick bringing this up to Eloise. What if we had actually been trying, and it was just harder for us to get pregnant? He was being an insensitive prick, and regardless, it was none of his business.

It was none of anyone's business.

"A baby wasn't in the contract." I add, making sure that he knew that whatever this plan was he and Harold had agreed on wasn't coming to play anytime soon.

My father rolls his eyes and gives me a shrug. "Well, regardless of whether there's a baby or not, the contract was signed. The CEO position is yours with or without a child. If you refuse to have a child, we'll just have to wait for Harold to meet his end." My father lets out a chuckle, and Eloise shifts uncomfortably in her chair.

I'm sure that even though she's not the biggest fan of her father, she doesn't wish any harm on the man.

"Oh, Donovan, don't be so damned insensitive. There will be no more talk about work or family matters. Do you hear me? You've made everything uncomfortable now." My mother huffs, pushing herself out of the chair.

"Eloise, come with me. There's no reason for you to have to listen to this type of nonsense. Besides, I want to show you some new silk scarfs that came in today from Thailand."

Eloise gives me a look that lets me know she wants to get out of there as soon as possible but follows my mother out of the room.

My father's stare bores into me, but it does nothing. My father has seemed to have forgotten that I helped him, not the other way around. He was a failed businessman and I had to come and help him. The least he could do is be on my fucking side.

"You don't bring this up to Eloise or myself ever again." I grunt and throw back the rest of the whiskey that's sitting in the cup.

"I'm looking out for you, William." He sighs.

"You should've looked out for yourself when you did a shit job at running your company." I bark, my father's eyes darken at the comment, and I know I've hit a sensitive area.

"I helped you, not the other way around. I gained us money and saved your company the only way I could. I broke up my previous engagement for you—"

"Oh please, Jasmine, and you were just a fling." He scoffs.

"We were in love! We had a future together!" I shout, utterly oblivious to Eloise walking back into the room.

She clears her throat, and my father and I both turn our heads to look at her.

"I forgot my phone." She pointed over to the phone near

my fist that I hadn't even realized I had slammed against the table.

I grab the phone and tuck it into my pocket.

"It's alright, we were just heading out." I declare my tone sharp, but not towards Eloise, but rather at myself for having said that aloud.

I had a past, and I had a relationship with someone I thought would be my forever. But that didn't take away from what Eloise and I had now.

Eloise nods and waits for me to gather my things before leaving. Mother comes in right as I make my way towards Eloise.

"What's going on? Are you leaving so soon? I was just about to show Eloise my silk scarves." Mother pouts, holding on tightly to Eloise's arms as if that'd stop us from leaving.

"Maybe next time, mom." I kiss her on the cheek, and Eloise gives her a quick embrace before following me to the elevator.

I had driven us here so there'd be no Cory in the car, which would have made talking to one another easier.

The elevator leads us down to the garage, and we walk over to the guest parking lot where I had parked. I open Eloise's passenger door and wait for her to get settled in before walking over to the driver's seat.

I had no idea how to bring this conversation up. I didn't want her to take what I said to heart. Even though it was the truth at some point in my life, it wasn't true now.

Things had changed.

We had changed.

"Eloise, what you—"

"I'm not offended by your statement, William." She cuts me off, giving me a gentle smile.

"May I remind you that it was I who tried to use your love for Jasmine to break up our wedding?" A chuckle leaves her lips, and I can't help but join in the laugh.

"You played one hell of a part, huh?"

Eloise shrugs, "I was scared, and some small part of me hoped I could find someone that would love me for me, not for my family's money or my father's company."

Silence fills the car; I wasn't entirely too sure how to answer that. Sure, I cared about Eloise more than her father's company and more than money. But in the beginning, I hadn't.

I hadn't even loved Jasmine enough to choose her over my own personal gains. And Jasmine hadn't deserved that. But she had found love with her best friend, whom I hadn't seen as much of a threat until after our breakup.

I guess some part of me still held onto that love, and jealousy that had riled up inside me enough to get into a fight with the guy weeks before my wedding.

"Do you wonder what could've been?" She asks, adjusting her head on the seat's headrest to look at me.

I take my eyes off the road for a second just to look at her.

"Before us? Yes. Now, during us? No." I make a turn onto our busy street and make a right into the garage. I park the car in our designated area and remove my seatbelt to face Eloise.

"My decisions brought me to this moment. And so far, I like their repercussions. At least the ones involving you. There's no reason to wonder what could've been when I'm very content with the way things are now." I stretch over the middle console and press my lips to Eloise's head.

"Your mine, Eloise," I whisper and feeling more than ready to bring her upstairs to our bedroom and fuck her.

"I'm yours, William."

We exit the car and make our way to our penthouse, our lips and hands locked onto one another.

Eloise's lips on my own. Her hands roamed from my arms, up my shoulders, and down my back.

My lips on hers, my hands tightening in her hair and then making their way down her back and tightening on her ass.

We stumble into our home, drunk on our yearning for one another.

"Whose room?" She murmurs between kisses.

"Our room." I respond, not fully grasping that before Vermont there hadn't been an *our* room.

Eloise pulls away in a fit of giggles and looks up at me.

"And which room would that be, Mr. Wren?"

God, the way she says my fucking name like that makes me want to bend her over and redden that little ass of hers.

"Yours is now ours," I say, choosing the room that was the biggest but also the most convenient for her so that she wouldn't have to move a single thing.

"Our room it is." She whispers, pulling me down by my neck and merging our lips together once again. I give her ass a slap and tighten my grip around them, forcing her to jump into my arms.

I leed her towards our bedroom and set her down on the bed, mesmerized by her beauty.

"You can trust me, Eloise," I murmur as I unbutton my shirt, one by one.

A sincere but worried look crosses her face, and I'm sure it's because she's unsure whether she can truly believe me.

"I will always choose you, I promise."

Eloise smiles, though it looks sincere, I also notice a hint of wariness in her eyes, but she gives me a nod and grabs my wrist to pull me over to her.

"I believe you, but I'd rather feel how much you mean it."

I quickly remove the rest of my clothes and then help Eloise remove hers and entangle myself with her beneath the sheets of our bed.

I was devoting myself to Eloise and her happiness and I knew she was opening her heart and trust to me.

Chapter Twenty-Six

Eloise

My ride to Ulysses's home makes me feel guilty. It almost feels as if I'm cheating on William. But this meeting was nothing like an affair. I just needed answers, and Ulysses was the only person who could give them to me.

I look down at my phone and open my bank's app. I had more than enough money to withdraw. But this was a joint account, and William would know immediately. And how could I possibly lie about one hundred and fifty thousand dollars being withdrawn from the account?

William had defended me to his parents last night. He had threatened to break their contract if they didn't stop harassing me about the pregnancy. He was ready to give everything up for me, and here I was keeping a secret. I was sure that he had found out about the video when he came back home from work yesterday.

But the dinner with his parents proved more than enough that my father was trying to puppeteer our marriage as he did me. But even I knew now that he had no power over me. The only person that seemed to have that power was this blackmailer.

"We have arrived, Miss Wren." Cory, my driver, announces. I look over to my right and realize that Cory was waiting with the door wide open for me to come out. I quickly shut off my phone and shove it into my bag.

"Thanks, Cory."

"Anytime, I'll wait for you here."

I give him a brief nod and enter the tall building. I didn't have to worry about keeping Cory quiet because we'd never driven here before, so he had no idea that I was meeting with Ulysses. And I'm sure William didn't have Cory track around all the places I went to.

Or did he?

I make a mental note to question Cory about it once I'm back in the car. I shrug off the anxiety and try to relax before it turns into a panic attack.

There's no need to panic, Eloise. You're just going to meet with Ulysses because it's just as much his name on the line as much as it's yours. I go up to his apartment and knock on the door. Ulysses is quick to open the door and greet me with a smile. He opens his arms, asking for a hug, but I just walk right past him.

I was already going behind William's back to meet with Ulysses. There was no point in twisting the knife by hugging him now.

Ulysses brings his arms down and shoves his hands right into the pocket of his slacks.

"We need to talk." I spit.

I wasn't sure why I was angry with him. It's not like he was the one blackmailing me.

No, Eloise, but he was the one who had the video in the first place and allowed it to end up in the hands of others.

"So your message stated. But I didn't think you meant out of anger." Ulysses closes the door and turns to look at me.

"Why else would I be here?" I ask, trying hard to hold back the look of distaste out of respect. Not that he deserved any of that.

"I'm not sure, Eloise. When your ex-girlfriend texts you that she wants to meet up and talk to you after having told me that I needed to back up, it doesn't really seem like it'll lead to an argument." Ulysses grumbles.

He makes his way to the fridge and takes out two bottles of water. He twists the cap of the water bottle and slides it over to me like he always did with all of my drinks before handing it over to me.

"Yes, and wishing I was with you on my birthday really respects those boundaries I put up."

Ulysses lets out a sigh and rolls his eyes at me before taking a sip of his own water.

"I wasn't aware I couldn't share my thoughts with you."

"That wasn't just any thought, Ulysses."

Ulysses runs his fingers through his hair and stares into the air in deep thought. Finally, his eyes find my own, and I'm shocked to see them brimming with tears.

"I'm sorry it's easier for you to leave us behind, more than it is for me."

Good job, Eloise. You've made a grown man cry.

I put my hand on his arm and try to console him. Our eyes were still glued to one another. This wasn't what I came here for. I needed answers. This blackmailer wasn't going to go away, and now they had a video that could ruin me.

That could ruin us.

"Ulysses, despite the turn of events. I didn't come here to reconcile our relationship." I drop my hand from his arm and take out my phone from my bag. I pull up the messages and show Ulysses.

His face pales and his Adam's apple bobs as he tries to find his voice.

"Do you know anything about this?" I ask him.

Ulysses shakes his hand and pulls out his own phone to show me.

"I only know that they're blackmailing me with the same fucking shit."

I take the phone from his hand and read the messages, ones that are identical to what I've received. Well, it was great to know that I wasn't the only one going through this and that someone would be getting a great load of money.

"Ulysses," I sigh and give him back the phone. "How did this person get ahold of that video?"

We could at least narrow it down to someone he sent it to or showed it to.

"Eloise, I have no clue. I didn't show it to anyone. You have to believe me." He brings his hands to my arms to hold me in place.

"Not even when we broke up? When you were so upset with me for choosing William over you?" Ulysses lets go of me and paces back and forth, dragging a hand across his hair again.

"Fuck, Eloise, I love you. I only ever wanted to get back with you after our break up. And the last thing I would want is for any man to look at you naked. Let alone while you're coming." He growls.

Well, I don't actually think I came in that video or much in our relationship. But this wasn't the time to bring that up or hurt his ego.

"Fuck just the thought of William seeing that makes me go ballistic. Has he? Have you—"

"Okay, that's enough. I think I've gotten the information I need." I make my way back to the door, ignoring where this conversation was trailing off to.

"Goodbye Ul—"

"Wait, stop." Ulysses runs past me and blocks the front door.

"What are we going to do about this?" He asks, his eyes begging me for an answer.

I stand in front of Ulysses and give him a shrug, unsure if there is anything else to do.

"What else is there to do but give them the money."

I could figure out a way to do this without having William find out. I just had to come up with an excuse for that amount of money.

"Fuck, I'm sorry, Eloise. This is all my fault. If I hadn't come up with that stupid sex tape idea, they'd never have something to hold over our heads." Ulysses takes a step forward to comfort me, but I back away. I didn't need his comfort; I needed his answers.

Besides, I think we'd done enough touching in my short

presence here. And I was already starting to feel guilty about it.

"We both decided on it. I just hope that this person doesn't get too greedy now that they have something they know we don't want to ever see the light of day."

I pass by Ulysses and make my way out the door. I take the stairs rather than the elevator this time. I needed to get out of here quickly. Even if it meant running down a bunch of flights of stairs. The minute I reach the last step, I push myself out of the staircase and towards the exit.

Cory stands by the car, looking at something on his phone.

I take a moment to catch my breath before walking over to him. He looks back up at me and gives me a nod before opening up the car door for me. I stop and look at him before entering the car.

He lifts his brow in question, and I give him a shy smile because somehow this felt even worse than seeing Ulysses.

"Would you do me a favor, Cory?"

"Anything you need, Miss Wren."

"This visit here," I say in a shaky tone, nudging my head over to the building. "Stays between you and I."

I made sure not to make it sound like a question but rather a statement. I was demanding his silence, and fuck, I hated acting like a prissy bitch. I can count on one hand the number of times I used that stupid persona to get something I wanted, and that never worked out. I mean, William ended up marrying me anyway.

Cory clears his throat before giving me a slight nod.

"As long as you're not in any harm, Miss Wren."

"I'm not, but William just wouldn't understand."

"Understood, it stays between you and I." With a final nod, I finally enter the car, and Cory closes the door and makes his way around the car to enter the driver's seat.

I guess this interaction answered my previous question. William definitely kept track of me. And even though Cory agreed to keep this between us, something told me that he would continue to be loyal and honest with William. So, I had to make sure that I followed through with my plan all by myself. No, Cory or William in sight.

The ding of my phone jostles me a bit and Cory meets my eyes from the rearview mirror. He's definitely cautious and worrisome now. I smile at him and look down at my phone. The message hitting me in the gut completely.

UNKNOWN

Tick. Tock. Eloise, I'm getting impatient. I want the money handed to me in two days tops. I'll be sure to send you the coordinates of where to leave it.

There was no time to think. This had to get done. I would have to deceive William, but it would be for the better. I just had to hope that this person wouldn't come back for seconds because if they did, my hands would be tied tighter than they already were.

Chapter Twenty-Seven

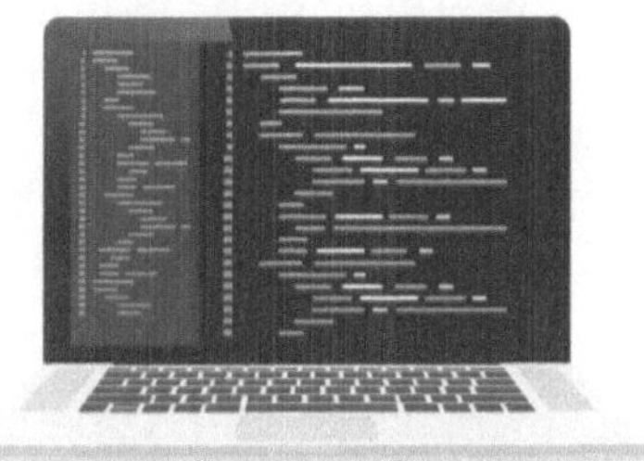

William

"What the fuck is this? I hear about you leaving the fucking company?" Harold barks through the phone's receiver. I see my dad was quick to inform Harold of my threats. I wouldn't be surprised if they were fucking too.

My dad followed that man like a dog.

"Exactly what you heard." I make sure to keep my voice steady. I didn't want him to get any emotion out of me.

"Listen here, you bastard. You're nothing without this business—" I'm quick to cut him off before he gets the chance to belittle me and my work.

"No, you're nothing without me in your business, Harold. I graduated from MIT at the top of my fucking class. I only did this for my father. And now I'm doing this for me."

That wasn't necessarily the truth. At first, there was

some selfishness involved. I broke up with my then fiancée to have this opportunity. I agreed to take Eloise's choice of being with someone she loved for my own selfish reasons.

And I guess I was still a little selfish because I didn't regret being able to have Eloise all to myself. And even now, I wasn't leaving the company for me; I was doing it for us. I wanted Eloise and I far from our archaic families.

"There's plenty of men I can give my fucking business to, William." He tried to make it sound like a threat, but we both knew he needed me.

"You're right, Harold. You can give your fucking business to anyone. But you've already given your only daughter away. And without her, there's no heir to your corporate kingdom. And I'd love to break it to you: I'm not letting that woman go. She's all mine now." I was acting like a territorial prick, but I didn't fucking care. Eloise and I were married, and there was no going back from that unless she genuinely felt differently about our relationship.

If she wanted to leave because of her feelings towards me, then I'd let her go. But if it's her father's words being spoken through her, then I'd have to grab her and fuck sensibility into her.

"I wouldn't be so sure of that." That is the only thing he says before hanging up the phone. I remove the phone from my ear and toss it on the table. My gaze lifting up to meet Liam, who was sitting across from me, sipping his scotch with a smug look.

"What?" I bark.

"You love her." He states, sucking on his teeth.

"No, I don't— I don't know—" I stop for a moment and gather my thoughts.

Was that what I felt for Eloise? Was it love? I'd only been in love one other time, and it hadn't felt the same way. But I guess not every love was the exact same.

"Stop overthinking it. You wouldn't give up a whole fucking company for her if you didn't." Liam places his scotch on the table and leans back in his chair. "And you also didn't have us meet up at the Maplewood for no reason. You're a man that plans. So, tell me, William, what's next for us?"

Liam was absolutely right about everything.

I was in love with Eloise, and I would do anything for her. I wanted this marriage to work not because we were forced to be together and it would make our relationship more manageable but because this woman found a way into a heart I wasn't sure even existed anymore.

I hadn't graduated at the top of my class for no reason. I was fucking brilliant, and I worked hard to be just that. And maybe I allowed my father to use me as his puppet, too. And I was fucking greedy; I had an easy grasp of a CEO position without having to do much for it. But even if I had to, I know I'd still be able to make it.

"Let's branch out and start our own company." I keep the offer short and sweet.

"You and me? Or are you just dragging me along to be your CFO?" Liam asks, taking another sip of his scotch.

"I'm dragging you along as my best friend. And you'd be Co-CEO. If we do this together, we're both moving up, and we're going to steal Harold's clients right from under his fucking nose.

Liam smirks and looks at me as if he's pondering the idea.

"We'd be starting from zero." He argues.

"We're too affluent to be starting from zero."

Yes, it'd take time, and we'd have to look for an office space, take out loans, find employees, and get clients in order to make money. But we had enough connections and money to make this work.

"You're fucking crazy. Wouldn't it just be easier to conceive a child?" Liam was playing devil's advocate right now. I knew he was in. He never played it easy, and I was sure his position as CFO was starting to bore him. He liked being challenged, and a new company would challenge him.

"Yes, it would be. I'm quite good at the actions that need to be taken in order to conceive a child. But if my wife doesn't want a baby right now, then we won't be having a baby. It will also be a big fuck you to Harold when his daughter and I have a child while I'm taking down his company."

Liam lets out a chuckle and shakes his head at me. The smile on his face already gives me the answer I need. Regardless, he tells me it anyway.

"Fuck it, I'm in." Liam extends his hand in agreement, and I take it. We shake on the agreement and order another scotch for the both of us. Liam was just the beginning of this project, and once we started getting more people on board, we would be able to play our cards right.

Liam and I continue to discuss the plan before I'm interrupted by a call. I see Cory's name flash on my phone's screen and quickly pick it up. I knew he had taken Eloise somewhere today. I wouldn't say I stalk her, but I do like to keep track of where she is in case of an emergency or if she ever needs me. Usually, I'd get a text to update me, so a call from him worried me.

"Is everything alright, Cory?"

"Everything is fine, Mister Wren. I've just dropped Miss Wren home now." He replies, but I know there has to be something else. He wouldn't just call for a mere update like that.

"What's going on?" I ask, my annoyance clear in my tone.

Cory clears his throat before finally speaking again.

"We stopped at Ulyssess's apartment today, sir." My grip tightens on the phone, and I bite the inside of my cheek to stop myself from lashing out in anger.

"What for?" I asked, even though I was pretty sure Eloise didn't say a thing to him. She probably thought Cory had no idea where he had even taken her. But I made sure to give Cory the information of all of her friends including where they lived. And, of course, I made sure that on that list, Ulysses' name was highlighted.

"Why didn't you call me when she was there?" I bit out angrily.

"I did, sir. It went straight to voicemail." I roll my eyes and send out a mental fuck you to Harold and his annoying ass calls.

"It couldn't have been too long of a visit then." I presume.

"No sir, she was in and out."

I doubt Eloise would meet with Ulysses for no apparent reason. There had to be something behind this. And even a quicky couldn't be that quick. Fuck, if she were trying to fuck him, I think she would take some precautions and go alone.

"There is something else, sir," Cory whispers at the end of the line.

"Well, spit it out, Cory." I was starting to get annoyed by this whole conversation, and that meant I was starting to think of firing a man that hadn't even done anything wrong.

"She asked me not to say a thing to you."

"Is that all?" I ask.

"Yes." He replies.

"Okay, thank you for the information, Cory. From now on, I want constant messages of where she is and what she's doing. Follow her if you must. She doesn't leave your sight, understood?" I bark out the orders, and Cory quickly agrees before hanging up the call.

If she asked Cory not to tell me anything, then some part of her must've known that I kept tabs on wherever she went and that Cory might've already known where it was that she was going or who she was visiting.

If this was an affair she would have been much more careful. There was something else to this, and I was going to figure this mess out.

"Trouble?" Liam asks, but there's not a smidge of smugness in his tone. Even he knows when not to fuck with me.

"There is, but I'm going to figure this all out and get to the bottom of this. Something tells me someone is still trying to fuck with Eloise, and I'm not going to have it."

Liam brings his glass of scotch up in the air with a cheer and shoots it back. "I'd hate to be the fucker that messes with what's yours."

I scoff and shoot my own scotch back.

"You have no fucking idea."

THE MINUTE I STEP FOOT BACK INSIDE THE penthouse, I hear Eloise's hums coming from the living room. She was probably humming one of those country songs she loves so much. I walk over and see her snuggling underneath a cozy blanket. A lavender-scented candle is lit on the coffee table, and she has her tea in hand, her book in the other.

"Nervous?" I ask her, causing her to jump and spill her tea.

"Oh my god, you scared me." She says, pressing her hand to her chest and setting the mug on the coffee table. I walk over to our kitchen and grab some napkins to clean up the spill.

"Sorry, didn't mean to scare you." I walk over and kiss the top of her head before bending down and cleaning up the tea.

"You don't have to do that; I can do it." She tries to take the napkin away from me, but I push her hand away.

"It's alright, take a seat. I'll make you a new tea." Eloise is hesitant but finally takes a seat back down on the couch.

"Thank you." She gives me a smile before spreading the blanket over her once again.

"So, what's got you so nervous?" I ask.

"What makes you think I'm nervous?" Her voice is teasing, but it lacks the playfulness she usually has.

"This is what you usually do when you're anxious. I assume it calms you." Eloise's eyes glaze as she takes me in.

That's it; c'mon tell me what's going on, blondie. Be open with me. There's nothing I can't help you with.

"Yeah, I guess I do that, don't I?" Eloise gives me a shrug before looking back at her book.

"I don't know. I guess being back here really makes me sad in some ways."

I set the wet paper towels inside the empty mug and slide onto the couch beside her.

"Why's that? What's going on, Eloise?"

I bring her into my arms, and she instinctively lays her head down on my chest. I didn't want to grill her for answers, but I wanted her to know that she could trust me with anything. Whoever was making her feel this way had to have some sort of leverage over her. And by the looks of it right now, my biggest suspects were her father and her ex.

I lift her chin up to look at me, her glossy eyes holding back the tears she so desperately wants to let out.

"You can tell me anything, Eloise. There's nothing I won't do for you." Eloise smiles and finally lets a tear stream down her cheeks.

"I almost believe you."

"Why almost?" I ask, feeling close to the actual revelation.

"Because you're only human like any of the rest of us. Not everything can be in your control."

"What's going on, Eloise? Speak to me, is it your father? Is he holding something over you? We don't have to do shit for him. You hear me. I'm not following through with this agreement. I'm going to quit and start a new company. I fucking love you, Eloise, and nothing is going to ruin our relationship, not even our families." I hold her head between my hands and watch as her face lights up at my words.

"What did you just say?" She finally whispers, leaning her face closer to mine. Her eyes were sporadic, looking at what seemed to be every detail of my face as if she wanted to make sure that no detail was ever forgotten.

I swallowed, and finally, her eyes met mine.

"I love you, Eloise."

Eloise lifts her hand to cup my cheek and runs it up my scalp. Her lips touch mine in a passionate kiss, and I bring her onto my lap. The kiss is sensual and loving. Nothing like the sexy and lustful ones we're used to sharing in these kinds of moments.

Eloise pulls away and finally looks down at me.

"I love you too."

I pull a strand of her blond hair away from her face and pull it back gently to the back of her ear to take a good look at her. My heart feels like it's going to beat out of my fucking chest. I don't think I've ever felt this way before. Eloise is my wife; she's all mine. And it's not because of some stupid contract. It's because she really wants to be here with me.

"Is everything alright, Eloise?" I ask, wanting to make sure that whatever was making her feel this way was cleared up by my words.

Eloise nods and pecks my lips one more time before saying, "It will be."

I deepen the kiss, and her grip around my waist tightens. Lifting her up, I move her towards our bedroom. A room that had been just hers before the trip. Even something as simple as sharing a bed was new in our marriage.

We were still just beginning, but somehow, this love had tied us together, and suddenly, it felt like we'd known each other for an eternity.

I break from our kiss and toss her on the bed before hovering over her. Our lips find themselves again, never wanting to break away from this pull we have.

"Eloise," I whisper, trailing tender kisses down her neck.

"Yes," Her breath is heavy, and she lifts her hips up to grind against me.

I rip away at my clothes, and Eloise follows. I take in her nakedness, watching as her perky tits rise with each breath and the way her pussy glistens for my erection.

"I love you," I say, aligning my cock with her entrance. Eloise nods, and her eyes glisten as I push into her slowly. Taking in the feeling of her pussy tightening around my cock.

"I love you." Eloise whispers. Suddenly what we're doing feels different and maybe that's because it is. This time, it's not about kinks and lust. This is love. It's our feelings, fears, and trust given to one another. And it scared me shitless, but Eloise made this feel right.

I hover my body over hers and thrust into her. The city's lights shine through the bedroom window, illuminating Eloise's beauty. Those crystal blues glowed in the night, and her swollen lips practically begged to be between my lips to be sucked and kissed.

Her eyes flutter as I adjust myself to hit her sweet spot.

"Yes, Will, right there." Her back arches, and I can feel her pussy clench itself tighter around my cock.

I lift myself up and deepen my thrusts. My thumb finds

her swollen and nub and begins circling the sensitive bundle of nerves. Eloise's moans only increase in volume.

"I'm going to come deep inside of you with just the thought that there will never be anyone else after me. It will only ever be us, blondie. Now that I have you, I'm not letting you go."

Eloise wraps her legs around my waist and matches up with my thrusts. I rub her clit faster and deepen my thrusts. And the minute I feel her tighten around my cock and that angelic moan leaves her lips, I come deep inside her.

I lower myself to hover over her body, press a kiss to her lips, and then let my body drop right beside her. I wrap my arms around her and bring her closer to me.

"That felt different." She says.

"Good different or bad different?" I ask, moving the strand of hair away from her face.

"It was good, but it was different. It was sensual." She says, scrunching her face in deep thought to try and find another word.

"It was love, blondie." I press a kiss to her temple, and Eloise furthers her head into the crook of my neck.

She stays silent and calm as I rub her back up and down, and just before falling

asleep, I hear her whisper the words, "Love's a funny thing."

And that it is, Eloise.

Chapter Twenty-Eight

Eloise

Love was a funny thing. I woke up with that thought rooted deep in my mind. Some part of me had always hoped to experience that moment when a person becomes enthralled by someone. And I finally got to experience that with William. It hadn't been intentional, but it slowly morphed into love, and now it would come to an end. A moment that should have been simple, filled with romance, was filled with fear and secrets.

I take one last look at William sleeping beside me before finally getting up and leaving. I get dressed quickly, too scared that if I didn't leave soon, he would stir awake and ask too many questions.

Even yesterday's questioning made me nauseous. Granted, he thinks this is all because of my father. But it's all because of me.

My past decisions had repercussions, and they were catching up to me. I take an Uber to the bank and make a quick prayer before walking in. I had never taken that much money out of a bank, and I wasn't sure if I was even allowed to do that. Surely, if my name was on the account, then I would be able to take out any money I needed.

I knew William would ask questions as to why I took that much money out of an account. My excuse was going to have to be as basic as shopping because not even I could fathom why anyone would need that much money in cash.

I step up to the teller and let her know exactly how much money I need to withdraw. She does eye me curiously but ultimately only ends up asking for an ID and social security number to confirm my account information. It takes a couple of minutes before she shows back up with a bag in hand and as she does a call from William comes through. I press deny and take the bag from the teller before walking out.

I clench my hands around the bag and look around, paranoid of being seen. Even more paranoid about having the money get stolen. There's only one reason a woman is coming out of a bank with a secure black bag that she didn't have on her when she was going in. I take out my phone and place an order for the next Uber. William sends me a few texts, but I don't even bother to look. They would only cause me more anxiety. I'd deal with the lying aspect of things the minute I delivered the money.

I swallowed and let out a shaky breath as soon as I got into the car. The blackmailer had sent instructions on where to hide the money. Ulysses texted me to let me know that he was sent the same coordinates. He had dropped off his money yesterday and said he hadn't heard back from the blackmailer since. I was hoping I'd be granted the same graciousness.

The Uber brings me two blocks down from where the Maplewood is. The instructions stated that I should enter the alleyway between the two red buildings and leave the bag of money in the green garbage bin that was left out for me.

I enter the alley, hoping there's no one there to fucking kill me. I count my breaths and try to focus on going home to William. That's the only thing that's pushing me through this. I find the green garbage bin and open the lid. The trash bin is empty, so I just slide the bag of money into it and take a quick picture as proof.

I make my way out of the alley and begin walking towards Maplewood. I send off a text to the unknown number, along with the picture I took. It's not until I finally get to Maplewood and enter it that I get a reply back.

ELOISE

It's done.

UNKNOWN

Love to see it. Thank you, princess.

My face pales immediately at the message, and I stop to look around. My eyes catch the culprit laughing away with their friends. All I see is red. My phone begins to buzz again, and I'm sure it has to be William, but right now, I have something more important to deal with.

I make my way over to the table and get an abundance of greetings from everyone. I try to stay calm and greet them back before turning back to Ulysses.

"Can we talk?" I ask.

"Sure," Ulysses replies but doesn't make a move to lift himself away from the table.

"In private," I add.

Ulysses sighs and pushes his chair back, and I walk away towards an empty hall. Ulysses is quick behind me and begins chatting about how scared he was when he entered the alleyway alone last night.

"I'm sure you were," I mutter through clenched teeth.

"I think we should've gone—" I'm quick to cut him off before he infuriates me even more with his fucking lies.

"Cut the acting, Ulysses. I know you're the blackmailer. The only thing I don't know is why?" The smile on Ulysses's face drops instantly, and a sly smirk replaces it.

A smirk I want to slap right off his face.

"Because you fucked me over, Eloise."

I take a step back, furrowing my brows at his statement.

"What the hell are you talking about?"

Ulysses lets out a deep chuckle, biting his lip as he takes a step closer. I move back until he's cornered me into the wall. Ulysses grabs my chin and brings my face up to look at him.

"You were supposed to marry me, Eloise." I shake off my head from his touch and push him off of me, but he doesn't budge.

"Let me go, you fucking prick. You're insane; this is all because of a contract that my father set up for me?" Ulysses's grin widens as he continues to peer down at me like I'm some sort of prey he's ready to sink his teeth into.

"You didn't fight for us, Eloise." Ulysses lowers his face, bringing himself closer to mine. His lips are now hovering over mine.

"And good thing I didn't, you fucking psycho." I'm quick to spit in his face and knee him in the balls before escaping his hold. Ulysses falls to his knees, clutching his groin.

"Go ahead and run from me, Eloise. I still have that fucking video, and I'm going to make sure I drain you of every bit of money that you have."

I don't stay around any longer to hear his threats. I needed to get the fuck away from him. The phone in my pocket continues to ring as I to run out of Maplewood.

I come to a stop the minute Cory stands there in front of the car.

Is William here?

I finally pick up the ringing phone and don't even bother to look at the caller ID.

"Hello?" I answer, my voice still shaking from my confrontation with Ulysses.

"Eloise." William's voice isn't like usual. It's rough, it's stern. He's angry.

"I think you owe me a huge explanation." He says, his breath is shaky, which tells me he's trying to control his anger as much as he can.

Fuck, was this about the money, the messages, or Ulysses? I hold back the ball of emotions that's beginning to consume me completely. The only thing I want to do right now is cry, scream, and beat Ulysses into a pulp. But I don't think doing any of the sort would help my position right now.

"It's not what you think." That's the only thing I can think of telling him.

"Get in the car, Eloise."

Those are the only words William utters through the phone's receiver before hanging up on me.

I look back over to Cory, who opens the car door for me to enter. I comply with William's demand and enter the car.

As I sit in the back seat, I try my best to prepare how I'm going to explain everything to William.

But even I'm smart enough to know that it doesn't matter how much I prepare. What William and I have has been broken.

The only thing I should be preparing for is how to mend my heart back once it shatters.

Chapter Twenty-Nine

Cory follows me up to the penthouse, which is unlike our usual routine. He usually goes around and does whatever he wants until either William or I need him. But he's never acted as a bodyguard.

"You told him, didn't you?" I ask on our way up the elevator. Cory stays silent; he doesn't even move an eye towards me. I shake my head and scoff at his silence.

"You didn't have to promise me your silence, you know." I know I asked him to keep the secret, but if he hadn't planned on keeping it, then what the hell was the point in acting as if he did? Acting like I could trust him, as if I could believe him.

"I had to tell him. It's part of my job." He finally admits as we make it to the top.

"That's a description of your job that not even I had a clue about. So I guess I'm not the only one keeping secrets around here." I walk out of the elevator with Cory hot on my trail.

"I know my way to his office. You don't have to follow me like some lost dog." I snap.

"I'm just following orders, Miss Wren."

I roll my eyes and stop directly in front of William's office door. I give it a knock and wait for William's "come in" before opening the door and stepping inside.

William is sitting at his desk, engrossed in whatever he seems to be typing into his computer. He doesn't bother to look up at me, but by his disheveled look and intense glare at the screen, I know that he hasn't calmed down since our talk on the phone.

I look behind me to see Cory standing in the hallway, not yet taking a step inside the office.

"What? Is the office off-limits for you?" I snap back again, but Cory doesn't seem to care one bit.

He doesn't even deserve my anger; he is only following William's orders.

"Thank you, Cory. You can return to your tasks, and I'll let you know if we need anything." William announces, but he doesn't take his eyes away from that damn screen.

"Yes, thank you very much, Cory, for being my shadow. I'll give you a call when I need you to follow me into the bathroom since it seems I have no actual privacy." Though my words are directed at Cory, my eyes glare at William, who finally bothers to look up at me.

Cory must close the door behind me because I hear a click and footsteps walking away.

"This isn't the best moment to act up, Eloise." William's voice is emotionless, which is easier to deal with than the strict CEO voice he puts on.

"Act up? You're the one that's keeping tabs on me and having Cory tell you every little detail about what it is I do." I can feel my cheeks redden from the anger burning up within me.

It's not just anger but betrayal that I feel.

William leans back in his chair, lifting his brows up at me. His right hand remains positioned on top of the table, and all he does is tap his index finger on the mahogany surface, not bothering to take his eyes away from me.

"It seems that it was well needed. I mean, suddenly, you're meeting up with Ulysses and then withdrawing a large amount of money from the bank and leaving it behind a sketchy alleyway." William leans forward in his chair and clasps his hands together as if this were some big fucking corporate meeting.

"What the fuck is going on, Eloise?" William's ice-cold gaze burns a hole through my chest, and I feel guilty for keeping all this from him.

"Now, Eloise." He demands.

I bring myself to the front of his desk and take a seat in front of him.

"Before I tell you anything, I just want you to know that I didn't know that this would turn out the way it did. And I only kept this a secret from you because I was ashamed of what you'd think of me when you found out."

William's eyes soften as I hold back any tears from spilling out.

I tell William how I thought the first message I received

was an accident and how the minute I was being black-mailed with an old sex tape, I realized just how real this whole situation was.

"I didn't realize it was all Ulysses until a few moments ago. That's why I was at Maplewood. I went to confront him. But he said that he would continue to threaten me with the video until I give him what he wants." I wipe away tears and struggle to breathe throughout the conversation. I didn't want this to lead to a panic attack. I was doing so well, and now wasn't the best time to have it strike back up again.

William's gaze is dark, and his body is completely stiff.

"He's blackmailing you with a sex tape?" William asks through gritted teeth.

"Yes, I know it's so stupid that I even made one because now it's going to ruin me and also you because you're married to me."

"You think I give a fuck about my name?" William growls.

I give him a slight shrug before nodding my head to his question. William stands up slowly from his chair and walks around his desk and stops right in front of me. I lean my back into the chair as William grips both hands around its arms and leans in closer to me.

"Eloise, I couldn't give a fuck about what people think of me. But you, blondie. No one fucks with you. No one threatens you. And they sure as fuck won't be blackmailing you, understood?"

I only nod and wipe away another few tears that slip away.

"Because I'm your wife?" I ask, rolling my eyes at the thought of starting back at step one again. Our Vermont trip had been for nothing because my mistake found a way to crush it all.

William's hand caresses my cheek, and I look back up at him, waiting to hear his rejection and hurt over my betrayal.

"No, Eloise, not just because you're my wife, but rather because I love you." William reaches down and presses a kiss on my forehead.

"Still?" I ask.

William tugs a strand of hair behind my ear and shares a smile with me.

"I'm afraid finding a way to unlove you is impossible, even if I wanted to."

"But aren't you mad?"

William lets out a hardy laugh but quickly brings his face back to a serious expression.

"Oh, Eloise, I'm fucking furious." The darkened gaze and angered-fueled tone are a huge juxtaposition to the caresses he gives my cheek.

"I would love to do nothing more than bring you over my knee and slap your ass until it's bright red." William's thumb grazes my lips, and I give it a kiss, but by William's intense stare, it seems that isn't enough.

I raise my eyebrow, confused as to what he wants from me.

"Come." William raises himself back up and puts out his hand for me to grasp. I link my hand with his and follow him back around his desk. William lifts me up and settles me on top of it. His lips hover over my own, and his eyes ask me for permission to continue. I give him the answer right away by smashing my lips onto his.

William's arms wrap around my waist as he pulls me

closer. Any anxiety I felt over our relationship dissipates now that I'm in this moment with him.

William grabs onto my hair tightly, making me gasp. He pulls away and looks down at me. "I'm so fucking angry with you, blondie." William lowers his head to the crook of my neck and sucks on that sweet spot that makes my body grind against his instantly.

"Why don't you trust me, Eloise?" He asks between sucking and kissing.

"I do trust you." I declare, sliding my hand up his head and gripping his hair, encouraging him to continue pleasing me.

"You don't." William pulls away to slide his desk chair across the room. He grabs ahold of my waist and pulls me right off of the desk to stand in front of him.

"You trust me?" He asks, his fingers hovering over the buttons of his shirt, and slowly, he begins to unfasten each one.

"Yes." I wasn't sure where he was getting at with this, but I didn't want to give him a reason to doubt my trust in him.

"Then why didn't you tell me?" His dress shirt falls to the floor, and his hands find his belt. But he doesn't remove it. Instead, his eyes intensify on me as he waits for my reply.

"I felt ashamed," I managed to choke out.

"I didn't want to disappoint you." I finally add, trying my best to control my anxiety that was begging to break loose from the vulnerability.

"I'm not your parents, Eloise. You can't disappoint me." And just like that, he unclasps his belt and pulls it right off.

"You said you trust me." He repeats.

I give a slow nod, and William closes the space between us.

"Get naked, Eloise."

I'm hesitant at first, I'm not sure what he has in mind. But I know I can trust William, and he needs to know that I mean it. I remove my clothes slowly until I'm fully naked in front of him.

"Sit on my desk, legs wide open for me, blondie."

I raise an eyebrow in question, trying to figure out what exactly he has up his sleeve. I take a seat on his desk and widen my legs. My pussy bare for him to see. I look at William's hungry stare and watch as his pants begin to tent up.

William opens up a drawer and pulls out a remote that controls the blinds of the room.

"You trust me?" He asks again, but this time, I knew what he was really asking. And the answer was still the same.

"More than ever."

William presses the button on the remote that has the blinds come up. He makes his way around the desk and hovers behind me. His hands find my breasts, and he gives them a tight squeeze before bringing my nipples between his fingers.

"They'll get here soon." He whispers in my ear. "And when they do, I want you sopping and ready to take my cock like a good girl right in front of them." He growls, his hand moving lower and giving my pussy a slap.

I jump at the contact and further myself into him.

"Yes, sir." I pur, my nipples hardening from excitement.

Was this right? Should sex even be on our minds during an argument?

William comes around to stand behind me, and I hear the unbuckling and drop of his belt. The sound of his zipper opening up follows, and I'm sure his dick is hard and out already.

"Open those pretty little lips for me, baby," William whispers from behind me. I lean back on my head and comply with his demand, opening my mouth wide for him. His spit falls down to my tongue, excruciatingly slow. Before I can swallow it down, his hand grips my throat, stopping me.

"Don't swallow it; you're going to need it. And you better be thankful I'm helping you after the secrets you've been hiding from me, understood?"

"Yes, sir," I manage to squeak.

William gives my face a delicate slap before commanding me to lie down on the desk. I do as he says and let my head hang on the side, my face now in front of his large member.

"Open your mouth and show me how sorry you are."

I follow his order, and William thrusts his cock down my throat.

"Relax that throat, baby, because I'm not stopping any time soon."

I focus on relaxing my throat and seem to forget to keep my legs open because William pushes himself further into my mouth to stretch over and pull my legs apart.

His hand smacks against my throbbing clit. I try to yelp in disapproval, but William's fingers circling my clit stops me. He brings his cock in and out of my mouth, and I continue to suck him, needing to satisfy him. Needing him to forgive me.

His hands move back up to my breasts, and he flicks his thumbs over my pebbled nipples. I close my legs again to use the friction to my advantage. A growl escapes William's lips as he pulls them apart. My disobedience earns me another smack.

"If you want to come, you better start listening, blondie." He removes his cock from my mouth with a pop and grabs my face tightly.

"You're going to keep those legs open for the skyscraper cleaners to get a good view of what's mine, and if you're a good girl, I'll let you watch them as I fuck you, understand?"

"Yes, sir." William drops his grip from my mouth and lines the crown of his cock with my lips again.

"Good, open your mouth and take my cock like a good girl."

He slides his cock into my mouth, and this time there's no waiting around. William thrusts in and out of my mouth. I try my best to control my gagging but can't help it when he goes in so fucking deep.

"That's it, pretty girl, take my fucking cock. Show me how sorry you are."

Fuck I was so sorry, but this punishment only made me want to keep doing bad things. I moan and push myself further into him.

"I'm going to play with these sensitive nipples until I see a puddle over my fucking desk, baby. These guys are so jealous, blondie. I bet you want to see how they look at you while I fuck that tight pussy of yours."

I groan and move my hands down to my pussy, needing

to find some kind of release. William pinches my nipples, and I let out a yelp that gets covered by his dick, thrusting deeper into my throat.

"No pleasing yourself until I say so; why don't you use those hands to grip my cock, baby." I listen to William instantly and wrap my hands around his member. The sooner I pleased him, the quicker I'd have his cock filling my pussy.

"That's it, baby, fuck, you're doing such a good job." Spit begins to accumulate in my mouth and spread all over my face. It's practically dripping down my face. William grips my breasts tightly before pushing back completely.

"Fuck baby, that's it." William moves his palm over my face and smears the spit all over. "God, you turn me on so much, blondie."

He brings his hand over to my pussy and inserts two fingers into my dripping cunt.

"You're so ready for me, aren't you, my beautiful Eloise?"

"Yes, please. Please fuck me, sir." I don't even realize I'm moving my hips up and down to meet with the thrusts of his fingers inside my pussy. Fuck I needed him so badly.

"Stand up, baby, and keep your eyes on the floor." I follow Williams's instructions and lift myself up from the table. My eyes remain on the floor as I get up and stand in front of the windows. I can see the shadows on the floor, so I know that the window cleaners are definitely fucking watching. And that excites me even more.

"Move up and bend over, blondie."

I take a few steps forward and bend over. William moves up behind me, his dick pressing up against my ass. He runs his fingers up and down my back, goosebumps lift, and I don't realize I'm shaking until William steadies me with his touch on my hips.

"Nervous, baby?" He asks as he aligns his cock with my entrance.

"No, just incredibly horny." I admit.

"I love hearing you speak those dirty words to me, baby; now look up and enjoy the view while I fuck you." William grabs my arms to hold me steady and thrusts into my dripping pussy. I bring my head back and moan. His cock feels like it was meant to please my pussy.

My eyes lock onto the windows where two men hang there, watching my husband degrade me like a whore. William grabs my hair with one hand and holds my hands back with his other. His thrusts remain rough and deep, and I can feel my orgasm rising.

"You see how they fucking look at you, baby? They wish they were in my shoes. But guess what, baby?"

His grip tightens on my hair, and then he finally lets go of my arms and brings his arm around to stimulate my throbbing clit.

"What?" I finally moan, bringing my hips back to meet his thrusts. William's touch on my clit deepens, and I begin shaking with need.

"They can look all they want, baby, but you're mine. You'll always be mine. This pussy gets wet for me, it clenches down on my dick, and it fucking creams on it too. Come on, baby, come right in front of them and show them who owns your fucking pussy." My legs begin to shake as I hold onto my climax before finally releasing it. I can feel my pussy clenching down on William's cock, and the minute his groan fills the room and his pace begins slowing, I know his cum is deep inside me.

William holds on tight to me and stretches over to the desk, his dick still very much inside me. He grabs the controller for the blinds and lowers them once again, and the cleaners pretend they didn't just see my husband rail me all the way into next week.

William slides himself out of me, but his hands still remain around my body, holding me close to his chest.

He takes a few seconds to gather his breath before sitting me back on top of his desk.

"Eloise, look at me." I look up to meet his eyes, not even noticing that I was ignoring his stare.

"I'm your husband, Eloise. I'm your support. There's nothing you could ever do that would make me think of you as anything less than the brilliant woman that you are." Tears brim my eyes at his words because even without saying the actual words William is telling me, he forgives me.

"I was just so ashamed." I probably look like shit right now, and he's still looking at me with those eyes that make me feel like I'm his world.

"Eloise, there's nothing to be ashamed about. You did something with someone you trusted. It's not your fault he's a fucking loser with no moral values. Let's get you cleaned up, and then I'll figure out the rest."

"But–"

"No buts," William lifts me into his arms, walks me out of the office, and over to our bathroom, setting me down on the vanity.

"Just let me take care of you, okay?" He asks, turning on the shower for us.

"Okay." That is all I say, but to myself, I let out a prayer in hopes of all this chaos somehow resolving. But even if it doesn't, the only thing that matters is Williams's opinion, and he doesn't see me as anything less.

"I love you, Eloise." He whispers in the shower as he massages my scalp with shampoo and leaves kisses down my shoulder blade.

"I love you, Will."

Chapter Thirty

I hadn't realized how much I missed coding until this very second. Granted, what I was doing wasn't too hard. I was just a bit rusty. This whole fucking time, I've been focused on achieving that CEO position that should be mine regardless because there was a contract. But this new goal of taking over as CEO took away the whole reason I got into tech in the first place. I'd have to thank Ulysses for bringing me back to something I loved.

After our shower, I encouraged Eloise to go to bed and told her I would take care of the rest. Money was given to Ulysses today, so it's not like he would be publishing this video anytime soon. He wanted to get as much money out of Eloise as he could, and deleting that video was the only thing that could keep that money coming.

The only thing that makes no sense to me is why would a

multi-millionaire need to blackmail someone for money. And if he was willing to go that low to obtain that money, it means that he's done other things to gain wealth.

It took me exactly two hours to find out that Ulysses and his father have found themselves in a tight space when it comes to owing money. It is so tight that tax evasion does not seem to be of immense help. It then took me another hour to hack into Ulysses's personal texts to find out that Eloise was sadly not the only victim of his blackmail.

I lean back in my chair and peer down at the evidence, and fuck; it feels good to take down the fucking dick. And I was going to take them down hard.

I pulled out my phone and made a quick call to Cory who might've gone home for the evening but would quickly drop everything to come by and help me with the next task I had in mind.

"I'm downstairs." Is his immediate response is as soon as he answers the call, and I can't help but smirk at his readiness. I get my things and make my way to the bedroom before leaving. Eloise lays there in a calm sleep.

Good.

The last thing I needed was an Eloise freaking out. Tomorrow, when she wakes up, this will all be over. Well, it will be over for us. It'll be just the start for Ulysses.

I shut the bedroom door and take the elevator down to the garage, where Cory is already waiting for me.

"Where to?" Cory asks, opening the door for me to take a seat.

"You wouldn't be waiting here if you didn't already know our destination." This is the only response he needs before getting in the car himself and driving us to Ulysses's home.

ULYSSES'S SMUG FACE IS IMMEDIATELY WIPED OFF HIS face the minute he opens the door and meets my fucking fist.

"What the fuck!" He groans as he tries to pick himself back up from the floor. I give him a kick to the gut before lifting him up by his pretentious polo shirt and slamming him against the wall.

"I don't really need to do any of this shit because there are more punishments coming your way, but no one takes advantage of Eloise, especially not her prick of an ex-boyfriend who couldn't even make her come. Even if I didn't already know the sweet sound of her climax, a mere fucking idiot would know that she faked it with you."

Fuck, it hadn't been my intention to watch the tape. But it was right fucking there, and though it pissed me off to know that this leech had his hands on my Eloise, it felt a little better knowing that the sex seemed bland at best and obviously wasn't as pleasurable for her.

Ulysses spits out blood onto his hardwood floors and peers back up at me. His smirk makes its presence again, but it won't take me long to swipe it right off again.

"So the princess ran into your arms and showed you our film. That's a shame. I was going to formally invite you to the premiere."

Fucking bastard.

I tighten my grip on his collar and slam him onto the floor. My fists meet his face, one after the other. Fuck me, all I see is red, and I'm unsure if it's because of my anger or the amount of blood that bursts out of this guy's face with every hit.

Ulysses catches my fist in his hand and aims his left fist up at my face, but I grab it before he can manage a hit and force my weight down on him so that he's held down.

"You're a sorry fuck of a human. You're a shit brother, a shit son, and you were a shit boyfriend to Eloise." I don't know why I feel the need to rub it all in his face because, by tomorrow, he'll be behind bars for sure. But sometimes not even jail time can make up for the harm someone has caused.

Fuck, Eloise's panic attacks were diminishing, for godsakes, and this fucker didn't give a fuck. He acted like he loved and cared for her and then caused her more pain.

I contemplate his murder right now, knowing no one would fucking miss him, maybe Charlotte but that's because the girl was loyal to her family, and despite Ulysses being a monster of a human, I doubt he was born like this. Just like all of us, he was just a mere puppet under his parent's hold.

"Why are you looking at me like that, man?" Ulysses's voice is shaking, almost as if in fear.

Good. He should be fucking scared.

"I'll delete the video and leave you guys alone. I'm sorry, okay? You've already hurt me enough. You going to kill me now, too?"

I very much should.

But despite the urge, I've never killed anyone, and I won't start dancing with the devil now just because his spawn is a major piece of shit.

A deep chuckle escapes my lips, and I know it only makes him even more uneasy.

"Your little promises don't mean anything to me, Ulysses, because the video has already been deleted. And all your truths have already come out."

Ulysses's eyes shift from side to side as he gathers my words.

"What the fuck are you talking about?" He growls, shaking underneath my grip. I push down on my weight and hold him still.

"If you're smart enough to blackmail, then you're smart enough to understand the ramifications. You're going to pay for what you did to Eloise."

"You think you're any better than me?" He challenges.

"You're just like me, William. We both had the same goal set; you just beat me to it and got that ring on her finger. But you are no better than me. You're still her father's little bitch, and she'll hate you forever for that."

He's bating me.

But he's right.

So I clock him in the face one last fucking time before getting off of him.

"You're very right, Ulysses; you and I are more similar than I'd like to admit. But the difference between you and I is that I learn from my mistakes, and I see Eloise's worth."

Ulysses lifts himself up from the floor and smiles up at me.

"Just like you saw Jasmine's worth?"

My hands tighten into fists, but I try my best to take a breather and focus my thoughts before I kick his teeth in.

"Jasmine deserved better, which is why I won't be

making the same mistake twice." I turn my back on Ulysses and almost make it out the door before I hear a call from what must be from God to turn back around and kick Ulysses's teeth in.

Which is exactly what I do.

Ulysses falls back in pain, and I turn around. This time, I actually take my leave.

"You and the rest of these elitist fuckers can suck my dick. Eloise's father included."

It was all going to end.

Chapter Thirty-One

The next morning, I woke up to a vacant bed, and by the looks of it, William didn't even come to bed because his side of the bed remained untouched. I grab my phone from the nightstand and see that I'm bombarded with a bunch of missed calls and texts from my parents and Charlotte. I scroll through the countless of notifications from news outlets and social media.

My stomach sinks to the floor at the thought of my sex tape being out in public. I wanted to believe William could do it. I had hoped that somehow he'd figured out a way to delete the video. I turn off my phone and pull off the comforter. I didn't want to see my face plastered all over the media. I'd rather just ask William how bad it all is.

"William!" I call as I enter the living room.

"In here." His voice leads me into the kitchen, where he's sitting with two plates and coffee mugs.

"You're up, great. Come, I made us breakfast." William stands up from his seat and pulls out the chair beside him so I can take a seat.

"I don't really have much of an appetite," I say, but I take the seat anyway.

William presses a kiss to the top of my head and takes a seat beside me. He grabs the cutlery and digs into his plate.

"Are you not worried about how this will look?"

William shrugs his shoulders and takes a piece of bacon into his mouth. How could he not be worried about how this video would portray our marriage? Shouldn't we be talking to a lawyer right now?

"How would their issues affect us, blondie?" William asks, furrowing his eyebrows in confusion.

"God, William, could you at least be a little bit more empathetic about how this makes me feel? For Christ's sake, it's my fucking face and body on the internet." I push off from the table and pace the kitchen. My panic attack was already rising within my chest.

Fuck me.

"Hey, hey, hey, Eloise, look at me." William stands over me, his hands holding onto my arms as I try my best to control my breathing.

"What are you talking about? There is no video. There's actually no trace of it anymore." He says.

"What do you mean? But the messages." I reach over to the table, pick the phone back up, and look through the messages.

CHARLOTTE

Eloise, please call me! Ulysses and my
father have been arrested!

MOM

Such terrible news with what happened to
the Hawthornes. It's best to avoid
Charlotte as much as possible.

"William, what the hell is going on?" I look back at him,
needing answers.

If my tape wasn't released, then what the hell was
released about the Hawthornes that was so terrible? William
grabs my hands and brings me to the living room. He grabs
the remote and turns on the news, where I'm met with a
video of Ulysses and his father walking out of their homes in
handcuffs. Ulysses's face looked beaten and bruised. I face
William, and look down at his scabbed knuckles, and raise
my brow.

"Would you care to explain what's going on, dear?" I ask
as I bring his hand to my face to observe the damage.

"Well, as I was looking for any remnants of the video, I
happened to fall under some evidence of tax evasion. And, it
seems that not even the tax evasion could help them pay off
the enormous amount of debt they owed, so I found that we
weren't the only people getting blackmailed, blondie."
William cups my cheeks and caresses them gently, waiting
for my response.

"And your knuckles?" I ask, grabbing them and giving
them a gentle kiss.

"He blackmailed you, Eloise. He should be dead." I roll
my eyes at how nonchalant he was about the whole thing.

Tears stream down my face, but this time around, they're

not out of anxiety or pain. It's out of pure joy and relief. I wasn't sure if this made me a terrible friend. Charlotte must be freaking out, and here I am, relieved that I got out unscathed.

"Oh crap, I should probably call Charlotte. She's probably freaking out." I run a hand through my hair, and take a seat back down on the chair, and search for Charlotte's name on my phone.

William brings his hands over mine to stop me from continuing my call.

"You should know that she's quite upset over the situation. It'll probably be hard for her to understand that her family is in the wrong."

I let out a scoff and shake my head at William's assumption.

"I get that this isn't the best news for them, but there's no reasoning that could make Ulysses and his father look like they're in the right. I think Charlotte will understand."

She was my best friend, and she had always taken my side, even when I was with Ulysses. She was the first to always admit when Ulysses was in the wrong.

"Dev called me today, Eloise. He said that Ulysses was stating that I was framing him. And the bruises on his face make a nice touch to his story. Of course, Dev knows he's lying, but Charlotte isn't sure what to think. You're obviously her best friend, but I'm just a man you married."

"You're my husband! And Ulysses is a leech who won't get off my ass." William cups my face and grins as if this were something to be happy about.

"If I were on your ass, I'd try my hardest to stay there

too." I slap away his hand and pick my phone back up to call Charlotte.

"I'm going to try to defend our name anyway. We did nothing wrong, and Charlotte will have to realize that sooner or later."

"Later then, let's just enjoy our breakfast, blondie. We will worry about this shit show after. I want to enjoy my morning with my wife."

I put my phone down, and William kneels in front of me so our faces are in front of each other.

"I'm sorry I didn't tell you sooner." I'm not sure why I apologized again, but it felt right to do so. "I can't believe you left the house to go punch him in the face." I was sure that William did more than just punch him in the face by the look of his knuckles and Ulysses's face. Nonetheless, a chuckle escapes my lips at the thought of this man running outside of the house to avenge me.

"You do realize that it's somewhat ridiculous, right?" I ask him, his eyes still hooked on mine, a sliver of a smile slowly rising on his face.

"Eloise, nothing is ever ridiculous when it comes to you. I never want you to doubt my love. I would do anything for you. I don't care about the money or the tape. I only care about you and what you want. I punched that fucker because he thought he could make you feel worthless, and then I nearly killed him because he had you first, and I can't help but feel jealous about that." I let out a shaky breath and chuckled at his stupid admission.

"Eloise, I want to give you peace, I want to give you calm, and I want to give you the life that *you* want. And I'll do anything to get you that." His words fill me up with a warmth I've never quite felt before. I can only compare it to a warm blanket protecting you from the cold during a cold winter.

And I knew that even if we couldn't exactly get the alternative life that I wanted far away from the one we had, it would all still be okay because William would be here with me.

"You are my peace and calm, Will. I don't know how or when that happened, but it did." William's lips find mine, and we stay in the kitchen like that for a while. Our lips interlocked, our hands wandering over each other's bodies, and our hearts beating in sync.

Chapter Thirty-Two

Eloise

"Do you think she'll be upset with us?" I ask William as the elevator lifts us to Dev and Charlotte's penthouse. Dev had spoken to William after our breakfast. He had called and stated that Ulysses was making all sorts of claims in regard to being framed by William.

I had followed William around our home like a lost puppy, begging him to ask Dev how Charlotte was. He finally caved and Dev informed him that she was confused and not sure what to believe. Ulysses and his father weren't exactly the most truthful people, and the evidence that came out proved that to be true.

"We don't have to tell her it was me who exposed her family."

I scoff and slap Will's arm, "we shouldn't stoop to her

family's level. She's been lied to enough. The last thing she needs is more lies and secrets."

William nods and presses a kiss to the top of my head, and I know that's his way of letting me know that he'll follow my lead. When Dev began asking questions, Will said it was best that they speak in person because the truth was much more complicated than just answering a simple yes or no question.

"She's going to hate me." I groan as the elevator door dings open.

"She's going to have to get over it," William grunts, waving a hand forward for me to take a step inside first.

"Eloise, is that you?" Charlotte's voice calls out. By the sound of it, I know she's been crying.

Charlotte turns the corner from down the hall and comes straight to the foyer to meet me. Even when breaking down, she still manages to look put together.

"Oh, Eloise. What the hell is happening?!" She marches straight into my arms and breaks down into sobs. So many times, it has been the other way around.

Charlotte had always been there for me before there was William, and the guilt of being the one causing her this pain is breaking me.

I rub a gentle hand on her back and give a slight nod to Dev, who passes by us to speak to William, who stands behind us.

"How about we take a seat so we can talk." I suggest.

Charlotte breaks away from our embrace and gives me a nod before pulling me towards the living room by my hand.

Dev and William stay put in the foyer to speak amongst themselves. I'm sure William wants to explain everything to

Dev so that he can see some rationality in his decision to put all of Ulysses's secrets to the media.

"Eloise, Ulyssess is pissed. He says William is setting him up because he's jealous of your guy's relationship. I told him he needed to shut the fuck up and that this wasn't the time to deal with a stupid high school crush on you." Charlotte continues to ramble on about her frustration with her brother and father's decisions.

"Mom is so broken. I'm trying to get her to come here, but she's so broken, Eloise. She just wants to remain alone. Dev got her a hotel to stay at for the rest of the week because the authorities practically ransacked our home. God, Eloise, they took everything."

Tears brim my eyes, and I want to be able to tell her that everything will be okay, but I know that things will no longer be the same.

"Charlotte, I have to tell you something." I bite my lip and rub my sweaty palms against the fabric of my dress.

"What is it?" Charlotte intertwines her hand with my own and sets it onto her lap, looking at me for some sort of comfort or reassurance, but instead, I'm about to kick my best friend when she's down.

"What your brother did is real." I start, and Charlotte immediately pulls back and shakes her head.

"You don't know that. He could be framed, and my dad has been in this industry for a long time. He wouldn't have made such a big mistake. This is all just a big mistake. How could you believe any of this?" Charlotte lifts herself up from the couch and begins pacing around.

"Charlotte, I know it's real because I was one of his blackmail victims." Charlotte stops and looks down at me, and for the first time, she doesn't look at me like a friend but rather an enemy who's just threatened to shoot her in her own home.

"Your name wasn't on the list of blackmailers." I sigh and nod.

"That's correct because William wiped it away."

William had wiped any evidence of Ulysses having been in contact with me and made sure that any evidence he shared with the media didn't involve me.

"You're lying." Charlotte accuses, her voice coarse and full of anger.

"I'm not, Charlotte. Your brother threatened me with a fucking sex tape we had made and said he would publicize it to the media if I didn't give him money." I get up and try to reach out for her. But Charlotte just takes a step back.

"You're lying. Why wouldn't you have come to me? I would've told him something."

"What would you have done, Charlotte? Nothing you would say would stop him from either denying that it was him or stopping him from doing it at all. There was nothing that you could've done."

Charlotte scoffs and shakes her head at the truth I had stated. I had to admit that I was aware that this truth would be hard for Charlotte to wrap her head around, but some small part of me hoped that she would believe me. That she would choose my side and deal with this together.

"Get out." She spits out through gritted teeth.

"Charlot—"

"Get out!" She shrieks, and that voice of pain is all that's needed to have Dev run into the room to calm Charlotte down.

"I think it best if you two left for today. There's a lot we're having to deal with right now. It's best we all talk when things have calmed down a bit." Dev says, his voice calm and comforting.

William wraps his arm protectively around my waist and pulls me towards the exit. It doesn't take long for the elevator to open, but right before we enter, I hear Charlotte say, "I never want to see them again."

I clear my throat to relieve the painful knot tightening in my throat.

"She doesn't mean it. She's just going through a lot. She will forgive you. Dev sees reason, and he will help her find it, too."

I nod and blink away the tears building up in my eyes.

"Just give it time, blondie. This will all blow over soon." William pulls me into his chest and holds me close as I sob into his shirt.

I was sure that this would pass, but I wasn't sure that it would ever be the same again.

Chapter Thirty-Three

A week had passed since the big reveal of Hawthorne's family secrets. A whole week since I'd spoken to Charlotte, who had still refused to speak with me. Dev had called a few times to talk to William. There was no bad blood between them, and Dev assured him Charlotte would see reason soon. She was just dealing with everything all at once.

And that was fine because I could wait as long as she needed me to. It couldn't be easy finding out that your family isn't as good of people as you think they are.

If this groundbreaking news came out about my own father, I wouldn't have been too shocked. It would actually please me much more to see him behind bars.

It's not like anything he did was clean and legal. I'm sure there must be some sort of law prohibiting him from marrying his daughter off to anyone he wanted. But out of all the wrongs he's done, that would probably be the last thing I'd want him behind bars for.

I flip the page of my book and take a sip of the chamomile tea I had begun making frequently every morning to calm my nerves. William had been gone often or in his studies most of the time, working on a big project that was coming up.

I was sure he was probably trying to distract his mind from everything that was happening.

The vibrating of an incoming call pulls me away from my thoughts, and I put down the book that I wasn't entirely focused on to pick up the call.

"Hello?" I answer, not having read the caller ID on the screen before picking up to respond.

"Eloise, it's nice of you to finally answer your parent's call." My father's voice sounds through the phone.

Crap.

I roll my eyes and sigh to try to prepare myself for this conversation.

"Hello, father, things have been busy."

"Yes, I'm sure it's been quite busy for an unemployed, childless woman." He digs at my insecurities, and I clear my throat, trying my best not to show that I care.

Fuck, that kind of hurt, but then again, he wasn't wrong.

And whose fault is that? He's the one who forced you to study something that you didn't even care for.

"Well, it's time to come out of that cave of yours, Eloise. You can't live in that house forever. Come meet me for lunch today. My assistant will send you further information."

My grip tightens on the phone, and I roll my eyes at his

demand. Even when he's given me off to another man, he still wants to hold some sort of reign over me.

"No, thank you. I'm a bit busy." I hadn't ever said no to my father before, and I wasn't sure what made me think that denying him would even work.

"That's cute, Eloise. But I wasn't asking; I was demanding. Be there today at one. Goodbye." My father hangs up the phone before I can deny him again.

What would happen if I didn't show up?

It's not like he has any real power over me, but just the thought of him making William's life a living hell at work frustrated me. I mean, I hardly see my husband. I was sure it was punishment for not following his plan of having a child.

And as beautiful as it would be to be able to carry William's child, I wanted our kids to be far away from our family. I couldn't protect myself growing up, but I could protect my kids.

I'd go to this dumb lunch, but I wouldn't give my father the satisfaction of getting what he wanted from it.

"I knew you wouldn't disappoint me, Eloise." My father chuckles as I take a seat across from him. No hellos or hugs were exchanged. We've never done so, and we definitely wouldn't start now.

Now that I think of it, I don't think I can recall a time in my life when I had ever been embraced by my own parents. Sure, our staff hugged me and had practically raised me. But

I had never experienced that type of comfort from my own mom and dad.

"Why are we here, father?" I ask, wanting to cut it short. The quicker I left, the higher the possibility of not ending my day with a panic attack was.

"Don't be rude, Eloise. I've invited you to a nice lunch. I bet that Hawthorne girl wishes she could spend a time like this with her father, and instead, he's locked behind bars." My father mocks.

"Charlotte, her name is Charlotte, dad. We've been friends for enough time for you to remember her fucking name." My father's eyes darken as he peers up at me through the menu he had opened the minute I sat down. He sets the menu down for a second and lays his elbow down on the table to point his finger at me.

"Watch your damn tone with me. I'm not happy with you one bit, and your fucking attitude isn't helping." He snaps.

I tighten my grip on my knees from under the table. I had never heard him speak to me in that regard. Most of the time, my father used my mother as a medium to speak to me. But it seemed that now that I no longer listened to my mother, he had to take time off his day to speak to me.

I had only ever heard that tone with his employees. Not even Mom pissed him off enough to have him speak to her in that manner.

"You know you're a beautiful woman, Eloise." My father begins, and I can already feel my stomach churn the way he begins this lecture.

"And beautiful women don't struggle when it comes to getting what they want. Let alone getting their husband into bed." His eyes bore into mine, and I knew exactly what he was trying to get at because it was the same thing he'd wanted since I came back from my honeymoon.

The waitress stops by to take our order, and I settle for the most expensive thing on the menu just to fuck with my father because I know that I won't be touching anything on that damn plate. And as soon as he got this little lecture over with, I would be running back home.

My dad takes his time with ordering. He doesn't bother having some respect in front of me when outwardly beginning to flirt with the waitress.

Jesus Christ.

"You know I could use good service like you on my yacht." My father says, caressing the wrist of the waitress, that I had no idea how the fuck he got ahold of.

Use a different word to hint at sex; check.

Bring up something that only rich people have to state you have money, check.

Touch her like the creep that you are and watch her giggle because she's too uncomfortable to say anything to you; check.

"Okay, that's enough. You can act like you aren't married some other time, father. Preferably when I'm not around." I shoo the waitress away with the flick of my wrist, and I don't miss the look of relief that passes her face when she walks away.

I'm not sure what had gotten into me to finally be brave enough to stand my ground, but fuck I was proud of myself for just doing it. No one should have to deal with my father, not the waitress and not even myself.

"I don't know what's gotten into you, but some sense and

respect needs to be smacked back into you." He growls, taking the cup of scotch to his lips and taking a sip.

"Why are we here, father?"

The answer was obvious, but I needed this conversation to be over as soon as possible. I could also hear my phone ringing from my bag, and I was sure it was William trying to find out where I was after sending him a text that I was meeting my father up for lunch.

"Don't you want to get that?" My father asks..

"I'd rather get this over with," I mutter.

"This might be the reason William is just so hesitant to have a child with you, Eloise. A woman should be submissive to her husband, and that means picking up the phone when he calls."

I was sure he was assuming that William was calling, but I had a mental note to ask William once I got home to make sure no one was lurking through my phone on my father's accord.

"If you're encouraging me to be a submissive wife, then it's best I go, seeing that my husband wants me home and far away from you." I grab my purse and make my way up to leave, but my father's hold on my arm stops me.

"Sit your ass down, Eloise. It's best you don't piss me off more than you already have."

I look around the restaurant, and though there are not many people around, the ones that are have their eyes on us.

I clear my throat, take a seat back in my chair, and give my father a nod to proceed.

"I'm not asking you to be submissive, Eloise. I'm asking you to stop playing coy and open your damn legs for the man and make sure he finishes inside. And you better hope I don't find out that you're on the pill because there will be hell to pay, Eloise. I need a fucking heir." My dad pours down the rest of his scotch before smacking the glass back on the table.

My grip tightens on the purse in my hands. For the first time, I truly fear my own parents. All the other times that something had been demanded of me, I would bend backward to fulfill it. I wanted to please them and make them happy. But nothing would ever make them happy with me because they never wanted me to begin with. That's why my father was so insistent on finding a man to marry me off. He wanted a man to pass down his company to, and now he wanted to make sure he had a grandson who had his blood.

And the look on my father's face told me he would do anything to get me to do exactly what he wanted.

"And what if we don't want to have children?" I challenge.

"Make him want to."

"But what if *I* don't want kids right now."

I don't know why I'm trying to get him to see some sort of reason; maybe it's just silly hope, maybe some part of me thinks that my father will suddenly give a fuck about me and my feelings.

"Let me make this clear for you, Eloise. Maybe I don't have much of a say in how to manage you, Eloise. But I sure as hell have a say in how to manage your husband at work. And I will make his life a living hell, I promise you that. I'll make sure he leaves work hating me so fucking much that he can't help hating my daughter too. Men like Will and I need an outlet, and when our wives aren't there or just don't do it for us anymore, there's always better all around. So just keep that in mind when you change your mind on this whole bearing a child idea."

My father raises his scotch glass over to the bar, gesturing for another drink. I take this chance to get up and leave. I hear him call my name, but I don't bother to stop.

My father made sure to go in for the kill, and I hadn't known he observed me enough to know how much being in a loveless marriage like the one my parents were in was a fear of mine.

And I couldn't bring a child into this world with the possibility of that happening, and the truth is, somehow, my father would figure out a way to drive William away from me because, in this lifestyle, it was inevitable.

And the only way for this to be fixed is for it to end.

Chapter Thirty-Four

Eloise

Cory is silent during the car ride home, and I'm sure he's informed William of where I was and that I was heading home. I'm sure he's also told him how I haven't stopped bawling my eyes out since I've stepped foot in the car.

"We're here, Miss Wren." That is all Cory says as he parks the car in the garage and makes his way out of it to open my car door. But I don't wait for him to make his way around the car. I open the door myself and make my way toward the elevator.

"Thank you, Cory."

"Anytime."

I tried to formulate what exactly I was going to say to William, but there wasn't a simple way of doing this.

The minute I enter the home, I make my way to his

office. I know he's there because he had sent me a text while I was at the restaurant letting me know that he would be home, working in his office, and to give him a call as soon as I could.

I knocked on the door, and William calls me inside. I open the door and watch him on the call as he looks back at me back at me from his screen.

"Good, we can move forward with the plan then. I'll give you a call later, but let me know if anything else pops up, thanks Liam." William hangs the phone up, immediately and stands up from his chair to makes his way around to me.

"What's going on, blondie?" William asks as he hugs me. A sob escapes my lips, and I'm sure he's so fucking tired of seeing me break down every four to five business days, but I'm sick and tired of feeling the need to.

"My father wants us to have a child." I manage to say between sobs.

William doesn't say a single thing. Instead, he rubs my back, trying to calm me down. I push away from his embrace and wipe away any remaining tears as I try to calm myself down.

"William, he'll make our lives hell," I explain.

"He won't be doing shit." William was so sure of his reply, but he hadn't seen how pissed my father was.

"William, you don't understand. You should've heard how he spoke to me. His tone— I just don't think I've ever heard him speak to me in that way."

William takes a step closer, trying to bring me in his arms again. I just shake my head and take a step back. Being in his arms will only make this harder than it has to be.

"If I don't give him what he wants, he's going to make it

his goal to destroy our marriage, William. And I can't give you a kid. Not now, not like this. I refuse to bring a child into a marriage that can end up like my parents."

William scoffs and shakes his head at my statement. He tries to reach out to me, but I don't let him.

"Eloise, first of all, we don't have any children. I don't care what your dad says. When we decide to have children, they will be born into a family where their parents love and care for each other. We won't end up like your mom and dad." William voices his opinion with confidence as if he's seen our future through some magic crystal ball, and if that were true, I want to see the crystal ball instantly.

"William, you don't know that." I sigh, wanting so badly to forget my plans to end this and move on with our relationship.

"Then what is it that you want, Eloise? What are you trying to get at?" William clenches his jaw, and I'm sure he already knows what I'm trying to say to him.

"I'm saying that the only way out of this is for us to end. My father can't screw you over if I'm the one ending things."

He would be upset with me, but he'd leave Will alone.

William stands there for a few moments. Nothing is said between us, and it doesn't seem like he's upset about my declaration, and I'd be lying if I said that wasn't upsetting.

William sighs, making his way back to his desk, and takes a seat in his chair.

"I don't understand what you're saying." William finally speaks, typing something into his computer.

Was he fucking with me?

Suddenly, I wasn't sad anymore. I was annoyed.

"Are you listening?" I ask.

This time, I stomp over to his desk and lay my hands down on the table.

"I heard you." He replies, not bothering to look at me.

"I'm saying we need to break up." I clarify.

William looks up at me and lets out a chuckle.

"Eloise, we're married. We don't do break-ups." He states, as a matter affectedly.

I throw my hands in the air out of frustration, "Ugh, you know what I mean, William, divorce."

William's jaw tightens again as he peers up to look at me again. He stands up very slowly and makes his way around the desk, which feels way longer than normal. I try to move back again, but William grasps my waist and pulls me in.

"Let me make something clear, Eloise. Obviously, I didn't fuck you hard enough the other day to drill it into you that I am in love with you. Which means that I have chosen you. I vowed to be with you through everything and anything."

"But my—"

"Your father is a nuisance, and I will deal with him the same way I dealt with Ulysses if I have to."

"But, Will—"

William shuts me up by pressing his lips against mine, and I instantly melt into his arms. This wasn't the plan at all. William pulls away from the kiss and gives me a delicate kiss on the head.

"You're worried, and you're anxious. But I need you to trust me, and I need you to finally set some boundaries when it comes to your family. They no longer have reign over you, blondie. And you have the free will to decide what you want to do." He murmurs, brushing his thumb against my cheek. I hold his hand close to my face, give him a gentle kiss, and nod my head.

"I'm sorry."

William smiles and kisses my lips once more.

"Head over to the bathroom and get undressed. I'll meet you there shortly to run you a bath. No worries should be in your mind, blondie. I can, and I will fix everything for us." He promises.

And I believe him.

Chapter Thirty-Five

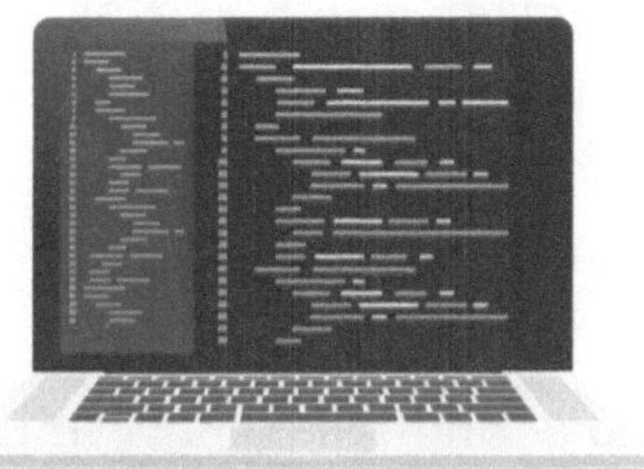

William

The minute I see Eloise make her way out of the office, I pick up the phone and give Liam and Dev a call.

"Please tell me you're done waiting around." Liam pleads the minute he answers the call. He's been on board since the beginning, and Dev was too. I was a little unsure about his continuation of the idea after the Hawthorne scandal, but he had assured me that he was still all in.

"Honestly, starting fresh is what we need right now. So I'm down to expedite this little idea of ours as soon as we can." Dev adds.

His voice sounds tired, and I'm sure he is. He knows that what Charlotte's family did was wrong, but he still feels obligated to help them for Charlotte's sake. But the truth of the matter was that no matter how good of a lawyer they got,

Ulysses and his father would be doing time, and there was no way out of that.

"Harry has started to threaten Eloise and me. And though I don't personally give a fuck about what he has to say to me, I do fucking care what he says and does to Eloise." I explain, rubbing a hand through my face.

The plan was stable, but it wasn't ready.

"I get you, man. I'd do anything for Charlotte." Dev sighed into the phone, and I knew he was thinking of all the other issues that were going on in Charlotte's and his life.

"That's because you guys are pussy whipped." Liam chuckles.

I roll my eyes but don't deny his statement. I wouldn't say I'm pussy whipped, but I would say I'm in love, and I don't ever want to let that go again.

"So, what are our moves? Leave him high and dry? I'm ready for Boston when you are. I've got the location down, Dev has started the hiring process, and we're ready to get this started."

Fuck, it was time. I was hoping we had a little more time to gather everything together and really sit down with Eloise and speak to her about this change. But I can't sit here and wait. This stupid contract with her father will get in the way of our marriage at some point.

I had done this for my parents. I had accepted the contract in order to make my father happy and save him from his own mistakes, and now I have finally realized that it is time to do something for myself.

"Tomorrow it'll be done. We'll walk into work like any other day and leave knowing we're making better moves for ourselves." I declare.

"That's what I'm fucking talking about!" Liam hollers over the phone.

Dev chuckles on his end and agrees with our decision. He also lets us know that he'll be speaking to Charlotte about the upcoming changes.

The minute I end the call, I make my way to our master bathroom, where I know Eloise is probably growing impatient at my absence.

I walk into the bathroom and see Eloise sitting at the edge of the tub. Her light yellow robe tugged snuggly around her curves. Her hand reaches down to touch the water that's filling up the top.

"Didn't I tell you to wait for me?" I ask, removing my shoes to leave them by the door. I make my way over to Eloise and slowly unbutton my dress shirt.

"You were taking too long, and I was getting cold in only my robe." She declares, reaching over to pour a bottle of lavender scented bubbles into the water.

A single strand of hair falls from the messy bun on top of her head, and I swipe it behind her ears so that it's out of her way.

Who the fuck am I kidding? I just really wanted to touch her.

"You look beautiful, blondie." I run my thumb across her cheeks, which are still a bit red and puffy from crying.

"The bags under my eyes beg to differ." She snorts.

Eloise leans back over and closes the faucet before standing up right in front of me. I take that to my advantage and give her ass a slap.

Eloise lets out a yelp and tries to swat my hand but misses.

"Don't talk about yourself in that way; as a matter of fact, one says thank you when receiving a compliment, got it?" I ask, using the tone I know gets her all hot and bothered for me.

Eloise crosses one leg over the other, and I know she's trying to keep that horny pussy calm right now.

"Answer me, Eloise," I demand, awaiting her submissive response.

"Yes, sir." She says, her eyes boring into my own, and fuck, she looked at me with those innocent blue eyes that somehow also begged to have me rail her in every place of our home.

"You getting in the tub, blondie?" I ask, finally picking at the rest of my buttons, opening up the dress shirt, and letting it fall to the ground.

Eloise gives me a nod, never once takes her eyes off of mine as she unties the bow of her robe and lets the silk slide off her delicious skin.

Fuck me. I've never been jealous of an inanimate object, especially not a fucking piece of fabric.

"Are you going in with your pants?" Eloise snickers, taking in my half-naked body as if it's her first time.

"Get in the tub," I demand.

Eloise follows my command and steps into the bath. She arches her back and leans back into the bath, her perky tits peeking through the water's surface, the bubbles adorning her creamy skin.

I get completely naked and slide in right behind her. Eloise places her head in the center of my chest and lets out a moan.

"I haven't even begun to touch you, blondie, and you're already moaning." I tease.

I cup the water in my hands and lift it gently to the top of her body above the water, dumping the warm water over her.

"I really thought this would end today." She murmurs.

I continue soothing her with the warmth of the water and kiss the top of her head.

"I just think that we won't ever catch a break here. There will always be people here trying to control us, trying to control me. God, William, Vermont was just so different." I smile into her hair, thinking of how much that trip had altered our whole relationship.

This marriage hadn't been the toughest, but it wasn't easy. Vermont somehow felt like a home, but maybe that's just because we were far away from all the chaos.

Eloise moves her head up to face me, and I look down so that I can look at those eyes.

"It's unfair of me to ask you to leave this all behind for me. To let go of what you were promised out of this marriage and just choose me." A tear slides down her cheek, and I'm quick to wipe it away.

"Eloise, I married you because I was a puppet to my own parents to some degree. I left a relationship that I thought I would be devoted to for the rest of my life to fix my family's name and finances. I married you in hopes of being able to make my family's name mean something again. But things have changed now. You've changed it all, blondie." I press a kiss on the side of her head and bring my hands up to her breast.

I squeeze them gently and flick my thumb over her

nipples. She instinctively moves in closer to me like the good little minx that she is.

"Eloise, you are mine," I murmur in her ear.

"Fuck the company and fuck our families, you are all I want."

A gasp escapes her lips as I tug on those needy nipples that are practically begging to be sucked and bitten.

I bring my hand down to her pussy that I know is craving my touch. I slide fingers in her center and pull her beautiful lips apart, a slight hiss escapes her lips, and I know her clit is adjusting to the warm contact of the water.

"I'm going to fuck you in the tub, Eloise. And I'm going to make you bathe in my cum. I'm going to make sure you realize that you're my fucking wife."

Fuck I wanted to mark my territory somehow. I wanted everyone to know that she was my fucking wife and that her pussy was only mine to fuck.

"Please, Will, I need you." She moans, arching her back and positioning her head at the crevice of my neck and shoulder.

I rub circles around her clit before pushing two fingers into her pussy. The bath tub was big enough to not only fit both of us in here but to give Eloise enough space to part those long beautiful legs of hers.

Eloise moans as she leans back into the crook of my neck, licking the sensitive spot and sending shivers down my body.

I crook my fingers inside her a bit more and a muffled curse comes out of her mouth. Eloise bites down on my neck and continues sucking on the spot that quickly intensifies my hard on.

"Turn around, baby." I moan, removing my fingers from her tight pussy so that she can turn around and straddle me.

Fuck she looked gorgeous standing above me with her legs on either side of me. Those perky tits made me want to ram my cock deep inside her and watch them shake with every thrust.

I grab her hips to steady her as I move in closer and bring her tits into my mouth. Eloise grinds on my aching cock and pushes my head closer to her, moaning as I skim my teeth against her sensitive nipples.

"I love when you ride me, baby." I growl, sliding my nails down her back and gripping her ass tightly and lining her up with my cock.

"You ready to take my cock, baby?" I grab my dick and slide it up and down her perfect pussy lips. I give her clit an extra bit of attention before lowering it back down towards her entrance and shifting my hips up to enter her.

Eloise grips the sides of the tub and moves her hips up and down, causing slight movement to the water and for those bubbles on her chest to start sliding down onto her delicate breasts.

"Come on baby, I know you like it harder than that. If you can't do it yourself then all you have to do is beg like a good girl." I murmur.

Eloise mews as I grab onto the sides of the tub and begin thrusting my hips up deeper into her.

"Oh god, yes!" She moans, bouncing up and down on my cock. My hips move faster and deeper into her. Eloise grasps my shoulders and digs her nails in them as she clenches her pussy around me. Trying her best to hold onto her orgasm.

"Beg, baby." I demand.

"Please let me come, sir."

I don't get to answer her before she's begging me again.

"Please, fuck please, please, please." She begs, tightening her grip and shooting her head back to look at the ceiling.

"Come all over my cock, blondie."

Eloise lets out a single moan and by the slight shake in her legs I know it's a good one. I only last a few more strokes before I pull out of Eloise completely and shoot my load all over her abdomen, some of my cum even reaching her tits.

"Good thing I'm already in the bath to wash it off." Eloise jokes, grabbing the loofah and soap. I grip her wrists and remove the body wash from her hands.

"I meant what I said, baby." I take the loofah from her hand and use it to smear my cum all over her skin.

"I want you covered in my cum, I want you bathing in it." I bring the loofah around her body and take her nipple that's covered in my cum into my mouth. I moan at how good my cum tastes on her skin. Fuck I needed her to taste us like this. I bring my lips onto hers and Eloise moans into our kiss, obviously loving the taste of us together.

I pull away and take her closer into my arms.

"This is just the first round of many tonight, blondie."

Eloise practically purrs in my lap and brings her lips to mine again.

"Is that a promise?" She giggles.

"No, baby. It's a vow."

Chapter Thirty-Six

William

"This is actually fucking happening," I say to myself as I adjust my tie while looking at myself in the mirror. All the planning that had been done was for this very moment.

There would be no more waiting, not now that they'd started threatening Eloise. And I had just enough of this fucking city. I was getting out of here and starting a life far away from all of this.

I had called my lawyer again late last night once Eloise had fallen asleep just to confirm that this wouldn't come back to bite me in the ass. But in truth, Harold had been so egotistical to believe that someone would want his company so badly that they would never make the crazy decision of committing to his daughter and leaving his business behind.

There was no clause that held me accountable for leaving.

I could back away from the contract and continue my marriage with Eloise, and the fucker wouldn't be able to do a thing.

No amount of threats or paperwork would be able to fix the mistake that had already been made the moment we signed that contract.

"What's happening?" Eloise yawns.

I look at her reflection in the mirror and watch as she stretches into the mattress and lets out a breathy moan as if the minx hadn't had enough of what I had given her last night. I walk over to her and sit by the edge of the bed.

Her perky breasts are out in the open, and the air conditioning is cold enough to have her nipples pebbling.

I let out a groan in annoyance.

I wouldn't be able to stay any longer than I already had. It had taken me a bit longer to get out of bed this morning when my morning wood was so close to Eloise's bare pussy.

But nonetheless, I had to get ready. I sent out an email last night to Harold and my father stating that there would be a meeting at the office at around ten.

"There's just going to be some big changes at work, and I'm not sure anyone is ready for what's to come. Hell, I'm not sure if I'm even ready, but I know it'll be worth it."

"Hm, I'm sure it will be." She murmurs as she rubs her hand up and down my arm to comfort me

I chuckle at her closed eyes and know she's fallen back to sleep the minute her hand drops to the mattress. I had worn her out last night. After the bath, I laid her back down in bed and fucked her again and again until her legs were shaky and she physically couldn't take me anymore.

I press a kiss on her cheek and cover her body with the

comforter. When I return, everything will have changed. Finally, we will be able to start the life we want.

The moment I walked into the board meeting room, my father and Harold were already sitting there discussing their next strategies. I'm sure their next big idea was to poke holes through condoms or replace Eloise's birth control with placebo pills.

And as dark as that thought was, I wouldn't put it past them to get it done.

"Will, what's going on? I don't like being pulled away from my current plans for the day." Harold snarls, leaning back in his chair and furrowing his brows as if I owe him some sort of apology.

"I'm sure I'm doing your secretary a favor by cutting into your fuck time." I walk towards the end of the table and stare at both men.

Harold scowls, and my father follows, obviously upset that I'm disrespecting someone who holds the future that he so desperately wants for me.

"He doesn't mean that, Harold. Why don't you apologize to the man, William." My father's jaw tightens, and I can practically hear his teeth grinding together.

I scoff and shake my head in shock.

"I didn't come here to waste any time. So, I think it's best that I just cut our interaction as short as possible."

My father's face pales, and I'm sure he knows what's coming.

"William, don't be irrational." He mutters, trying his best to calm his voice. But I don't give a fuck.

"Eloise and I are done dealing with your shit. You can

keep the company and give it to someone else for all I fucking care. But I'm done with this."

My father stands up from his seat and slams his fist against the table as if that would intimidate me one bit.

"What the fuck do you think you're doing, William." He growls.

"I'm choosing Eloise," I murmur, the truth coming out before I can even think it through. And though they didn't deserve a response or honesty at that, it was simple and felt right to admit.

Harold lets out a heavy laugh. The fucker really sits there and cracks himself up like a crazed maniac before looking up at me.

"You think you can leave my company and take my daughter, too?" Harold lets out a tisk and lifts himself off of the seat to face me directly.

"My daughter is your connection to the company; in other words, any man who wants my company marries my daughter. And if you don't want my company, then you sure as hell don't get my fucking daughter." He spits, and I have to hold myself back from knocking this fucker out.

The only thing that's stopping me is knowing that the contract he wrote was worded in a way that lets me leave this company with Eloise still around my arm.

"I would do a better job at reading your contracts, Harold. Better yet, I'd do a better job at hiring a lawyer that knows what the fuck he's doing when writing these contracts out."

Harold furrows his brows in confusion, and I can't help but laugh at the guy's confusion.

"Harold, don't listen to him. He doesn't know what he's

talking about. He obviously still wants Eloise and the company. That was what was agreed upon." My father's fuming at this point, but it feels liberating knowing that I'm going to screw these two over big time.

"Shut the fuck up, Donovan." Harold snaps before looking back at me.

"What the hell are you talking about, William?" He asks, his mind elsewhere, probably trying to remember the exact words of the contract.

"The contract never says anything about the repercussions of not wanting to continue with the pursuit of the company. It only declares that I will get the company after you resign and if I marry Eloise. But there's no statement that says Eloise and I can't continue to be married if we decide not to take on the role of CEO. As a matter of fact, there's no statement that says I *have* to take on that role anyway." I suck my teeth and give Harold a smile, knowing I've beat him at his own game.

"That can't be possible." He murmurs.

I shrug and begin to walk away, ignoring my father's shouts.

"Wait a minute!" Harold shouts, and for some reason, I pause and decide to hear him out.

"How could you possibly want to leave this? Do you know what you're giving up? This whole company could be yours, William." Harold tries to reason as if that would be enough to make me stay.

"To hell with it. If you stay married to my daughter and guarantee a child in the near future, I'll retire now." He suggests, and I have to say that's one hell of an agreement.

"Take it, Will, you get the girl and the position." My father tries to remain calm, but I can tell he's freaking out.

I shake my head at Harold before meeting his eyes so that he takes in every word I'm about to say.

"It's not worth it; this isn't worth it. But Eloise, your daughter, is worth losing all this for. No amount of money or position could ever outshine the true gift that it is to have that woman in my life. And that's something that you lacked to realize."

With those last words lingering in the room, I make my exit and don't give them any clarity as to where I'm leaving to, or the plans I have up my sleeve. Liam and anyone else in the company who has chosen to leave and come work at our start-up will give their letters of resignation, one by one.

That will be a constant punch to Harold's face, and I hope everyone takes their sweet time so that he suffers a little while longer.

I WALK THROUGH THE CROWDED CITY AND MAKE A TURN on a street I had done my best to ignore this past year. But it was necessary for me to get it done in order to start something new.

My phone vibrates in my pocket, and I pull it out to read the message I'm sure I received from a couple of people.

Liam

Harold's going crazy! He is talking all sorts of shit about

you and how he plans on ruining you. He called his lawyers
and went off on how fucking stupid they were.

Dev

He's the bigger idiot for trusting a cheap lawyer like that.

But regardless, congrats, buddy. You're making a great
decision. Have you told Eloise yet?

I snicker at the messages and type out a quick reply,

Thanks, and no, she has no clue yet. I'm going to surprise
her later tonight.

I shove my phone back into my pocket and ignore any of
the other texts. I hadn't even received one from Eloise, which
meant that her parents hadn't reached out to her yet.

But they will be reaching out soon, so I have to make this
quick.

I enter the bookstore that has been completely revamped
and under new management since I've last been in here, and
I freeze at the entrance as soon as my eyes meet the head of
curls that belong to the woman who once held my heart in
the palm of her hands.

I open my mouth to call out her name, but as soon as she
looks over at the door, my own name escapes her lips first.

"William?" She asks, her eyes wide as if she's looking at a
ghost. I clear my throat and make my way over to her, trying
to maintain some space between one another.

Not only out of respect for her but also for Eloise.

I didn't enjoy her closeness with Ulysses, and it would be
hypocritical of me not to put some boundaries between
Jasmine and me.

"Hi, J." I greeted her with the nickname I had called her
throughout our relationship, hoping to make this interaction
a bit lighter.

"Hi, um, what are you doing here?" She asks, looking over my shoulder almost as if expecting someone to be behind me.

My guess is that she either thought Eloise would be here with me or expected her boyfriend, Oren, to show up any second now.

"I wanted to apologize." I take a deep breath and try to gather thoughts on the words that I had been planning on saying.

Jasmine lifts up her hand to wave me off, and I noticed the ring that's taken real estate on her left ring finger.

A smile breaks through my lips as I nudge my head towards her ring.

"You're engaged? To Oren, I assume." Jasmine blushes and covers her hand, almost as if embarrassed to have been caught with it.

"Yeah, it happened fairly recently, actually very shortly after opening up this place." She says, gesturing to the room.

The bookstore was way better than it had been when she was just a mere employee. I look around the shelves and down at the book table and spot a stack of books with her name.

I glance between her and the books, putting two and two together.

"Is this really your work, Jasmine?" I ask, picking it up and turning it around to read the synopsis.

Jasmine gives me a shy grin before nodding.

"Yeah, it is. It's a romance, and I published it this summer." I grab the book and keep it in my hands, knowing it's just up Eloise's alley.

Getting your wife a book written by your ex doesn't seem

like the most rational idea. But knowing Eloise, she won't even care and become a fan of her writing regardless.

"I'm sure romance books aren't up your alley." Jasmine chuckles and points at my grip around the book, probably unsure as to why I'm buying it.

"You'd be surprised. Eloise has introduced me to a multitude of tropes and romance subgenres I'm quite fond of. And I'm sure she'll love this book by the looks of it."

Jasmine raises her brows at the bringing up of Eloise's name.

"How is Eloise?" She asks, and I know she's genuinely concerned.

"She's good— we're good. Actually, we're really great." I smile, and Jasmine shares one back.

"Look, Jasmine, I'm not here to waste your time. I really came here to apologize. I meant that you deserved better. I should've told my parents to fuck off, and I should have ignored my own greed and instead should have been better to you. I should have chosen you." I clear my throat and try to figure out the best way to word my next sentence.

"That's very nice, Will, but—"

"But I don't regret it." I cut her off, not wanting her to draw her own conclusions. I'm not trying to get her back or show her that I regret my decision because I truly don't.

"My decision led us to the life we're currently in. You're here happy with Oren, newly engaged, and probably even more excited to marry him than you ever were with me." Jasmine keeps her eyes on me but doesn't deny my statement. And I knew she wouldn't because even though there was love between us, the true love she found with Oren was something rare and beautiful. Something I had found with Eloise.

"And because of my decision, I was granted a marriage with someone who deserved better than me. But I honestly became too selfish to want to give her away to anyone who could grant that better. So instead of working to be the man she needs, I'm working to be the man she deserves."

Jasmine's eyes shimmer, and I know she feels for me and my love for Eloise.

"I don't think we were ever meant to be forever, Will. We were just meant to be the relationship that would guide us into our final ones, and though our end was excruciating at that time. It gave us something even more beautiful and eternal at the end." A single tear falls from her cheek and from my own as well.

The door opens, and a singing song of swears follows.

There he is.

"What the fuck is going on here?" Oren growls from behind me.

Jasmine rolls her eyes, walks past me, and gives Oren a peck on the lips and a hug. Oren greets her, but his eyes stay glued to me.

I raise my hands up in surrender, not wanting him to think I was here to get Jasmine back.

"I just came here to apologize to Jasmine," I explain and point to the book in my hand. "And to buy her book, too."

That one was new, but it wasn't a lie.

"Apologize for what?" Oren looks between Jasmine and me for answers, and Jasmine only rolls her eyes and gives him a slap on the chest.

"Calm down, you caveman; he's happily married and in

love with Eloise. He just came back to apologize for our past. That's all." Jasmine walks around the counter and brings out her hand for me to hand her the book to scan.

"Is that so, William? Are we happily married and in love?" He interrogates.

I'm sure he's expecting a lie or a comeback, but I remain calm and nod my head.

"Yes, it's true." Jasmine scans the book and brings up the total. I hover my card over the terminal and wait for the chime of approval before sliding the card back into my wallet.

Oren looks at the book Jasmine puts in the paper bag.

"The sex in that book is based on our sex life, you know," Oren states, but it seems more like a warning rather than a rub-it-in-my-face kind of statement.

"Oren, shut up! Leave him alone. He's being kind." Jasmine hands me the bag and gives me a brief apology.

"I'm just warning him." He mumbles.

"Thanks, Oren; I'll make sure to let Eloise know." I wave them goodbye and leave the bookstore. I stop and take out my phone and call Eloise.

"Hello?" Eloise's sweet voice answers.

"Pack your bags, blondie. We're going on a trip."

We were going to start fresh.

Chapter Thirty-Seven

Eloise

I hadn't realized that packing a bag would mean a whole flight to an unknown destination. I had gotten multiple calls from my parents and even some from William's parents, and it had begun to worry me. But William assured me that nothing was wrong and that they were just trying to get to me in order to have William change his mind.

"What exactly are they trying to change your mind about?" I ask.

"I'll tell you everything soon; there's something I want to show you first."

I groan and shake my head at his perseverance. I would've given up and told him everything by now, so why couldn't he do the same?

"I promise I will tell you everything. I just want it all to be right. I've had this planned for a while, and because of the incident with your father, it's been rushed. Not that it's a big deal, but I want things to go right, especially this moment that I had planned for us." William interlocks my hand with his and gives it a firm kiss.

I sigh and keep my mouth shut throughout the plane ride. I didn't want to keep annoying him with questions that would go unanswered, and I also wanted to give him the respect of telling me the way he felt would be right. It had to be something important enough to have us on a flight.

"Vermont?" I ask as we step outside the airport.

What the hell were we doing here? Not that I was complaining. I loved it here, but I was still unsure what the point of the destination was. William had gotten us a key to the rental car and was now driving us to our destination, which he said was currently two hours away.

"Is this another romantic getaway?" I ask, his eyes still focused on the road ahead.

"No."

I slouch in my seat and think of another guess. It was too soon to be back here. Plus, he had been working on a large project for work the past couple of weeks, and today, he said big changes were coming to the company.

"Are we on one of your work trips?!" I exclaim, feeling like I got my guess right this time.

William remains deep in thought for a few seconds before finally answering.

"In a way, yes. But not really."

I roll my eyes and give his arm a slap. William laughs and shakes his head.

"Okay, blondie. No more questions. You are only allowed to play music on the rest of the car ride or talk about the latest book you read." I sigh and know that no woman would really mind that, but I so desperately wanted to know what was happening.

I shuffle through my playlist and stay quiet for the remainder of the drive. William wasn't budging, and I was sure that if I had guessed correctly, he'd just give me some confusing response like last time.

After what seems like forever, William finally pulls into a gravel road that leads to a large house surrounded by beautiful trees. And a few feet away from the house stood a little creek.

"This is so beautiful!" I gasp, taking in the beauty of the home and the land surrounding it.

William parks the car in front of the driveway, and I immediately hop out of the car to look. William follows me to the front of the house. After a few seconds of just admiring, I turn to look at him.

"What is this?" I ask, "Like, why are we here?"

William stands there smugly and raises his brows.

"You like it?" He asks, ignoring my question.

"This is very nice, William. But, what's all this about?" I ask, moving my hands towards the acres of land. A bed and breakfast was surely out of the way because the lights were off, and there was no sign introducing the home as that.

"This blondie is ours." He finally admits, and for a second, I feel myself swaying a bit, but I quickly gather my thoughts and balance and take a look at the house.

Had he gotten us a vacation home? A home away from home. But it was enormous for just a vacation home. And it would be a lot to maintain. We would have to make sure we had someone here weekly to trim the grass and keep everything nice and neat.

"Our vacation home? It's quite big, don't you think?" I ask, taking a step towards the door.

"No, Eloise. It's our home." He corrects, and I freeze in my spot.

I turn slowly, and William stands before me, the key hanging right in front of my face. I take the key in my hand, my hands shaky from the reveal.

This didn't make sense; our life was in New York, and the company was in New York.

"You mean— but what about—"

"I broke things off with your father. I left the company. Dev and Liam are both on my side. They're investing in my start-up. We're establishing it in Boston. It's about two hours from here, but I wouldn't have to be in the office every day. And it's worth it anyway. You're worth it, Eloise." His words squeeze at my heart, and I'm trying my best to grasp what he's just revealed, but I can't believe it.

"I don't understand," I murmur.

I shake my head in denial and try to gather my thoughts on what he's done. William pulls me into his arms, cups my face with one of his hands, and makes me look up at him.

"Is it so absurd that I would leave everything behind for you, Eloise?" He whispers it with love and devotion.

My god, this man did it.

"But what about the company? The money?" I ask.

"I have enough money to get by and good investments in my start-up. I'm positive it'll work out. But none of the other things really matter, blondie." He soothes and rubs my cheeks with the pad of his thumb.

"When I first married you, I was greedy and a fucking dick to you, Eloise. I'm so sorry for that, but I love you, and I never want to see you anxious or panicked because of our family, not even because of me. I want you to do whatever your heart desires. If that's teaching, then you have my support. I want our children to grow up around love and support. I want them to make their own choices and support their dreams." William clears his voice and takes a step back. His gaze is still on mine as he drops to one knee and pulls out the velvet box from his pocket.

"Will, what are you—"

"I want to give you the life you deserve, starting now. And I want you to make your choices and live your life with me because you want to because you love me." He croaks, and in this very moment, I know that William believes I could actually deny him.

"Eloise, I choose you over everything. No amount of money could ever buy me the love and friendship that we have. I want a forever life with you, chosen by us. So, will you please marry me again, Eloise?" A stream of tears breaks away from me, and I burst into a sob, not able to control my emotions.

"Yes, of course!" I manage to choke through tears.

William removes the current ring from my hand and

replaces it with a new Marquis ring, like the one I had pinned to my Pinterest board thousands of times.

William stands up and brings me into a loving kiss full of passion and desire.

"Forever with you starts today, blondie. And I'm so grateful for all the good and bad that has happened before this moment because it made you mine." He whispers, holding me tight in his arms.

"I vow to put you first, Eloise. And I vow to be yours forever. Nothing will separate us. I'll always be here." He declares it like an oath, just like he had done before our wedding.

"I vow to always be yours and put you first, Will. I love you, and I want forever with you." I whisper the words, but I'm sure he can feel the raw intensity of the emotions that are tied to every syllable.

These were our vows, the only ones we needed to move on in our lives.

A vow of forever.

Epilogue

Eloise

Seven Years Later

"Is it going to be a boy or a girl?" One of my students shouts from their seat.

"It's definitely a girl because she already has a boy." Another one argues from across the room.

"That doesn't matter. My mom has me and my brother." Someone in the back rebuttals.

"Okay, okay, that's enough," I say, shushing the class of rowdy second graders. For the most part, they were always a great class to teach, but at times, they got carried away when they got too excited. But today, I let them know that I would be leaving on maternity leave next week, and now they were all excited about the upcoming baby.

I had to admit when I first saw the positive test, I wasn't

as excited. But that was mostly because only a year had passed since I had given birth to our son, Warren. And just thinking about all the pregnancy symptoms and pushing out a human being from my body again made me want to puke and cry.

Then again, that reaction might have also been pregnancy symptoms.

William, on the other hand, was ecstatic, and that had sent me into a wave of calmness. But William had always found a way to be calm when I was freaking out.

Even on our wedding day, he was there to soothe me. When I told him I was nervous but wanted to try and go back to school to pursue a degree in education, he was supportive.

Even when I found out about our first pregnancy with Warren, it was unexpected. William and I had decided we would wait another year or two, but Warren had other plans. And despite my anxiety, William somehow found a way to make me feel better about it all.

I sit back in my chair and rub my hand around my very round belly.

"Well, let's do a vote," I say, looking around the room to all my students.

"Raise your hand if you think it's a boy." Little tiny hands shoot up, but not enough to overpower the ones who are guessing that it's a girl. I take note of the number of hands that are up in the air before giving them a hand gesture to put them back down.

"Hmmm, now who thinks it's a girl?" I ask, most of the class shooting their hands up before I finish my sentence.

"Wow, so I guess the girl is the winner, but is it correct?"

I ask; my pregnant pause builds the tension within the room. I only wait a few more seconds before I finally respond.

"Those who voted for a girl... are... indeed... correct."

The entire class jumps out of their seats, excited about the reveal. I put a steady palm on my round belly that's currently being kicked and tossed in by our little peanut.

"I'm going to miss you, Miss Wren." One of my students shouts from their chair. A wave of little whines and agreement sounds throughout the classroom, and I'm quick to calm them down.

"I know, I know, and I'm definitely going to miss teaching you all. But I promise your substitute teacher will be phenomenal, and I'll even promise to stop by and visit."

The class erupts in a cheer, and I take a quick glance at the clock.

"Okay, everyone, let's make sure that we're all packed up and ready for dismissal. Please remember, just because I won't be here Monday doesn't mean that your homework isn't due." I get the exaggerated wines and sighs of despair but only chuckle as everyone heads outside to their lockers to pack everything up.

This moment felt just as bittersweet as the last time I was pregnant with Warren. I truly loved what I did, and leaving my kids behind to take care of my own baby sometimes felt wrong. But William said that just by seeing how much I cared for my students, he was sure I'd be a phenomenal mother.

That had been something I was even more fearful of. I hadn't had the best example of parents and wasn't sure how the hell I'd be around my own. But the minute I heard those cries during the birth, and they laid Warren on my chest, I knew I would do anything to protect him.

After dismissal, I was quick to gather my things and make it back to my car so I could be home quickly. One thing that this pregnancy had brought onto me was painfully swollen ankles, and all I wanted to do once I got home at the end of the day was sit back on the couch or bed and enjoy the foot massages that William gave me every night.

The minute I pull into our driveway, William's standing there with an overly excited Warren in his arms. He's waving at me as I pull in, and I can't help but laugh at his insistence on being put down. He tugs on William's shirt and points to the floor. William ignores him and instead walks to my car door and opens it for me.

"I still think you should've let me drive you today." I roll my eyes and hand him my bag as I unbuckle the seatbelt and make my way out of the car.

"Mama!" Wren lets out a whine as he reaches out for me with his arms. I take Warren away from William's arms and adjust him around my waist as best as I can with my belly in the way. William closes the car door and follows me into the house. I bombard Warren with kisses, making him fall into a fit of laughter.

I let out a sigh as I lay myself down gently on the couch. I try to adjust Warren to my side as best as possible. If William were to try and take him, he'd only burst into tears at our separation. While William and I were at work, we usually had a nanny who would come and take care of Warren until one of us arrived from work to take over. Mandy was our neighbor's daughter who had experience with nannying, and Warren was very quick to trust her and he felt comfortable around her. And better yet, she was amazing. It had been hard to leave him and go back to work, and even though William had told me that working wasn't an actual necessity for me but I loved teaching and I wanted to enjoy it as much as possible.

Will's start-up has become successful, and I'm extremely proud of him. It hadn't been easy. As much as he tried to stay in Vermont, most days, they needed him in Boston. It was even harder when Charlotte refused to pick up my calls. I knew it wasn't because she was upset with me, rather upset and embarrassed of her own family's action. At least that's what she said months later when I received a call from her sobbing and apologizing. Both she and Dev had come by to visit throughout the years, especially after Warren was born.

And even when they weren't here, I was constantly receiving packages from them, all for their godson. William and I did have to get them to stop after receiving a bike he wouldn't be riding anytime soon.

"You know, I missed mommy too." William groans, plopping down beside my feet and automatically bringing them onto his lap and into his hands.

"No," Warren spews, snuggling closer to my neck.

"If I were that close to her breasts, I'd say no to you too."

"Behave," I mutter, jabbing my foot into one of his ribs.

"Okay, okay, no more innuendos in front of the kid or soon-to-be kids." William presses his thumb against one of the knots, and I melt into the couch.

"You don't have to do this now, and I'm sure my feet are smelly."

My pregnancy with Warren had been completely different than now. With Warren, I had felt beautiful during my pregnancy. This time around, I was overly sensitive, in constant pain, swollen, and sweaty. Feeling pretty wasn't something I could even relate to. Granted, William did his best to assure me that he didn't care and that I was even more beautiful when pregnant. But I was sure that it was because he had probably developed a breeding kink.

"Eloise, you're carrying our baby. I don't care how you smell. I'm going to make you feel good in any way possible." He assured me, continuing his massage on my feet.

"Better yet, how about I go run you a bath." And while you soak up in there and relax, I'll order something for us to eat."

"No." Warren gurgles, tapping my chest for attention.

"I can already see how the rest of our years are going to be with him." William laughs as he gets up and walks over to give both Warren and me a kiss on the head before walking to the bathroom to start the bath.

I look down at Warren, who continues to sing-song a mumble of no's. That seemed to be his favorite word, and I had to agree with William that Warren's favorite word was going to stick throughout the years.

Warren was going to be as stubborn as William; I mean, he was an identical copy from the hair to his nose, lips, and eyes. Warren was William's mini-me. I was kind of hoping that our little peanut would have a head of blond hair or something that was like me. It was only fair that after carrying them for nine months and helping to create them, I'd share some similar attributes.

"Obviously, you didn't get the memo." I tease, giving his back little rubs.

"What memo didn't he get?" William asks, coming back over to lift me up.

"The memo of sharing some of his mother's attributes," I say, leaning down to place Warren in his baby walker. He begins to fuss almost immediately, but William is quick to turn on the TV and distract Warren with his favorite cartoons.

William walks back over and bends down to give my belly a kiss. "I'm sure our princess Penelope will look just like you. I'm so sure of it I'd bet my whole company."

"Well, let's not do that." The last thing we needed was a daughter who looked just like her father and a lost business.

"Why don't you head upstairs and into the bath? I'll join you in just a second." He says, pressing a kiss to my lips.

"Join me? But what ab–"

The doorbell's ring cuts me off, and William lifts a finger up for me to hold my thoughts. The minute he opens the door, I hear our nanny, Mandy's voice.

"Mandy?" I ask, peering my head over to take a quick glance around the hall.

"Hi, Eloise. How're you doing?" She asks, pushing her light chestnut hair behind her ears. She was a great nanny, and even after almost a year, she was still quite shy and reserved.

"About to feel better the minute I enter the bath." I look between Mandy and William as they step back into the living room. Mandy makes her way over to Warren, who immediately starts asking for her to pick him up.

I lift a brow up at William, confused as to why Mandy's here. William wraps his arms around me, bringing me close. "I asked her if she'd be okay coming here in the evening instead so we could have some time to ourselves before we add another one to the mix and our schedules become hectic again." I try to hold back the tears that are beginning to burn in my eyes. This had been so sweet of him to do. I had been panicking over handing two under two for a while. The only reason I hadn't mentioned my worries to William was because I didn't want to terrify him either.

"Everything is going to be just fine, blondie." He soothes me, his hand coming down onto my lower back. "Come, that bath water is probably getting cold."

I say a quick thank you to Mandy and let William lead me up the stairs to our master bedroom. The bathroom smells divine, like a warm sugar cookie. I look at the multitude of candles scattered around the bathroom and focus on the scent on top of the vanity. I was sure that William had taken that from my holiday stash, but I didn't mind one bit. I walk over to the filled bubbly tub, push my hand through the surface to feel the water's warmth, and let out a delightful hum.

"Still warm?" William asks, bringing his hand under my shirt to help pull it off.

"It's amazing. Quickly help me get out of these," I say, reaching my hands above my head so that he can pull the fabric off much easier.

"God, I love how beautiful they look when you're pregnant." William's gaze lands straight onto my already full breasts. He moves his hand behind my back, unhinges my bra, and eases it off, being extra careful not to toss them around. Even when we had sex, he made sure to be careful because they had become overly sensitive.

William removes the rest of my clothes and helps me settle into the warm bath. The water soothes my achiness instantly. I close my eyes and lean my head back on the edge of the tub. William runs his hands through my hair, leaving gentle kisses on my face.

"How's my beautiful wife feeling?" He whispers in between kisses.

"Better now." I hum in delight as he continues to trail his fingers through my scalp.

"Don't get me wrong, I love being pregnant, but when we start getting closer to the date, I am more than ready to be done with the pregnancy. That and our little peanut hasn't been easy." I rub my hand in circles around my belly. It was crazy that our baby would get here pretty soon.

"Soon enough, she'll be in our arms, and we'll have two babies under our belt," William says, bringing his hands away from my scalp and down my neck.

"What are you doing?" I say as his fingers tease my pebbled nipple.

"I'm going to enjoy some us time while we still have it. I think you need some destressing. It's not good for you or the baby." He murmurs, pressing kisses down my neck. I move my face towards him and capture his lips with mine.

God, I needed this. I can't remember the last time we even had a moment alone like this without being disrupted. And now, with two, it was just going to get more complicated.

"Our sex life will be nonexistent when this baby comes." I manage to speak through our kiss and his advancement down my body.

"Trust me, blondie. I don't think you'll even be thinking about sex after this baby is born." a giggle escapes my lips at his stupidly correct remark.

"Besides, when you're ready and up for it, I'll be here to deliver." He assures.

That was something William had been amazing at the get-go. I think that's what I found most attractive. I finally had someone I could trust. Someone who calmed my anxiety rather than causing it. It was William who encouraged me to continue my studies and pursue a degree in education. I was so worried about what kind of mother I'd be when Warren came into the picture, and William was there to comfort me and let me know that I had the best example of what kind of mother I didn't want to be. And that I was already far from the woman she was. My parents had practically pretended I didn't exist until they heard I was pregnant. That's when I finally got a call from them, acting like nothing had happened. William was quick to cut ties when they kept bombarding me with calls and causing me even more stress. After that, I never heard from them again.

"Hey, what are you thinking so deeply about?" William asks.

"Nothing, I'm just thrilled we're together." William presses a kiss to my forehead and lets his gaze fall into my own eyes.

"I am too, blondie. But just in case my words aren't enough, let me prove it to you in another way." William's hand finally reaches down between my legs, and I lean my head back and let myself fall into the pleasure of his touch.

"You, Eloise, will forever be the best thing I ever agreed on." I open my eyes to find him peering down at me.

"You, William, will forever be the best thing I failed to fight against." William's lips find my own, and I kiss him, knowing that William and I are forever.

Acknowledgments

Firstly, I want to thank all the readers who have supported me since The Muse. It's never easy to self-publish, and I'm genuinely my worst enemy when it comes to my writing. But you lovelies pushed me to continue. So thank you!

To @Isisreadss — Thank you for your support! Readers like you who constantly promote indie authors like me help make our dreams come true.

To @teafromtya — I've been a fan of your Booktok from the beginning, and seeing my book on your feed made me feel like I was one step closer to accomplishing my dreams. Thank you!

To Kim — Thank you for all the love and support! It means the world to me. Please don't share my books with our boss. I fear it could obliterate our friendship.

To AnnMarie — It makes me so happy to hear you tell everyone that you know an author and be such an immense support. Now you can tell everyone that you're in the acknowledgments of a book, too!

About the Author

Eliana Vazquez is a self-published author from Kearny, New Jersey. She graduated from the University of New Haven, where she majored in communications, her concentration being in Film and Media Production. When she's not at her desk writing you can find her enabling her coffee addiction and buying more books than she could ever read.

instagram.com/elianavazquez.author
tiktok.com/@elianavazquez.author